The Poet's Funeral

The Poet's
Funeral

John M. Daniel

Poisoned Pen Press

Poisoned Pen Press
6962 E. First Ave., Ste. 103
Scottsdale, AZ 85251
www.poisonedpenpress.com
info@poisonedpenpress.com

Printed in the United States of America

Author's Note

Except for the literary celebrities who walk in and out of this story in cameo roles, the characters in the book are all fictitious and should not be confused with any real people, living or dead. And although the American Booksellers Association convention was held in Las Vegas in 1990, I have invented all of the events described in this story.

I wish to thank Pete Reynolds of the American Booksellers Association for confirming the dates of the Las Vegas ABA trade show, Saturday, June 2 through Tuesday, June 5, 1990. I also want to thank the Rock Bottom Remainders for allowing me to have them perform at that convention, even though the band didn't yet exist at that time. (As far as I'm concerned, no ABA or BEA convention is complete without the Remainders.)

I want to gratefully acknowledge the help and encouragement I received from many people, including participants in my pirate workshop at the Santa Barbara Writers' Conference; members of Santa Barbara's Community of Voices; the Great Intenders of Arcata, California; and Robert Rosenwald, Barbara Peters, and the Poisoned Pen Press Posse.

Finally, I gratefully dedicate this novel to two of the best friends a writer could hope to have: Meredith Phillips, my partner in crime, and Susan Daniel, my partner in everything else.

—John M. Daniel

Preface to the Trade Edition

What you have in your hands is the trade edition of *The Poet's Funeral*. If you're looking for the Ongepotchket Press edition, complete with pictures of the dead poet and all her friends, and including a bunch of previously unpublished, posthumous poems of obscure origin, let me know and I'll give you your money back. This is the first and perhaps the only sincere tribute to the poet Heidi Yamada.

Included are eulogies by several of Heidi Yamada's associates, people who knew her well, some even before she became a celebrity. I have annotated these testimonials with what I know about those speakers, and I have also tied the speeches together with the thread of what really happened during the last few days and evenings of Heidi's life.

Finally, I must say I take umbrage at John Daniel's statement that the characters in this book are fictitious. Believe him if you want to, but I'm telling you that what happened in Las Vegas was real and the characters you're about to read about are real. I ought to know.

—Guy Mallon

Obituary

Heidi Yamada (1950-1990) was born and raised in Los Angeles, California, the only child of Tetsu and Megumi Yamada, survivors of the Manzanar Internment Camp during World War II. Mr. Yamada, who died in 1965, was a gardener for the Huntington Library; Mrs. Yamada, who died the same year, was self-employed as a housecleaner.

Heidi Yamada attended the University of California, Santa Barbara, on a full scholarship, from 1968 to 1973, majoring in environmental science. It was there that she became fascinated by poetry, taking classes from and eventually working as personal assistant to poet-professor Arthur Summers. Under his mentorship, she became a serious poet and pursued a literary career with remarkable success.

Her first poetry collection, *And Vice Versa,* was published by Guy Mallon Books in 1980. *Jump Start* (1982) and *Second Helpings* (1983) were both published by Random House. A deluxe "art book," *Love From My Velvet Slipcase,* was produced in 1988 by Ongepotchket Press of Santa Barbara.

Yamada wrote in a style of her own that some criticized as ornate to the point of opacity; others called it brilliant and innovative. Her work sold remarkably well, and she became a celebrity of considerable fame. Her striking looks, outspoken personality, and flamboyant behavior were even more famous than her poetry, which, no matter how one interpreted it, could not be dismissed or ignored.

Ms. Yamada died of an apparent drug overdose on June 2 in Las Vegas, Nevada, during the American Booksellers Association convention. A memorial service will be held in Santa Barbara on July 10. Memorial contributions can be made to the National Endowment for the Arts.

—*Publishers Weekly*

List of Speakers

Guy Mallon is the proprietor of Guy Mallon Books, a literary publishing company in Santa Barbara, California.

Arthur Summers, Professor of English at University of California, Santa Barbara, is the author of many collections of poetry and has been named United States Poet Laureate for 1991.

Beatrice Knight is a literary agent based in San Francisco.

Charles Levin is a senior editor at Random House, Inc.

Taylor Bingham was book review editor for *Newsweek* from 1971 to 1983.

Linda Sonora is the author of *Desert Nights: Stories; Violent Ink;* and *Very Hot Plate.*

Maxwell Black is the author of *The Yellow Bandanna; Howdy, Mr. President;* and *Gol Dern It.*

Mitzi Milkin is the founder and president of Ongepotchket Press.

Lawrence Holgerson is a noted collector of modern American poetry.

Guy Mallon

She Made Me Become a Publisher

I know that Heidi Yamada had a profound, lasting effect on every one of us who will be speaking to you today. Every one of us was changed by knowing her. She was that kind of person: beautiful, stylish, funny, original to the point of being unique, and disruptive in the best possible sense: she turned our lives around.

As for me, it is no exaggeration to say Heidi Yamada made me what I am today: a publisher. If Heidi had not walked into my life in the spring of 1980, I would no doubt still be a small-town, small-time merchant, selling used books and barely getting by. But, by the grace of Erato, Heidi did walk into my store, and into my life, and she offered me a manuscript that was to become her first published book, and mine as well.

In the ten years that have passed since that spring day, Heidi went on to publish other books with other publishers, and I went on to publish other books by other poets, and both of us made names for ourselves. Heidi Yamada is right now, today, perhaps the most spoken name in the world of poetry. My name is barely known outside the city limits of Santa Barbara. But I have no regrets except for one: that Heidi Yamada is no longer with us, will no longer visit my office and fill it with smiles and arresting phrases.

Happy is the man who has found his work. Heidi helped me find mine.

I had a small used bookshop in downtown Santa Barbara when I first met her. I got into that business mostly by accident, having collected first editions of post-WWII American poetry all through college and then through my twenties and early thirties, working for a big bookstore in Palo Alto. By the time I got tired of the traffic in the San Francisco Bay Area, I had acquired enough books to constitute a fine collection. Perhaps the best private, individually owned collection in the country, although Lawrence Holgerson would no doubt dispute that claim.

I quit working for the Palo Alto Bookshop, a job I'd had too long anyway, and packed all my books into a U-Haul trailer and pulled them out onto the road. My plan was to drive south to Los Angeles, where I had a few friends. I never made it that far because my car threw a rod in Santa Barbara and I had to stay there for a few days. I found a third-floor walk-up room in the Schooner Inn, a cheap hotel on lower State Street.

It was February 1977, and the weather was gorgeous. I spent the first day out on East Beach, where everyone was naked, including myself. The second day I walked around town and knew I'd found the city I was meant to live in, a place of red tiles, blue skies, erect birds of paradise, and cascading bougainvillea.

On the third day, I stumbled onto one of the three major finds of my life among books, the Santa Barbara Used Book Factory, a hippie store in an old Spanish courtyard on a side street lined with skirted palms. I never pass up a bookstore, and the sign in the window said: "Going Out of Business. ALL BOOKS ON SALE."

I walked through the door and went straight to the front counter, where a tall young bushy-haired man was staring dreamily into space, plucking a nonexistent guitar.

"Hi," I said.

"Hey."

"You got a stepladder I can use?"

"What for?"

"I'd like to browse your stock."

"Be my guest," he said. He smiled at the ceiling and continued playing guitar riffs in the air.

"I need something to stand on," I persisted. "I'm only five feet tall."

He shrugged. "Plenty of books on the lower shelves," he informed me.

"Can I see your guitar?" I asked.

"Huh?"

I held out my hands. "I play a bit myself," I said. "Lemme see your axe."

He gave me a quizzical smile and held out the pantomimed instrument. I took it carefully, looked it over, and said, "If you don't mind, I'll play a few tunes while you go get me a stepping stool."

The dude nodded and grinned. "Whatever, my man. Oh, I got an open tuning on that. If you want to change it, feel free." Bobbing his mop, he shuffled off to the back of the store. He returned a few minutes later with a small stepladder. I thanked him as we made the exchange.

I poked around in that store for two hours, moving my stool from aisle to aisle, picking up a few books and then putting them back, reminding myself I had enough books in my life, and then, misshelved in the European History section, on a top shelf, I came across a copy of Jack Kerouac's first book, *Lost in the Old Country*, a self-published collection of poems, which Jack had inscribed to Allen Ginsberg, with the title poem hand-written by Jack on the front flyleaf.

Lawrence Holgerson had told me about this Holy Grail of a book. Ginsberg himself was offering a small fortune to anyone who could find it. Holgerson was prepared to match his offer.

I put the book back in its hiding place, went up to the front counter, and asked the young man if I could speak with the owner of the store.

"Go right ahead," he told me with a bow.

"You own this business?"

"It owns me."

"How much you want for it? The business, I mean, including all the inventory."

He named a figure that was slightly less than I had in my bank account and in the world, and I got out my checkbook.

That was the beginning of Guy Mallon Books. I did all the necessary things: business license, DBA, State Board of Equalization, bank account, liability insurance, Chamber of Commerce, Better Business Bureau. I paid for a month's rent at the Schooner Inn. I was set: thirty-five years old and in business for myself. I was lonely, but I knew that in time I'd make friends. I was also horny, but that was nothing new. Most important, I was in business, and I was glad to have a permanent home for my first editions, which had spent too much time in a trailer.

I auctioned off the Kerouac autograph quickly—Holgerson outbid Ginsberg—before I got too fond of it, and I was funded. Then I started cataloging my collection and bought a year's worth of ads in *Antiquarian Bookman*.

The front room was full of the previous owner's inventory, the usual second-hand bookstore staples, mostly crap, and the back room had my trailerful of poetry firsts. Over the next three years I improved the front room until it could pay for itself—the rent and my one employee, who dusted the shelves and ran the cash register.

And she, my employee, who joined me in early 1980, was the second great find of my life in the book business.

She walked in off the street one bright, warm winter day, this knockout lovely young Asian-American woman (actually, we said "Oriental" back then). She was short (not as short as me, but who is?), and she wore sandals and cut-offs and a UCSB tee shirt, and her hair flowed like black liquid satin over her forehead, beside her cheeks, around her shoulders, and down her back. She flashed me a sassy smile and told me she had come to pick up some books for her boss, Arthur Summers.

Yes, *the* Arthur Summers. By that time he was one of my best customers. He was also a former Yale Younger Poet (that would have been decades ago) and the Chairman of the English Department at UCSB and had won the Bollinger Prize earlier that year. And, knowing of his reputation as an aging Lord Byron and having enjoyed the steamy sensuality of his verse, I was not surprised to learn that he had an assistant as lovely and lively as Heidi Yamada.

I took her into the back room and proceeded to fall in love with her.

I showed her the gems of my collection, the J.V. Cunningham, the Yvor Winters, the Janet Lewis, the Edgar Bowers, the Thom Gunn....

"Thom Gunn?" she said. "Sounds like a cowboy star. Who's this guy Winters? Is he related to Summers? What kind of a name is 'Yvor'? Poets are a weird bunch, boy."

"I'm boring you," I said. "Sorry."

"Boring? You're not boring. These books are a bit moldy, but you..." She looked into my face and gave me the first of hundreds of glittering winks, each more glittering than the last.

"I what?"

"You ain't boring, pal. Keep talking. Tell me about poetry. Or about anything else. Smile at me again. Hire me."

"Hire?"

"I'll put Guy Mallon Books on the map. I promise. I can do it. Watch." She spun around, flipping her long black hair, stretched out her slender arms and snapped her fingers and wiggled her shapely butt.

"What about Professor Summers?" I asked. "Don't you work for him?"

"He'll be glad to be rid of me," she answered. "But you won't," she quickly added. "I mean you'll be glad to have me. If you'll take me. I've always wanted to work for a publisher." She took my hand. "Let's go across the street to the Paradise Cafe for lunch. We can discuss my salary and all the many things I'll be doing for you."

"I'm not a publisher," I reminded her.

"Yet," she said. "That's one of the things I'll be doing for you."

I've heard it said that short men fall in love too easily. Affection from a woman, almost any woman, is taken as a miracle: that this beautiful woman, in spite of my height, thinks I'm grand, and I'd better take advantage of this gift because it doesn't come along more than once in a lifetime and it makes me feel a foot taller, that kind of thing. I like to think I'm wiser than that. And so I'm careful. But here was Heidi Yamada making eyes at me, and I knew I had been careful too long.

Twelve hours later, in my room on the third floor of the Schooner Inn, between the second and third times we made love, Heidi Yamada propped herself onto one elbow and smiled down on my face. The golden candlelight made her face shine, her teeth glow, her eyes sparkle, her hair ripple with ebony luster. I held one breast while I stroked her arm, and the breast seemed to respond to my squeeze.

"Guy," she said.

I kissed her shoulder.

"Guy, I want you to publish me."

"I'm not a publisher," I reminded her.

"We can fix that," she said. "I want you to publish a book of my poems. I don't want any publisher but you. Guy Mallon Books, Publisher. Will you do it?"

Shine, glow, sparkle, ripple. Squeeze.

"You're a poet?" I asked.

"No, but I could be. It's about time I did something with my life. I'm thirty years old, and I've been a professor's assistant for almost ten years, ever since I was an undergraduate."

"Have you ever written a poem?" I asked.

"No, but how difficult can it be?"

I started to laugh, knowing all at once that for the first time in months if not years I was neither lonely nor horny.

"Huh," she said. "You laughin' at me, bucko?"

"No, of course not."

"So you'll do it? You'll publish me? You'll make me a postwar American poet?"

"Sure. How difficult could that be?"

"Yes! Oh man, Professor Arthur Summers is going to shit a brick!"

She fell back and held my hand, and we both giggled at the ceiling until I started to get just a little bit horny again.

And that is how I became a publisher, and how Heidi Yamada became a poet. She wrote her first poem the next day, on the job, between sweeping the floor and counting out the change in the register before we opened the door. She brought it to the back room and handed it to me and watched me read it.

"Nice handwriting," I commented.

"Yeah? And?"

"Well…"

"Do you like it?" she asked.

"Maybe you need to warm up a little bit. This is your first poem ever, right?"

The smile left her lips. She nodded. "You said you'd publish my book," she said.

"And I will," I said. "This poem shows me you have a way with words, your images are arresting, you have an ear for language and an eye for detail, and before long you'll be writing real poetry. Heidi, Babe Ruth didn't hit a home run his first time at bat."

"I have an ear for detail?" she asked.

"Eye for detail. An ear for language."

"Yeah?"

"Yeah."

"Too much!" The smile had returned. "I'll have a book of poems ready for you by the end of the week I promise."

"Well—"

"As Thom Gunn would say, time's a-wastin', pardner."

So she delivered a book-length manuscript in seven days. The handwriting was still beautiful, but unfortunately she wanted the book set in type.

I chose Caslon Old Style. She got to choose all the words, and she refused editing. She let me choose the font because I was the publisher.

Her publisher.

By the time the book came out in the fall of 1980, we were no longer lovers. When the book went back to press for a second printing, spring 1981, she quit the store to write full-time. She got Beatrice Knight to be her literary agent. The following year, spring 1982, Heidi's second book was published by Charles Levin Books, an imprint of Random House. It was reviewed by Taylor Bingham for *Newsweek* and she got on the Carson show and made the cover of *People*.

By that time, Guy Mallon Books was publishing three other poets, real poets who wrote real poetry, including Arthur Summers.

We continued to grow through the 1980s. It got to where Guy Mallon books were being reviewed regularly by the major poetry journals, and we were packing up our wares every Memorial Day weekend and hauling them off to display them at the annual American Booksellers Association convention. The conventions gave me a chance to travel all over the country, but of course I liked it best when they came west, which usually meant Los Angeles, Anaheim, or San Francisco.

Most of us in the business of literature pretended to be appalled that the American Booksellers Association had chosen Las Vegas for their convention in 1990. Was this what the nineties were going to be all about: schlock, insanity, waste, high risk, tits and ass? And then most of us winked and shrugged and said, well, that's what New York publishing has become in the eighties anyway, so let the new decade roll. Viva Las Vegas.

Besides, the ABA convention, known simply as the ABA, whether it's held in Chicago or Washington D.C. or New Orleans or San Francisco or Anaheim, is wilder and goofier than Las Vegas anyway. It's a four-day roller-coaster of hard work and wild parties, wheeling and dealing, free books, free booze, literary celebrities to bump into (literally), deals to make, nonstop noise, lines to stand in for tasteless hotdogs, hospitality suites, shuttle-buses, hands to shake, backs to slap, a lot of standing around in utmost boredom until another friend walks by and you're off for another beer, more shmooze, more noise, more party invitations, more lies and hype....

Tell me again: why is it I love the ABA?

Carol, my partner, thinks the ABA sucks out loud, and of course she's right. If you're a bookseller you're having a wonderful time wandering the aisles, gazing at the new season's splendid goodies, catching sight of Stephen King or the Pillsbury Doughboy or Ed Meese or Barry Manilow, being treated like royalty by the publishers who want your business. But for those of us actually working the booths, it's a lot more standing than walking, and the smiles get to feeling forced by eleven in the morning and there's still at least twelve more hours of smiling before the day ends and you get to sleep a few hours to prepare for the next morning's hangover and hard work.

Yet I love it.

So there we were, Carol and I, Friday afternoon before the show opened, setting up our booth. We had driven over from Santa Barbara that morning in a rented Ford station wagon, and by the time we got to the outskirts of Vegas, where a new casino was being hoisted, a version of Camelot built out of Lego Blocks, we were already hot and tired and cranky. Then for about three hours we'd been rolling our hand truck back and forth between

the car and our booth at the Convention Center, then slaving
under the fluorescent lights, which were turned up to nine. A
boom box blared rock from our neighbors in the next booth,
who were frantically fashioning a life-sized model of the Arc
de Triomphe out of papier-mâché. The music, if that's what it
was, was intermittently interrupted by the whir and beeps of
teamsters' trolleys and forklifts. Our tee shirts were sweaty and
we'd gone through the six-pack. It's this way every year, the back-
breaking backstage setup. But we were almost finished, and our
booth looked great. I was catching a second high as we hoisted
our display panels. Carol spread our tablecloths over the rented
tables, then arranged flowers and stacks of books—giveaways
of backlist overstock and display copies of our forthcoming fall
list—while I started to hang the posters.

"Not again," Carol said. "She doesn't get the center panel this
year, Guy. It's been ten years since you published that book. Give
it a rest. Give me a rest. I'm tired of looking at that woman."

"We still have a lot of copies to sell," I reminded her. "And that
book's our main freebie for the show. Besides, Heidi Yamada's a
big star this year. Again."

"Bullshit. She's a has-been."

"That's right," I conceded. "And now she's making a come-
back. At least she has been somebody."

"She has been a lot of things," Carol said. "She has been your
plaything, for one, and all the world knows it, and you like to
rub my nose in it."

I stepped back and surveyed the display. There she was, on
a blown-up cover of *And Vice Versa,* bigger than life and still
beautiful.

"But that was my first book," I said. "She put Guy Mallon
Books on the map."

"She put Guy Mallon on the mat." She gave me a grumpy
scowl and gave the finger to the poster.

"I can't believe you're jealous. Of Heidi? Come on."

Carol finally cracked up, bent over laughing. I knew she
couldn't keep up the jealous act with a straight face. She kissed

my forehead. "I'm glad she gave you a good time, baby," she said. "She's screwed half the publishing industry, so there's no reason you shouldn't have had a turn."

"So can I keep the poster?"

"If you don't want that poster, I'll take it," said a voice from behind me, out in the aisle. I knew that voice. That whine.

"Hello, Lawrence," I said, turning around. There he stood in a self-deprecating slouch, his wispy goatee jutting forward. I shook his clammy hand. "Have you met Carol Murphy, my business manager?"

"Of course, of course," Lawrence said, with a broad smile and a bow. "A pleasure to see you, my dear."

"Likewise," Carol answered. "Guy, give me a hand with this table. It needs to go back about three inches."

"May I help?" Lawrence asked, rubbing his hands together. "I'll give you a hand, or I'll go get you a beer or whatever. Really. My pleasure. And I mean it about that poster. If you're not going to use it, I'd love it for my collection." He pulled a pack of Salems out of his shirt pocket and shook one into his mouth.

"Can't smoke in here," Carol told him.

"Those guys are smoking," he said, nodding at a couple of men pushing a loaded dolly.

"Those guys are teamsters," I said. "You're not."

Lawrence put his cigarette back into the pack and put the pack back into his pocket. "Anyway, about that poster—"

"You collect posters too now?" I asked.

Lawrence shrugged. There was a mustard stain on the lapel of his rumpled linen jacket. He couldn't help being a shlimazl, but I wished he'd go away.

"You know I'm addicted to Miss Yamada," he admitted. "An ABA poster would look nice on my wall. I could pay you for it. But if you're not planning to use it anyway, well, I mean how much did it cost to have made? I could reimburse you for that, I suppose, or I could help out here in the booth." He started to take off the jacket.

"Don't strip, Lawrence," Carol said. "We don't need any help. We're almost finished. What do you say, Guy? Give the lucky man a poster?"

"After the show," I said. "Sorry, but I want that thing up. Heidi's finally getting a lot of attention again this year."

"Really?" Lawrence said. "I can have that poster after the show?"

"Yes," Carol said before I answered. "Guy and I have just struck a deal."

"How did you get into the building, Lawrence?" I asked him. "The convention's not open to the public till tomorrow morning."

"I'm not public." He pulled an exhibitor's red badge out of his pocket and showed it to me. His name all right, and the name of the company, Ongepotchket Press.

"You're working for Mitzi?" I said.

"Just during the show. I volunteered."

"For a price, I bet."

"Let's call it a swap. An energy exchange is how I like to put it."

Carol said, "I thought Mitzi decided not to display after all."

"That's right," Lawrence said. "But she'd already paid for the booth and we already had these badges, so even though the booth will be empty, we're here."

"I'm sort of sorry Mitzi isn't displaying," Carol said. "Just think of what she might do with an ABA booth. Ongepotchket indeed!"

"What does 'ongepotchket' mean, anyway?" I asked. "I've always wondered."

"Overdecorated," Carol said. "In a word, Mitzi."

"Anyway," Lawrence continued, "that leaves me available to help you out. By the way, are you going to the WESTAF party tonight?"

"Sure," I said.

"Ugh," Carol said.

"Any way you can get me an invitation?" Lawrence said.

"I don't have an extra," I told him. "Can't Mitzi get you in?"

"She's not going," Lawrence grumbled. "She's embarrassed because the book hasn't come out. I said she still needed to be there, but she said no way. Heidi will be there of course, collecting the award even if the book didn't come out. Everyone will be there. Mitzi doesn't want to show her face. She tore the invitation up. That bitch."

"She's pretty pissed off at Heidi?" Carol asked.

"Wouldn't you be? This was supposed to be big time. He'll be there," Lawrence added, putting his pudgy finger on an advance reading copy of our new Arthur Summers collection, which will be published in September. "Professor Poet Laureate. He'll be handing Heidi the award. I want to see that! Please, Guy, isn't there somebody you could ask?"

Carol said, "Lawrence, we're not scalpers, we're publishers. And right now we don't have time to walk the aisles shmoozing and begging for tickets."

"But your booth is finished, and maybe…"

"And maybe it's time for us to go have a cool shower and a quick nap at our hotel. Sorry, Lawrence. Ready, Guy?"

"In a minute," I said. "Lawrence, maybe you should wander over to the Random House aisle, over in the three thousands. Maybe you'll find Charles Levin. He probably has plenty of party invites to give out. You should hit him up for the Linda Sonora party tomorrow night. Those invitations are going fast."

Lawrence nodded quickly, smiled quickly, and scurried away like an overdue white rabbit.

"What was all that about?" Carol asked me. "Levin won't be helping with the setup."

"I know. I wanted to get rid of Holgerson before we left the booth. I don't trust him."

"Come to think of it," Carol said, "I put out five advance copies of the new Summers book. Now there's only four."

We were staying in the Landmark Hotel, right across the street from the Convention Center. The good news was we didn't have to drive to the show and pay for parking. More good news was that the Landmark was cheap, forty bucks a night, which was because of the bad news: the Landmark was a dump. It looked like a mushroom from Mars from the outside; from the inside, a dump.

It had seen better days, even great days on the Las Vegas scale. Built by Howard Hughes back in the sixties, it was once the tallest building in town. Hughes lived like an eagle at the top, and nobody ever saw him leave; but his money was like a magnet that brought in the high-rollers and celebrities. After Hughes died the place was sold a couple of times and now nobody would buy it. It was bankrupt and there were rumors that it would be leveled by dynamite later in the summer. It had managed to stay open long enough to be in business during the ABA, but that was it. Half the staff had been let go, the rest of the staff was surly, the halls were dingy, the carpets were threadbare, the casino downstairs was oddly quiet, and our room reminded me of the Schooner Inn in Santa Barbara, which I remembered with nostalgia but not with admiration.

Who cares? It was cheap, and it was close. And it was air-conditioned, which was a blessing after the short hike across Paradise Road. Besides, the only reason we needed a hotel room was to crash when we were too exhausted to notice the peeling wallpaper or the rust stain in the sink.

We walked through the muted casino to the bank of elevators and pressed UP. We could hear the machinery grinding for a couple of minutes and then the door opened and we walked into the elevator and I hit the button for the twelfth floor. As the door slid closed, we heard a voice call, "Stop!"

I put my hand on the rubber just before the door closed, and it backed open again and another passenger got in with us. She was a young woman, a short redhead, pretty if a bit pudgy, sweaty and blown by the desert wind, wearing jeans and an I♥New York tee shirt, and she had four camera bags hanging from her shoulders.

"God," she said, with a toothy smile. "Whew. This is one hot town, I'll tell ya. Where are you staying? Oh, right, the

Landmark. Yeah, me too. Some place, huh? What's wrong with this elevator? How come it's not working?"

"What floor?" I asked her.

"Twelve," she said, shrugging a couple of her cameras off her shoulders and resting them at her feet.

"Us too," Carol said. "Probably the only floor they're using." She pressed the button and the door slid closed.

"I can't believe I'm staying in this piece of crap," the woman said. "It's all I could get. I just made my reservations yesterday." The elevator started its lift-off and she gave us another smile and stuck out her hand. "Marjorie Richmond," she said. *"Publishers Weekly."*

"Carol Murphy," Carol said. "And this is Guy Mallon."

We shook hands and Marjorie Richmond said, *"The* Guy Mallon? Publisher?"

I could see a reflection of my proud grin on Carol's face. She knows me too well, can do imitations of me that put me in my place and make me laugh out loud. Right now she was doing an aw shucks.

"God, this is so great," Marjorie went on. "I want to shoot you."

"Be my guest," Carol said.

The elevator bumped to a halt at the twelfth floor and the door opened. We got out and started down the hall, the three of us and all of Marjorie's technical baggage. "Hold on a sec," she said. "Guy, will you carry a couple of these camera bags for me? My shoulders are killing me. Straps are cutting off all the circulation in my boobs. Man, do I need a massage."

I took the heavy bags from her and we hit the dimly lit trail.

"I spent a couple of hours with your poet this afternoon," Marjorie said. "Heidi Yamada? She's so great. Totally photogenic."

"Taking pictures? Of Heidi?" I asked. "So are you doing a story for *PW*?"

"Yeah. It's a last-minute thing. We're doing a poetry issue in July and I'm here to follow some of the poets around. Are you guys going to the WESTAF party tonight?"

"Wouldn't miss it," I answered.

"Unfortunately," Carol added.

"Oh God, it's going to be great," Marjorie said. Another huge smile. There was lipstick on her teeth, and sweat was dripping off her forehead, but she was a dish and knew it. *PW,* I thought. And she's heard of Guy Mallon Books. She photographs poets. "So this is my room," she said. "Twelve twenty-four. You guys want to come in for a few minutes?"

"No thanks," Carol answered for both of us. "We're just next door. Twelve twenty-six."

"Hey, nice. Coincidence, huh? By the way, do you know if there's a shuttle to the WESTAF party?"

"I doubt it," I told her. "It's a pretty exclusive affair."

"Right," Carol said. "Only the wildly rich and famous stars from the small-press publishing world."

"Well shit," Marjorie said. "I guess I'll have to take a cab. That's such a pain. All this shlepping. I'll take those bags now."

I handed her the luggage and she fished around in one of them and pulled out a couple of business cards for Carol and me. Then she fished around in another camera bag and found her hotel key. While she opened her door, I read the card:

Publisher's Weekly
Marjorie Richmond
Photographer

Marjorie got her door opened and hefted her camera bags. Another smile, right at me. "Hey, why don't we share a cab? Save a few bucks."

"We've got our own car," I told her. "A station wagon."

"Oh."

"You can come with us, Marjorie," Carol said. "Meet us in the lobby downstairs, six-thirty sharp."

Still looking at me she said, "That's so sweet of you. See you then. Bye."

When we got inside our room, I said, "Well that was good of you."

"I can take a hint," Carol said.

"You think she was hinting?"

"Guy, get real. Didn't you notice all the circulation in her boobs? What a phony."

"I noticed her boobs, I guess," I admitted. "You think they're phony?"

"No, they're real. It's her that's a phony. Trust me."

"Is this your jealousy act to make me feel tall?"

"Believe me, I'm not jealous."

"Then why should I trust you?"

"Because I'm older than you, kiddo," she answered.

"By five years," I admitted.

"And taller than you."

"By eight inches."

"And I know a lot more about women than you."

"What makes you think that?"

"Heidi Yamada, for one thing." Carol peeled off her tee shirt. "And I'm better at business than you."

"Granted."

"And I'm a better proofreader, by the way." Off came the bra. Wow. As always: wow.

"What's that got to do with it?"

Carol glanced at my crotch and said, "You're getting too big for your britches, big guy. Are we going to take that shower or what?"

"What," I answered. I reached for her and she stepped back.

"I'm pretty hot and smelly," she said. "I'm stinkier than you."

"And older and taller and a better proofreader. As for hotter and stinkier, give me a chance and I'll catch up with you."

She grinned as she slipped out of her pants, then turned and bent forward to peel back the bedspread. Wow again. "This is going to have to be short," she told me. "We have a long shower to take and it's already five o'clock."

◇◇◇

Afterwards, as we stood together in the shower, Carol said, "Guy, I want to apologize. I don't know how you put up with me sometimes."

"What are you talking about?" I asked. "I thought that was delightful."

"Yeah, that was great," she agreed. "For a quickie. No, I'm talking about what a bitch I can be sometimes. I'm sorry I was so snide about Marjorie."

"No harm done," I said, soaping her belly.

"Yeah, well you know how I get at ABA. I know how much you love this event, all the parties, all the hype, but it puts rocks in my stomach."

I held my palm against her slippery skin. "I don't feel any rocks," I said.

"They're there all right. I just don't like crowds, and I can't stand phonies. Put 'em together and whattaya got?"

"Bibbity bobbity boo?" I guessed.

"That's right." She put her hands under her wet breasts and bounced them in front of my face. "Bibbity bobbity boo. I'll try my best not to get too negative." She finished rinsing and turned off the water.

"And I promise not to get manic," I replied. "We'll get through this weekend."

"I know," she said. "We always do, somehow. I may hate ABA, but I love you. Now let's get dried off. We don't want to be late for the show."

Arthur Summers
A Teacher's Pride

Mea culpa.

That's right: I am here to make a confession. I am guilty of the first deadly sin. Pride.

It's not what you think. Oh of course I am proud of my writings and my modest publications and the few small honors I've been fortunate enough to harvest.

But the source of my greatest pride is and always has been my accomplishments as a teacher.

What makes a teacher proud? What in fact gives a teacher the right to be proud? The success of his students, that's what. And the greatest pride a teacher can feel comes when he realizes that the success of one of his students has surpassed his own.

That is why, as sad as I am—as we all are—today to have lost the brilliant poet we knew and loved and admired, my heart will not let go of the joy and, yes, the pride of having been Heidi Yamada's mentor.

I am often asked, "Can the writing of poetry really be taught?"

The answer, of course, is of course not. All a teacher can do—must do—is recognize that brilliance and encourage it.

Heidi once asked me, "Professor Summers, do you think I could ever be a poet like you?"

"No, Heidi," I answered. "You could not. You must be a poet like you."

That is what she did, and that is why am proud to have been her teacher.

I admit I was amazed when Heidi brought me, along with the manuscript of her first book, a blurb from Arthur Summers.

"This is a startling first collection by a new poet I've had my eye on for quite some time. I can honestly say I've never read poems like these by any other student of mine—or by anybody else, for that matter."

"Isn't that great?" Heidi bubbled. "That Arthur is such a sweetie pie! He called me a *poet*." She kissed me, then kissed the blurb, then kissed me again. "A poet!" She set the sheet of paper down on my cluttered desk and said, "I want you to print that super big on the back of my book."

I set my coffee cup down on top of the famous poet's priceless words and looked up into her sweet, innocent grin. "Heidi—"

"Watch it," she said. "Don't spill coffee on that paper. I'm going to frame it."

"Heidi," I said, tapping a pencil eraser on the UCSB English Department letterhead, "this is meaningless. It's transparent bullshit."

"What are you talking about?"

"Read it again," I told her. "Find the praise and win valuable prizes." I handed her the blurb and watched her face grow a scowl.

"It's meaningless," she agreed.

"Meaningless."

"Which means what?"

"That it doesn't mean anything," I said.

"I know what 'meaningless' means, dodo. But what this piece of shit means is Arthur Summers doesn't like my work."

"Well," I shrugged, "there's no accounting for taste."

"I don't care if he likes my poems or not," Heidi said. "But that asshole owes me a better blurb than this." She crumpled the paper into a ball and threw it across the office at my wall of feminists. "You mind the store. I'll be back in an hour."

She was. She handed me another sheet of paper, again bearing the letterhead of the UCSB English Department.

"Buy this book," I read aloud. *"Read it and be amazed. Heidi Yamada is spectacular. She is a real poet."* I handed the blurb to the real poet and said, "Way to go. How did you do it?"

"Do what?" she answered. "Arthur did it. He made it all up, except the last sentence. I made him add that." The grin, the by-now-famous Heidi Yamada grin, was back again, lighting up that perfect face. God damn it.

"You're sleeping with him, aren't you," I said.

"Aw. You're jealous."

"Never mind," I said. "As long as it gets people to buy the book."

"You *are* jealous," she taunted, still grinning. "My jealous publisher."

"This isn't your publisher feeling jealous," I told her. "It's your lover. I think."

Heidi put her hand on the side of my face and said, "Arthur's just a friend. We were lovers once, yes, but that was years ago, back when I was an undergraduate. Oops."

"Oops?"

"I'm not supposed to say that. That's part of the deal."

"What deal?"

"Arthur gave me the first blurb because he likes me. He gave me the second blurb to keep me from telling the entire world that I used to fuck his brains out while I was taking his class on the Romantics."

"You took a class in the Romantics? Were you an English major?"

"No. Environmental studies. Talk about boring. I thought the Romantics would be fun. I was reading a lot of Georgette Heyer and Barbara Cartland at the time. I didn't know the Romantics were a bunch of dead English flits. But by then I was having a good time giving Arthur a good time, so—"

"So it's all over now between you and him?"

"Right," she said. "Ever since he told me I'd never be a poet. I figured if Keats and Shelley and those guys could get famous writing bullshit, so could I, but I planned to write stuff that was real. Arthur said I'd never make it. 'You'll never be a poet,' he goes. And now he's saying, in writing, that I *am* one, and I want you to print that on the back of my book, as big as it will fit."

"I was hoping to put a picture of you on the back," I said.

"No way. My face goes on the front. And another thing. I'm dedicating my book to him. 'To Arthur Summers, who taught me so much about the love of poetry.'"

"And vice versa," I commented.

Heidi clapped her hands. "Yes! That's great! That's going to be the title of my book. *And Vice Versa.*"

A couple of years later, by which time Heidi Yamada was the darling of the New York literary establishment and I was no longer either her lover or her publisher, I got up the nerve to ask him how and why he had written such effusive praise for such silly drivel as *And Vice Versa.*

We were in back room of Guy Mallon Books, which was still a used bookstore in the front but was now primarily a publishing company in the back. I was publishing four titles that season, all Santa Barbara poets. Julia Cunningham, Julia Bates, Perie Longo, and of course Arthur Summers. Arthur was still being published by major university presses, but he threw me his table scraps, recycled collections of his previously published poems about baseball, about Southern California, about academe. I brought these out in signed, numbered editions of three hundred each and sold them for a hundred bucks a pop to a list of subscribers. It was easy work for me, as long as there were addicted collectors like Lawrence Holgerson forever willing to buy poems they already owned in other collections.

It was after hours and Arthur and I had spent all afternoon planning the next Summers collection, a bunch of beach poems with etchings by a local artist he was currently bedding.

I closed up the shop out front and opened up a bottle of pinot noir in the back and we toasted the new project.

Then Arthur raised his glass again and said, "And here's to the little bitch who made all this possible."

"Hear hear," I said. "Did you read the interview she gave *Publishers Weekly* last week?"

"No! Heidi was interviewed by *PW*?"

"Yup."

"Did she mention me by name?"

I laughed. "No. It appears she's forgotten us both. We knew her when."

"Thank God."

"The interviewer called her the Judith Krantz of the poetry world and she asked, 'Who's Judith Krantz?'"

"That's to her credit, I suppose," Arthur said.

We each had another glass of wine, then we finished the bottle, and I said, "I've always wondered how you could have done that."

"Done what?"

"That blurb for *And Vice Versa*. 'Heidi Yamada is spectacular'? How could you say that?"

Arthur stuffed his bulldog brier with latakia and fired it up. Sitting there in my leather armchair, his legs crossed, he cut quite a figure, with his forest of unruly white hair, his face like the profile of a New Hampshire mountainside, a portable chimney clenched in his jaw. Filling the room with a delicious sour cloud, he replied, "Heidi Yamada *was* spectacular. I believe you had an opportunity to know that yourself."

"Oh that," I said. "Sure. But 'She is a real poet'? How could you say that?"

"Oh that. Well, because Heidi was…spectacular. Shall we open another bottle?"

Halfway through the second bottle of pinot, he volunteered more. "She had me by the short curlies, of course. It's in my contract with the university that I'm not supposed to shtup the undergraduates. I was fired from Stanford for getting a sophomore pregnant, and UCSB made it clear that I had to keep my dick out of the coeds' britches."

"I hate to tell you this, Arthur, but by now everyone has guessed that you and Heidi were lovers."

"I suppose," he sighed. "It's a bit embarrassing. That I screwed her and she screwed me into writing such stupid praise for her stupid book. But it's thanks to the spectacular Heidi Yamada that you have a publishing company, the only publisher of poetry that I know of to make a profit without grants, and thanks to her that I have a new publisher." He lifted his glass again.

"I'll tell you this, though," he added after a smoky pause. "I want that whole episode forgotten. It's done, and it's done with. Heidi doesn't need my support anymore, and if she ever dredges up that affair again, now that the world is for some reason paying attention to her, I shall personally, and I mean this, kill her."

I've never mentioned that promise before, not because I'm not a gossip (because I am a gossip, obviously), but because I never thought that promise had any promise. But poets have a way of telling the truth. The tricky part is knowing how much of that truth is literal and how much is poetry.

So come with us to the WESTAF party, Friday night, before the official opening of the Las Vegas ABA. Summers had just been named the next Poet Laureate, and it had gone to his handsome head in a big way.

We turned our station wagon over to a valet parker and approached the front door of the large ranch-style house. It was a warm desert night, loud with insects, and a waxing moon was flood-lighting

the manicured cactus garden in the front yard. The front door
stood wide open, and from inside we could hear cocktail chatter
and piano music.

Carol took my hand and said, "Here we go. Ready to boogie?"

"Always ready to boogie," I said.

"Shit," Marjorie said. "This fucking camera bag keeps sliding
off my shoulder. Guy, would you give me a hand?" Marjorie
was dressed to maim, her translucent white blouse covering a
bright red bra.

At the door we were met by a giant in a shiny suit who said,
"You got invitations?"

I fished the engraved WESTAF invitation out of my jacket
pocket and gave it to the goon. "Right," he said. "Two. You two
have a good time." Then he turned to Marjorie. "Yours, miss?"

"I'm with them," she answered.

"This invite says two. You make three. Doesn't compute. You
want me to call you a cab?"

"Wait a minute," she said, gaily laughing. "My mistake, okay?
I thought since I was coming with Mr. Mallon I wouldn't need
my invitation, so I left it at my hotel. I have all this camera
equipment, see, and—"

"Yeah, I see that. What I don't see is your invitation. You
want me call you a cab, like I said?"

Marjorie set down her three bags and crossed her arms under
her red breasts, took a deep breath and said, "Listen. I'm on
assignment. I'm from *Publishers Weekly.*"

"So? I'm from Winnemucca."

"Guy, help me out here!" By now there were two groups of
people behind us on the front stoop, waiting to pass muster.

"There you are!" was the lilting call from just inside the door.
Herself, dressed in skimpy silk, a gardenia in her inky hair, a
copy of *Second Helpings* in her hand. "Guy, Carol, you come on
in here! Oh, hello, Marjorie! Still alive after that long shoot this
afternoon? Oh, hey, I forgot to give you this." She opened her
book and brought out an invitation and handed it to Marjorie,
who turned it over to the doorman.

"You have a nice time, miss," he said, then he turned to the next party. "You guys got invitations?"

Marjorie hefted her bags and we followed Heidi into the beige living room. "Isn't this lovely?" Heidi gushed. "It's 'old Las Vegas,' which means it was built way back in the fifties. Isn't that cute? This place is gorgeous. All this art."

Indeed the walls were covered with what I assumed was trendy and expensive art. Paintings, lithographs, collages, woodcuts, photographs. All over every wall in sight. "These people are big supporters of the arts. They gave a million dollars to the Western States Arts Federation this year, so they got to host this party. Great people. Come on, I'll introduce you around. There's Arthur."

Marjorie had already spotted the Poet Laureate Elect and was hustling across the room, pulling a camera out of a bag as she went.

"Your big night, Heidi," Carol said. "You nervous?"

Heidi laughed. "I don't get nervous. Mitzi gets nervous enough for both of us. She's so nervous she didn't come to the party. That was her invitation I gave to Marjorie. She refused to come, so she asked me to let the photographer in, and I said what the hey, right?"

"I suppose Mitzi's upset," I said. "Her book delayed and all."

"It's her own fault," Heidi said. "She didn't send it to press. We had a disagreement, so what? She still could have sent it to press. Especially since it won the Western States Book Award. Don't worry, honey, that book is going to be published. If Mitzi won't do it, I'll find somebody else. The important thing is the poems, right? That's what this award is all about, right?"

"I have a certain affection for those poems," I admitted.

"Maybe you should publish the book if Mitzi bails," Heidi said.

"Spare me," Carol said. "I need a drink. Then I'm going to spend the evening draped across that grand piano listening to that hunk play Gershwin tunes."

She stepped down into the sunken living room and strolled off toward the music and I followed Heidi into a crowd of poets and publishers and publicists, most of whom I'd met at ABAs past. A drink materialized in my hand, good smoky scotch. Marjorie took photos of me shaking hands with Arthur Summers. I don't enjoy having my picture taken with somebody as tall as Summers, because it makes me look like a toddler instead of just a short person. But I'm a good sport. I smiled up into his craggy face.

Arthur Summers looks like a bald eagle. I don't mean he's bald; he has a great mass of slightly unkempt white hair. I'm talking about his commanding eyes.

"Congratulations, Art," I said. "It's about time."

Summers chuckled and put his arm around Heidi. "It's about time for this little lady, too, wouldn't you say?" Heidi grinned up at him and Marjorie kept her camera flashing.

It was about time for some shmoozing and boozing. I wandered around the house admiring art. I picked up another tumbler of single-malt scotch and a little brie and caviar sandwich, then stepped up some tile steps and wandered out into the back yard to admire the topiary juniper bushes in the moonlight. I found Maxwell Black out there sitting by himself by the swimming pool, a bottle of Bud in his hand. He looked up at me and said, "Howdy, Guy." He didn't stand, and I didn't sit down; we were fairly close to eye level anyway. He looked snazzy in clean faded jeans, a lavender chambray shirt with pearl buttons, and his trademark yellow bandanna ascot.

"What do you think of the party?" I asked him.

"Hmmph," he said.

"You don't care for this kind of horseshit?"

"Don't insult horseshit."

The free drinks and canapés were inside, so we were the only ones out on the patio. "So Max," I said, "what's the real story on *Out of My Face*? Is it ever going to come out, or is it dead in the water?"

"You got me by the seat of the pants," he answered. "The poems are all written, as you know."

"Indeed I do."

"So now it's up to Mitzi. But there's this standoff happening. One of them gals has to bend, or the world will be deprived of another fine collection of poems."

"What's the squabble about?"

"Two words," he said. "Heidi Yamada. Sorry, pardner, but that's all I'm allowed to say."

I chuckled. "It's always about Heidi. Everything's about Heidi."

"I didn't say it was about Heidi, exactly. I said it was about two words."

"You're a man of few words yourself, Max."

"Well, this is her night. She gets the prize anyway, and she spent all afternoon getting her pitcher took."

"That must have been fun."

"That photographer is one hot little chick."

"Marjorie? She seems pretty taken with Art Summers."

"Coupla sluts," Max snorted. "Made for each other. Somebody's going to get laid tonight."

"Well look at you two! Two of my favorite men," chirped Beatrice Wright, wending her way across the patio with a champagne glass in each hand. "Max, honey, you look stunning tonight. Love the bandanna."

"Shit," Max said. "Wisht old Heidi would let me stop wearing these damn things."

"It's all packaging," Beatrice said. "You're in good hands. Anything new coming out for you?"

"Naw. Heidi's pretty caught up in her own work these days."

"Maybe you need a new agent," she told him. "You know I'd kill to get a client like you."

"You'd have to," I said. "Max is Heidi's personal property."

"Shit," Max mumbled.

"I need another scotch," I said, and I moseyed back into the living room, which had become more crowded with bookish bohemians. I knew a lot of them and most of them knew me. I had to dodge my way across the room to keep from being talked to or stepped on.

I met up with Carol at the piano; she was singing along with the piano player, who looked spiffy in a powder-blue tuxedo and a Hawaiian shirt. The piano was quite a piece of furniture, a huge ebony grand polished to look like a black mirror.

"You doing okay?" I asked her.

She handed me her glass and said, "Would you get me some more gin?"

I did, then went on wandering.

I said hello to Robert MacDowell of Story Line Press, Randall Beek of Bookpeople, Tree Swenson of Copper Canyon. Bobbi Rix of Consortium was laughing with Eric Kampmann of NBN, each of them outsmiling the other. Marjorie Richmond bustled among us, urging us to just act natural ("God, I'm only *Publishers Weekly.* Smile!" *Flash!*) I chatted with Howard Junker, Douglas Messerli, Jim Hepworth, all the small-press western bigshots. Forgive me for name-dropping, but let me point out that they all said hello to me, too. Maybe it was because I was Heidi Yamada's first publisher, the one who discovered her talent for the first time. After Arthur Summers, of course. He'll always have that honor.

"I feel deeply honored," he said, finally, after the piano player struck a large chord and the cocktail crowd hushed to hear their next Poet Laureate. He stood on the steps that led out onto the patio and addressed the assembled audience in the sunken living room. "I feel deeply honored to be here tonight, and I want to thank the Western States Arts Federation for giving me this opportunity, and on behalf of WESTAF I also want to thank our gracious, generous hosts tonight, Pete and Carla Benedetti, for having us into their lovely home."

Gentle applause.

"This is the moment we wait for every year, the annual WESTAF poetry award presentation. There's no surprise this year; the winner was announced two weeks ago. That was before it was announced that the book itself is on hold and won't be published for a few weeks yet. But I think we all know about delays in this business. Authors blame them on publishers, publishers blame them on printers, printers blame them on God, and God is too busy trying to get Inland Book Company and Bookazine to carry the Bible."

Chuckles.

"The winner of this year's award, Heidi Yamada, is a remarkable phenomenon in the publishing world. You could say she's a significant sidestep in the history of literature, and I only call her a sidestep because she's taken poetry in a new direction that nobody else has dared to explore. In any case, her poems are unmistakably *her* poems, and all of us look forward to reading the new collection, *Out of My Face.* The judges who have read it assure me that we're in for some surprises.

"The Western States Arts Federation honors western authors and western publishers by awarding a handsome check to one poet and one publisher each year, to celebrate and help promote a book properly in a business world dominated by the New York Literary Establishment. To be eligible for this award, the author and publisher must each be from one of the seven Western states, which pretty much guarantees that the award also celebrates small and independent publishing, a tradition that is older than the New York Literary Establishment, older than New York itself.

"Some authors, like Heidi, start out with the small press and use their critical achievement as a stepping stone to the larger houses. And like Heidi, many of them find that the world of big-time publishing is not so devoted to literature as to sales. A few authors who make this journey become stars. Others leave New York and leave the writing life, disillusioned. Some return to the more comfortable and artistically rewarding atmosphere of small-press independent publishing. Tonight's honoree, Heidi Yamada, has done all three.

"Heidi and I go back quite a ways, as some of you know. That's why it's with affection and nostalgia as well as pleasure that I now award her this certificate and this check. Here you go, Heidi. Can't wait to read that book, doll!"

Heidi stepped up next to Arthur Summers and accepted his chaste kiss and the check. Still holding his hand, she beamed at her audience and nodded to their applause.

"Oh God," she breathed, when the crowd settled down. "This is so cool. I know there are a whole bunch of people I should be thanking right now, and some of them are in this room right now, and God, I'm really grateful to them, I really am, but since they're all in my book, well, you'll see when you read it, if you ever read it, I mean if Mitzi Milkin gets off her ass and her high horse and sends the damn thing to the printer, shit. Oops. Anyway, yeah Arthur here and I, we go back a ways like he said, in fact he gave me my first big break. Well maybe not that *first* break, that happened in high school in the back of Bob Snyder's Mustang, but anyway. Art Summers, our new Poet Laureate—hey, congratulations, baby!—he gave me some great advice when I was just starting out. 'If you want to get to the top,' he told me, 'you got to start on the bottom.' And then he said, 'Turn over.'"

Flash!

Marjorie probably gave up her one chance to sleep with a Poet Laureate by photographing Professor Summers at that moment, with such a horror-struck look on his bright red face. His wide grin turned to a scowl in what looked like time-lapse photography, and he looked over his snickering audience as if they were a classroom of misbehaving children. Then he strode down from the tile steps and the party parted as he headed for the front entrance of the Benedetti house and left without saying good-bye.

Back on the tiles, Heidi shrugged and said, "Well, he never did last very long, as I remember."

But she had lost her audience. The party was revving up again with cocktail chatter, and the piano man began to play some pleasant ballad and I decided to go check on Carol. She wasn't at the piano, but there were Max and Beatrice, holding hands. She clinked a champagne glass against his beer bottle and sang along with the piano: "I've got a crush on you...."

"Hey, what's going on here?" Heidi stormed over and pointed at Beatrice's left foot, which was outside its shoe and resting on the top of Max's blue suede boot. "You playing footsie with my man, Beatrice?"

The piano player played on. Beatrice gently put the champagne glass on the piano's shiny top and put her foot back into her shoe.

"Huh?"

"Aw, sugar, old Beatrice is just trying to show me how to flirt at a cocktail party so I can keep up with you, baby," Max said, grinning. He took a swig of Bud. "Okay, baby?"

Heidi ignored Max. "You keep your hands and your feet to yourself, Beatrice. Max is my property. Everyone knows you screw your clients. Well, Max is not your client, and you're not screwing him. Is that understood?"

"Aw, Heidi," Max persisted. "She wasn't doing any of that."

"Oh shut up, Max," Heidi said. To Beatrice she said, "Make yourself useful for a change. Go get me a glass of champagne." She turned to the piano player and said, "Quit playing that stupid song."

Flash!

Marjorie was back among us. Heidi quickly dropped her fury and smiled sweetly at the camera, then at me, then at Carol, who had returned to the scene with a fresh glass of gin, then at the piano player, while Marjorie kept pointing and clicking her camera. The grande finale was a big kiss on Maxwell Black's lips. Lovebirds, you gotta love 'em.

"Come on, Maxwell," Heidi said. "I've had enough of this. Take me gambling."

Carol and I got away from the piano and walked around the perimeter of the living room and out onto the patio. "Well," she said, "welcome to the ABA. Having fun?"

"What a crowd," I said. "That old gang of mine."

"Not to mention that little redhead."

"What do you have against Marjorie?" I asked. "So New Yorkers are a little different from us, big deal. I can't wait to see her pictures of this party in *Publishers Weekly.*"

"Don't hold your breath," Carol said. "Marjorie Richmond is a phony."

"You keep saying that. You're just jealous."

Carol chuckled. "She's too short for you, chum. Anyway, I want to get back to the hotel."

"What if Marjorie isn't ready to leave?"

"Maybe the doorman will call her a cab."

Back inside, the party had thinned out, and uniformed caterers were picking up glasses around the room. We found Marjorie on the bench next to the piano player. He was a good-looking man even if his taste in clothes was a bit odd, even for Las Vegas. The two of them were playing, and replaying, and replaying, the first eight bars of "Heart and Soul."

"We're ready to go," Carol told her.

"Big day tomorrow," I added.

Marjorie took her hands off the keys and lost her smile, then found it again as she turned to her piano partner and said, "Casey, can you give me a ride home?"

Casey grinned. "Sure. My place or yours?"

"Whatever. Now, where were we?"

They got back into "Heart and Soul," and Carol and I got back into the warm desert night outside the Benedettis' ranch mansion. I gave the valet ticket to one of the teenage goons standing around in white shirts and clip-on bow ties.

As we waited for our car, Carol ruffled my hair and said, "Tell me again, Guy. Just what is it you found so charming about Heidi Yamada?"

Beatrice Knight

Opening the Door for a Star

Unlike a lot of you here today, I am not a poet. I don't even read poetry for pleasure. When I read poetry, it's all business.

I am in the business of recognizing talent. I am also in the business of opening doors. I am a literary agent. I'm good at what I do.

But the humbling truth is that if I am considered the best literary agent west of the Hudson River it is not simply because I know how to open doors. No, if I am successful—and let's face it, I am successful—it is because of the talent I choose to represent. I do not sell schlock. I sell only the best writing and represent only the top writers. The stars.

For the most part, Heidi Yamada managed her own career. She found her first publisher without my help, and she found her last publisher by herself also. But in a move that was fortunate for both of us, she allowed me to advise and direct and represent her when she made the giant step from the noble but obscure world of small-press publishing to the major leagues. The New York Literary Establishment.

The New York Literary Establishment can be a frightening jungle. Heidi was a sweet young poet just crawling with talent, just waiting to be taken advantage of. I was her guide. I opened some doors. I made sure the powers that be took notice, paid attention, paid respect, and paid well.

I am grateful to Heidi, not only for the fifteen percent—I worked for that—but for the gift of her loyalty and friendship, and for the honor of having polished such a bright, shining star.

The first time I ever talked to Beatrice Knight was when she called me up from the Miramar Hotel during the Santa Barbara Writers Conference back in 1981. I had never heard of her before, which she found difficult to accept.

"Oh come now, Guy dear, you are a publisher, are you not?"

"I am."

"Well, sweetie, every publisher knows who Beatrice Knight is, so don't pretend not to be excited and intimidated by this phone call."

"What do you want, Ms. Knight?"

"I want to give Heidi Yamada the jump start she deserves," she told me. "Do you have any objection?"

"What are you talking about?"

"Do you have an option on Heidi's next book?" she asked.

"No way."

"Good. I'm going to make her a star."

People have asked me if I resented the fact that Heidi Yamada deserted Guy Mallon Books after her first book and went on to sign with Random House for her second.

Hah. The truth is, I didn't even want to keep *And Vice Versa* in print, but I couldn't very well get out of it, after the first printing sold out so quickly.

Fluke or phenomenon or fraud? All I know is she pulled it off. She still had a key to Summers' office on campus and shortly before the book was due back from the printer she spent a weekend there, typing his entire Rolodex onto Avery labels. And she stole a full box of English Department no. 10 envelopes.

We ordered a thousand extra covers to be printed, trimmed, and shipped with the books, and when the shipment arrived we had the backs of the covers printed with an order form. Heidi wanted to print one of her poems on the back too, but I argued her out of that. The picture, the blurb, that was enough, I told her, and reluctantly, mercifully, she went along with it.

We sent the mailing out into the world to the Summers list and to my own catalog list. I didn't want to use my catalog list, but Heidi accused me of being ashamed of her book, and of course I couldn't admit that. She told me Summers was proud to have us use his list, which turned out to be a total lie, but by the time I learned that, the orders were coming in like bees to the hive, and I was too astounded to care.

The first printing of five hundred copies sold out in three months, all to full-price mail-order customers. Lawrence Holgerson ordered ten copies. The price was ten bucks. I gave ten percent to my author, which left me with $4500. I had doubled my money.

So I couldn't very well say no to a second printing, even though by then I was beginning to wish I had never met this prima donna.

I take that back.

I'll never regret and I'll always be joyfully grateful for those first six months with Heidi, when we were in production on *And Vice Versa.*

For one thing, she transformed the front half of my business from a junk store to an elegant bookshop, bright and colorful, with fresh flowers on the table and customers lined up at the register. She did that all herself, leaving me free to work in the back room, cataloging my postwar American poets and learning how to be a publisher.

Second, she made me a publisher. Because she expected me to do things right, I read all the books and learned the vocabulary. I signed up for the CIP program, got my ISBN prefix, joined

COSMEP and PMA, and subscribed to *PW.* Most people don't know what any of those initials stand for, and maybe they're lucky, but I was having fun.

Third, Heidi restored my sexual self-confidence, which had taken a nearly fatal beating with the death of my second marriage. She made me feel tall again—or at least she made me feel as I imagine tall people feel all the time. I won't go into details, but let me tell you it was worth it all, even the embarrassing success of *And Vice Versa.*

While it lasted.

It formally ended in the back room, when I wrote her the check for five hundred dollars, her ten percent royalty for the sale of *And Vice Versa.*

"What's this for?" she asked.

"You earned it."

"What, for the sex?"

"The what?"

"You don't have to pay me for all the lovin', Guy. You paid me plenty by publishing my book."

"Are you telling me that you slept with me just to get me to publish your book?"

She glared back. "Are you telling me you published my book just to keep me sleeping with you?"

We glared at each other as long as we could stand it, then both broke out laughing together. "Yes," we both said at the same time.

"And it was worth it," I said.

She nodded. "But the next book is strictly business."

"What next book?" I asked.

"Wait here." She left the office and returned a few minutes later with a manila envelope, which she handed to me.

"No sex for this one, honeybunch," she said. "This time it's all business. And another thing. You're going to have to find somebody else to mind the shop. I have my career to think about. As of now, I'm a full-time author."

"Heidi, I'm not sure—"

"You can't back out on me now, Guy. I'm a real poet now, and I'm a success. You made good money on my first book, and you have to keep me going. We're on a roll."

I handed the manuscript back to her. "Tell you what," I said. "I'll order a second printing of *And Vice Versa*. We sold five hundred copies in a couple of months. If the second five hundred sells that fast, we'll talk about publishing this new one."

She pouted. "Okay. It'll sell, and we'll do another book. Meanwhile, though, I'm not working for you anymore and I'm not sleeping with you anymore, and if I find a publisher who has more faith in me—after all, I'm a known quantity—I'm jumping ship, no hard feelings."

"Okay."

"And another thing. I want my original manuscript for *And Vice Versa* back. That's going to be valuable some day. To collectors."

"Okay."

"You said I had nice handwriting once, remember? About the only nice thing you ever said about me."

The second printing arrived in February 1981, and that's when I found out that I had published exactly the right number the first time. The books sat there. We had used up the mailing lists, and that was it. I got the local stores to stock a few copies, but Heidi's friends, if she had friends, were all out in Goleta where she lived, and I don't think they read books.

Meanwhile, I was getting busy on other book projects while I also built up my business as a rare book dealer.

Thus ended the short, happy career of the lovely and talented postwar American poet, Heidi Yamada. I wish.

She blamed it on me, of course. It's always the publisher's fault. "How come my book isn't in all the bookstores? Chaucer's, Earthling? It should be right up there on the counter, next to the cash register. The only store that has a decent display of *And Vice Versa* is Guy Mallon Books, and that doesn't count. How come the *Santa Barbara News-Press* hasn't reviewed my book? Have any sold yet? Jesus, Guy, what kind of a publisher are you?"

A happy one. I had plowed my profits into a second printing, and that second printing had fizzled, and now I had no
obligation to publish Heidi Yamada ever again. So I wasn't at
all distressed to hear her say, "So long, pal. If you're not going
to do anything for my career, I'll go it alone."

In June she signed up for Barnaby and Mary Conrad's Santa
Barbara Writers' Conference, an annual event at the Miramar
Hotel on the beach in Montecito, where writers come to work
on their craft and wannabes come to work on their careers.

She had me place twenty copies of *And Vice Versa* in the
conference bookstore, and she geared up for a week of classes,
cocktail parties, panel discussions, and heavy-duty shmoozing
with agents, editors, and famous writers.

Halfway through the conference she phoned me in tears.
"Nobody's bought a single copy of my book," she cried. "The
poetry teacher doesn't understand my work. Ray Bradbury won't
even talk to me. Who the hell is Ray Bradbury, anyway? He's just
some jerk from L.A. is all. I can't even get an agent to read my
new manuscript. This sucks, Guy. What am I going to do?"

Was this the time to tell her the truth? What was the kindest thing
I could say? "Heidi, maybe this is telling you something."

"Yeah? Like what?"

"Like maybe you aren't cut out to be a poet?"

"Oh fuck you." She hung up on me and my ear still smarts.

The next day I got the call from Beatrice Knight, telling me
she was going to give Heidi's career a jump start.

"Are you sure you know what you're doing?" I asked her.

"Guy, honey, I happen to be the most powerful literary agent
on the West Coast, even if you've never heard of me. Of course
I know what I'm doing."

"Have you read anything she's written?" I asked.

"No, and I don't need to."

"Don't you want to?"

"Frankly, Guy dear, I can't stand poetry. I don't even like most poets. But this lady is hot. I just spent the afternoon drinking wine with her, and I'm telling you, I can make her a star."

Which she did. The gossip I heard later was that Beatrice was at that time sleeping with Charles Levin, who had his own imprint at Random House. Levin had sent Beatrice on a quest to find him a hot young California poet. Like Erica Jong, he ordered, but more West Coast and more exotic.

Hence Heidi Yamada, the newest headliner for the house that had published such immortals as Robinson Jeffers and Rod McKuen—neither of whom Heidi Yamada had ever heard of, much less read. You could say that it was neither talent nor hard work but just plain luck that earned Beatrice Knight her fifteen percent of Heidi's six-figure advance for *Jump Start* and two other books. But given the fact that shortly after the contract was signed Heidi fired Beatrice and stole her lover, I'd say Beatrice was entitled to whatever she got and still had plenty of cause to be plenty pissed off.

You wouldn't think a high-powered top-notch agent would have much to teach a rinky-dink ivory-tower publisher of poetry books that only a few people bought and even fewer people read. But I'll never forget the valuable lesson Beatrice taught me: when at the ABA, it's important, vital, even essential, to get your hands on two drinks at a time, one for each hand. With all that's going on around you, you never know when you'll have a chance to get back to the bar.

The 1990 ABA officially began, as it does every year, with the voice over the public address system, the same voice every year: *"Ladies and gentlemen, in just a few minutes the doors will open and our friends the booksellers will start pouring in here. They're the ones we do this for, people, so let's give them a wonderful welcome. Your booths all look beautiful, and so do you. Have a great*

time, and enjoy the show." I've never seen that man's face, but he sounds like a kind uncle.

And here they came, nine o'clock on the dot. With their shopping carts and tote bags, up and down the aisles like Visigoths, grabbing samples. It was good to see them, as always, and a lot of them even stopped at our booth to look at our display of western poets. This year we had a big poster of Arthur Summers, because we were so proud to have the incoming Poet Laureate on our forthcoming list. There was his hawklike face, brier pipe and all, smiling sternly from our display panel, as if to say, "Buy my book if you want to pass my course." And right beside him, his most famous student, the charming and beautiful Heidi Yamada, smiling like the Happy Hooker, as if to say, "Buy my book and you'll get your money's worth." Both photos were ten years old, but both still commanded attention. And on the front table of our booth sat several stacks of books: fifty copies of Heidi's *And Vice Versa* (second printing), ten freebies each of several other better poets, and the four remaining advance reading copies of *On Second Thought,* the newest Summers collection, which we had scheduled for September. The Summers advance copies weren't freebies, but they were important to display and I might place them in good hands if the right reviewers expressed interest.

"I must say, Guy, your booth looks tremendous. Just fabulous, as always." I looked up from my clipboard to acknowledge the compliment and saw before me a face almost familiar. He knew my first name, so presumably I should know his. I let my eyes drop to his lapel and read his brown badge. Brown for media. "Taylor Bingham. *Metropolitan Book Review.*"

"Hello, Taylor," I said. He looked shorter, older, shakier, and a lot heavier than the prestigious book critic I used to know. Yes, I had heard that he'd become a drunk.

"You had to look, didn't you? My badge, I mean. You didn't recognize me, admit it."

"Sorry. I mean my brain's kind of overloaded, and I, uh…"

Taylor gave me a sad smile. "It's okay. I haven't been on the scene very much lately. Where's Carol?"

"She's taking a walk. We spell each other throughout the show, one hour on, one hour off. That way we both get some exercise and get to see the books."

"Glad to see you doing so well, Guy," Taylor said. "I must say."

"You haven't changed a bit," I told him. "Looking fit."

"Wrong vowel, pal."

"So you're with *Metropolitan Book Review* now?"

"I'm a stringer, selling lies for peanuts. I do fifty-word reviews for them. I won't tell you what they pay me. And they only pay me for what they use, and they only print good reviews, and the books they send me are crap. Small press books. Oops. I'm sorry. I didn't mean that. I mean if they ever sent me one of *your* books, you know I'd give it a rave."

"Okay," I said. "Next time we publish a book by Heidi Yamada, I'll send you a set of galleys."

"You do that," Taylor Bingham said, the smile now a hundred miles away. His face was flushed and his hands trembled out of his cuffs. "You do that and I'll wipe my ass with it. Guy, how can you keep that woman's face on your display year after year? I thought you liked poetry."

"Would you like a free copy of her first book?" I asked him. I picked one up and tried to hand it to him, but he folded his arms and shook his head. "Have you ever read it?" I asked.

"I tried."

Time to change the subject. "Are you going to Linda's party tonight?"

"I didn't get an invitation," he answered.

"That shouldn't stop you. Go by the Random House aisle and ask somebody. Tell them you're old friends with Linda. And with Charles."

The grin was back. "Linda Sonora and Charles Levin. Two of my favorite people. Sure, I'll be there," he said. "They're having a special on cyanide at KMart, two for one."

"Better get three," I said. "I hear Heidi's planning to be there too."

Taylor giggled. "Great. Lovely. Free booze and literary assholes on parade. I can't miss that."

"You're still holding a grudge, huh, Taylor?"

"Why not? I mean look at me. The three of them pretty much ruined my life, Guy. See you later. Have a good show." With that he slipped into the stream and floated away down the aisle, just as Carol returned from her walk.

"You just missed Taylor Bingham," I told her.

"That's nice," she said. "How is Taylor?"

"He looks horrible."

"Last I heard he tried to commit suicide. Now he's at the ABA. What a glutton for punishment."

"See any good stuff on your walk?"

"The Bridge Publications booth is staffed by aliens on steroids again. The small press ghetto is nice and quiet. The women's rooms are clean. The Consortium aisle is very tasteful. Random House brought most of the city of New York. Your friend Charles Levin brought his office."

"I'd better get over there," I said. "I want to score us an invitation to their party tonight."

Carol opened her ABA program and pulled out a printed invitation. "I've already taken care of that. Charles Levin gave me one. It's for us, he said. You and me. Nobody else. He was very clear about that." She handed me the card.

"You Are Cordially Invited," I read aloud, "to Join Charles Levin and the Staff of Random House for a Celebration of *Very Hot Plate,* a new novel by Linda Sonora. Saturday Evening, Nine O'Clock. The Elvis Mansion. Shuttle Buses will depart the Hilton Hotel at 8:45 p.m."

"The Elvis Mansion," Carol said. "Such class. Bennett Cerf would have loved this. Charles keeps those invitations in his desk. Locked."

"He has a desk here?"

"I told you. He brought his whole office."

"Do you think he's trying to keep anyone in particular away from the party?" I asked her.

"Guess who," she said. "And I bet Linda doesn't want her there either, and after last night I don't blame either one of them."

"I'm going for a walk," I said.

"Have fun." She handed me our ABA program so I wouldn't get lost.

I strolled down aisle after aisle. The colors of the ABA are dazzling. The noise is like the steady roar of freeway traffic. The energy level is high and happy, especially on the first day, Saturday. The stacks of freebies, the gladhanding sales reps, the wandering horde. I ended up, as I always do, at the Random House aisle. A small press publisher can feel lost and insignificant at the ABA, but I don't worry about that much. Another way to look at it is to remember that I have as much right to be showing off my stuff as this overblown giant. I remember when Random House just meant Random and Knopf and the Modern Library and Vintage paperbacks. Maybe Pantheon. Now it's new publishers every season. Ballantine? What's Random House doing publishing mass market paperbacks? Crown Books, the king of instant remainders? Sierra Club calendars? Random House is the big top, and I felt like a kid at the circus walking into their aisle.

At one end of the aisle Julia Child had a full kitchen set up and she was cooking recipes out of her latest cookbook from Knopf. Huffing and grinning and chattering with honest charm, she worked hard, flanked on both sides by tall men in full-white chef's costumes and hats. The sous-chefs didn't do any cooking; I guessed they were just there for decoration or protection.

As the crowd gathered around Julia, I wandered on. I nodded at John Updike and Anne Tyler, who were sitting in armchairs against a wall holding hands, but they didn't nod back. On the wall above them was an enormous poster, a blow-up jacket of a book they had both blurbed, *Very Hot Plate*. I picked up an advance reading copy and moved on.

I saw Lawrence Holgerson coming my way, his goatee'd chin darting this way and that, so I turned my back and hid my face in my ABA program. He was carrying two Penguin Books tote bags; they already bulged with freebies and it wasn't even noon.

At the far end of the aisle, sure enough, was a facsimile of an editor's office, and there behind a large oak desk sat the most important hip-lit editor in the New York publishing world. On the wall behind his desk was another giant poster of the big book of the season for Charles Levin Editions. *Very Hot Plate.* And there was the big editor himself, seated at the desk, pretending to edit a manuscript. He wore a blue blazer and a floppy bow tie and tortoise-shell glasses.

I knocked on his fake door and he looked up and smiled. "Hey, Guy," he said. He stood up and walked around his desk, hand outstretched. "I saw Carol earlier. I hope you'll be coming to our little party tonight?"

"How could I miss it?" I said. "I feel honored to be invited. I hear you're being pretty stingy with those invites."

We shook hands. "I have to, Guy," he said. "Christ, everybody wants to be there, but Linda wants some control. So do I. You wouldn't believe some of the people who have been hitting on me for invitations. Lawrence Holgerson, you know that idiot? And Beatrice Knight? Well, nothing against Beatrice, but she told me she wanted to bring Maxwell Black, and you know what that means. Taylor Bingham even asked me for an invitation, for God's sake. Haven't seen that son of a bitch for years, and now he comes by like we're the best of friends, with his hand out. You've got to draw the line somewhere, right? ABA parties can be such bullshit. So phony, you know what I mean?"

"So this will be an intimate little gathering of—"

"A couple hundred, tops."

We walked out into the aisle. "Quite a display," I commented.

Charles grinned. "Yeah. My team goes all out." Then he lost the grin. "What's going on down there?"

Loud popping. Smoke was rising from the far end of the Random House aisle, down where Ms. Child was cooking, and shouts rose above the hum of the crowd. People were rushing toward whatever was going on, and others were running away, in our direction. Charles strode off toward the action, and I scurried to keep up with him.

We were halfway there when one of Julia's sidemen, in full dress whites, stepped into our way. It only took an instant. No longer wearing a chef's hat, this man had a shiny bald head and a grinning face with big nostrils and a huge bushy mustache. I saw the arm swing around from behind the man's back, and the delivery. The chef's hasty retreat, running back where we had come from at top speed. I noticed that he was wearing running shoes.

"Fuck!" shouted top editor Charles Levin out of a face covered with custard pie. "Get that asshole! Shit! Get him! Get him!"

But nobody was pursuing the attacker. Everyone in sight was standing around taking in the spectacle of Charles Levin, who was wiping his glasses and then wiping his face with his hand and then licking his fingers and finally smiling. Smiling for the camera. *Flash!*

"Hello, Marjorie," I said.

"Hi, Guy! Isn't this great?" *Flash!*

Charles was doing his best to be a good sport. He smiled politely, and then he said to Marjorie, "And who the fuck are you?"

"Nobody," she told him. "Just a civilian. That was great! And who are you?"

"You're not from the press?" he insisted.

"No way. I just like to take pictures."

"You're not wearing a badge," he pointed out.

"Bye!" she answered, and she was off.

Charles and I walked back to his mock office, where he took off his blue blazer and tossed it over the back of his chair. "I have to get to the men's room and clean up. I wonder who the hell ordered that assassination? I just have to...*Holy shit!*"

"What's up?"

"Somebody broke into my desk! Look!"

I went around the desk and looked. Yes, the top drawer looked as if it had been pried open with a crowbar. There were ugly scars on the finish, and splinters on the floor and the chair.

Charles Levin felt around in the desk drawer, red fury clashing with the lemon custard on his face. "Call security," he told me. "Now!"

"Something missing?"

"My invitations. They're gone. All of them. Didn't you hear me? Call security!"

◇◇◇

Invitations to the Charles Levin/Linda Sonora/Random House party may have been rare and sought after, but anybody could go to the Baker & Taylor cocktail party held in the Hilton main ballroom starting at six. Consequently it was a huge crowd, all taking advantage of the free drinks and munchies. Carol and I liked the B&T party every year, because the noise level was so high and the group so large that there was little danger of getting caught in a conversation with somebody who knew about Guy Mallon Books. I suppose the reason for these parties is to shmooze and do business, but Carol and I had been doing that all day, and it was time to wash out the brains. We had a big evening ahead of us.

The only hard part was getting enough to drink before they ran out of liquor, so we had to get there fairly early. That meant a couple of hours standing around with drinks in our hands, because the shuttles for the Random bash didn't depart till quarter to nine.

After leaving the convention center, we'd walked back to the Landmark. No sign of Marjorie Richmond this time. I wondered if we'd see her at the Random House party later.

"I doubt it," Carol said.

"Why not? Wouldn't *Publishers Weekly* be welcome?"

"Guy, you are so gullible." She kissed me. "Let's get cleaned up."

So we changed our underpants and washed our faces and brushed our teeth, and I put on a bow tie.

"My aren't we fancy," Carol commented.

"I want to look good in *Publishers Weekly*," I said. I picked up my Penguin bag and looped the handle over my left arm. I held out my right arm to her and said, "Shall we?"

The Hilton was a short walk, which seemed like a long walk in the hot Nevada afternoon, but the ballroom was air-conditioned, and sure enough, there was a crowd and there were free drinks at the bar and there was a table heaped with jumbo prawns, brie, grapes, hard-boiled quail eggs, and raw broccoli morsels to dip in roquefort. We gulped our first drinks and got our glasses refilled, then got our hands full of chow and wandered into a sea of loud strangers, glad not to have to talk for a change.

"Guy, Carol, darlings! I'm so glad to find you!"

We turned and faced her, the most powerful agent on the West Coast. "Hello, Beatrice," I said. "Can I buy you a drink?"

"I've already got two." She held up her hands, each containing a cocktail glass. "Gotta work this bar fast. So. Are you going to the Levin affair this evening?"

"Yeah," Carol answered. "You?"

Beatrice chuckled gaily. "Well, technically my Levin affair ended nine years ago, but yes, I'm going, probably to Charles' chagrin. I wouldn't miss this one."

"So were you on the guest list?" I guess my first drink was enough to give me a loose tongue. "Or were you part of the pie plot?"

She laughed. Agents laugh a lot. "I have an invitation, and I won't tell you how I got it. But I don't know who gave Charles the pie in the face, and I have no idea who stole the invitations. My supplier didn't tell me where they came from, and I didn't ask."

"They? You have more than one?" Carol asked.

"One for me, and one for Max Black. I slipped it to him on the ABA floor this afternoon. I hope he makes it."

"Are you really hoping to represent him?" I asked.

"I have a once-in-a-lifetime opportunity for him, if he'll take it. Gibbs Smith is doing an anthology of modern cowboy poetry, and he wants Max to edit the collection and write an introduction. I told Gibbs I was Max's agent."

"Which you're not," I pointed out.

"So? Agents are allowed to lie, that's understood. But they have to make good. I have to get Max on board. My reputation and my word are at stake here, not to mention a good piece of change."

"And Heidi's what?" Carol asked. "Jealous?"

"Heidi Yamada is possessive, grasping, bitchy, vindictive, call her what you will." Beatrice took a sip from each glass. "And

Mitzi's just as bad. I've got to get Max away from those two. It's for his own good."

"And yours," I said.

"What's this about Mitzi being in trouble?" Carol asked.

"Hah! I love it. That's why she's so in debt, you know. She has so much invested in this new Yamada book, and if it doesn't come out, she'll be totally screwed. I love it!"

"What's holding it up?"

"Hell if I know. Some disagreement. Some delicious catfight. Meanwhile, Mitzi's in hock big-time."

"It couldn't be that bad," I said. "The book hasn't gone to press yet, so she hasn't had to pay a printer or a binder."

"Well, from what I heard, she paid Heidi a ten-thousand-dollar advance, for one. Then there's the cost of her ABA booth, for two, which she's not even using. Then there's the WESTAF award, which cost her a pretty penny."

"What?" Carol said. "You can't buy that award."

Beatrice smiled a miss smartypants smile. "Mitzi didn't pay WESTAF, of course. But from what I've heard, she paid the judges plenty, and there are five of them."

"That's outrageous," I said. "She bought the judges? How much?"

"Not money, of course. That would be beneath even her, and even them. No, but there were crates of Santa Barbara olives and cases of Santa Ynez Valley wines. You'll see over the next year several full-page ads for Ongepotchket Press books in every issue of *Puddle City Review.* And one of the judges, who will remain nameless..." She winked.

"What?"

"Refused to accept money or gifts but told Mitzi he wouldn't say no to a blowjob."

Carol turned her back, gin snorting out her nose.

"So did she?" I asked.

"Heidi got the award, didn't she?"

Charles Levin

Do It Anyway

One of the dangers of being successful is the temptation to stop taking chances, to settle into a comfortable rut, just doing what you do until one day you wake up bored.

Ten years ago, I was on the brink of boredom. Drugged with success, I found it harder and harder to get up in the morning and go to my office. Random House was paying me well and my authors were a stable of thoroughbreds. I should have been proud and full of energy. Instead, I was smug and fed up. Why? Because I hadn't taken any chances in years.

That's the state I was in when Beatrice Knight introduced me to Heidi Yamada. It was late June, 1981. Beatrice called me from the Santa Barbara Writers Conference and told me she had discovered a star. "Exotic," she said. "Ethnic. You'll love her."

"Never mind that," I said. "Can she write?"

"Never mind that," Beatrice said. "She's gorgeous. She wants to meet you."

Beatrice had steered a lot of good writers my way, and I owed her one. "If you tell me she can write, I'll be glad to read her manuscript," I said. "Send me something to read."

So she did. She sent me a copy of that first book, And Vice Versa, *published by Guy Mallon, the one with the picture of the poet on the cover. I took one look at that face and gave Beatrice a call. "Bring her to New York," I said. "I want to meet her." I was kidding, of course.*

I took that book home with me that night and read it. I read that slim volume cover to cover, twice, without getting up from my chair. I was knocked out.

This was poetry unlike anything I had ever published. It was unlike anything I had ever read. It was, well, different. *It was outrageously different. Different to the point of being extremely risky.*

Was I making a huge mistake? If I were to publish this woman, this Heidi Yamada person, would I be gambling my reputation as a connoisseur of good writing on a book that nobody would understand?

Did that matter, if I understood the work? No. Do it anyway.

For that matter, did I understand the work? Did I understand the poems I had just read? No. Do it anyway.

Did I like them? Not really. Do it anyway. *I looked at that cover-girl face again.* Do it.

I picked up the phone and called the West Coast. "Beatrice," I said, "I want to meet Heidi Yamada."

"You already told me that," Beatrice said.

"This time I mean it."

The following Monday morning, Heidi Yamada walked into my office and into my life, and for better or for worse, I haven't enjoyed the luxury of boredom since.

My relationship with Heidi Yamada was, I'm the first to admit, stormy. She was, as you all know, a strong-willed woman with confidence in spades. She could be a pain in the neck. And I still don't understand a lot of what she wrote.

But by God she was something. "Different" hardly does justice to how different she could be, as well as how difficult. And I give her full credit for giving me the kick in the pants that I so desperately needed when I was wallowing in the doldrums of success.

Thank you, Heidi. Sleep well.

After signing her three-book contract with Charles Levin/
Random House, Heidi was suddenly rich. She bought a house
in Connecticut, so she could be closer to her publisher—and to
her editor—during the production process. I guess she had some
notion that the powers that be at Random would give her the
same kind of artistic control that Guy Mallon Books had given
her in the small press arena. And perhaps she was right about
that, because *Jump Start,* like *And Vice Versa* before it, featured
a full-bleed photograph of the poet on the front cover, this time
wrapped in silk and looking like a cross between Madam But-
terfly and Ava Gardner.

At any rate, for the next couple of years Heidi didn't spend
much time in Santa Barbara, although she bought a home here
too, a Spanish-style bungalow on the Riviera with an ocean view.
But she only came home when she was on book tour.

So most of what I know about her Random House years I got
from fairly reliable sources. Gossip, yes, but believable. During
those years, as I thought of myself less and less as a bookseller
and more and more as a publisher, I was busy hobnobbing
with the Santa Barbara literary community. I became a regular
at the Wednesday writers' lunch, a tradition started by Ross
Macdonald and kept alive by Barnaby Conrad. A bunch of us
writers and literary hangers-on would convene once a week for
lunch at the Miramar, where the food was second-rate but the
gossip was delicious.

Eventually, at least once a Wednesday, the gossip would get
around to Heidi Yamada.

When her third book, *Second Helpings,* made it to the *New York Times* bestseller list, mystery writer Wilson Williams was outraged. "It just goes to show you the hypocrisy of the East Coast Literary Establishment," he fumed. "I mean, for God's sake, how could a poetry book possibly make it to anybody's bestseller list?"

"It's not the poetry that sells the book," Lefty James remarked. "Did you see that one of her poems was printed in *Cosmopolitan?*"

"I don't read *Cosmopolitan,*" Paul Shelley said.

"I saw that issue at my doctor's office," Betsy Danforth said. She was our gang's one real poet. "I read Heidi's piece, but I wouldn't call it a poem."

"What would you call it?" Wilson asked.

"Words," Lefty answered for her. "Words on paper. That's all writing is. Helen Gurley Brown doesn't publish poetry. She publishes words. And this month's words are Heidi Yamada. She's the flavor of the month. Besides, I happen to know that Helen will print anything Charles Levin tells her to print."

"Charles Levin is a son of a bitch," Paul offered. "Everybody knows that."

"They're all sons of bitches," Wilson said. "All publishers are sons of bitches." He turned to me and said, "Not you, Guy. You're a good publisher."

"What I don't understand," Paul said, "is how Charles Levin has managed to turn that little no-talent into a superstar. It's no mystery, of course, why he published her in the first place."

"I'd like to know what her secret is," Lefty said. "He's rejected every book I've sent him. Helen won't buy my stories either. What do they want? I'll tell you what they want. They want me to write tell-all bullshit about the movie stars I've slept with, and I keep telling them—"

"Why do you think Levin signed Heidi?" Betsy asked Paul.

"Because he's sleeping with her, of course," Wilson said. "Why else would anybody publish a book of poems by Heidi Yamada?" He turned to me and said, "Not you, Guy. Not you, of course."

"No comment."

"Well, they've got good marketing, is all I can say," Paul said.

"You mean the cover?" Lefty said. "The bare ass?"

It's true. The cover of *Second Helpings* did not have a facial portrait this time.

"I wonder if that's her ass," Wilson mused. "Heidi's, I mean."

I realized that everyone at the table was looking at me for an answer. I kept my mouth shut.

"All publishers are prostitutes," Wilson Williams said. "I mean what kind of statement does that cover make? It just means 'buy this product.'"

"No," Betsy said. "It means 'kiss my book.'"

Those were two golden years for Heidi Yamada. The first Random House book, *Jump Start,* didn't sell especially well, although it did get reviewed by *Publishers Weekly* (the review consisted of a single punctuation mark: "?") and by *Newsweek* (that review made about as much sense as the book itself). The second book, though, the one with her bare buttucks on the cover (yes, they were Heidi's), was the bestseller, the one that put our home-town princess on the cover of *People.* Insiders were beginning to predict a bright future for Heidi Yamada.

"Maybe someday she'll learn to write," Paul Shelley said one Wednesday.

"She could enroll in the Famous Writers School," Mickey Raskin suggested. "If they'll take her."

"She could never pass the entrance exam," Paul said. "They wouldn't even let me in the Columbia Record Club."

It was all jealousy, of course. When Heidi came to Santa Barbara for the *Jump Start* book tour, we were all in line at the Earthling Bookshop. When *Second Helpings* was plastered all over the windows of Chaucer's and stacked up in towers on the front counter, right by the register, we were all on hand to kiss her cheek and buy her book, and vice versa.

Speaking of which, Charles Levin called me up in the fall of 1983, after *Second Helpings* had finally dropped off the *NYT* list, and offered to purchase the reprint rights to *And Vice Versa.* I

else knows who they are at the most exclusive party in Las Vegas. We suddenly knew for sure that nobody here knew us, knew about us, or cared to know about us.

We followed a stream of chattering, chuckling publishers and booksellers through the overdecorated living room and out into the back terrace, which had been converted into a moonlit ballroom with a guitar-shaped swimming pool in the center. A bar was set up at one end, above the neck of the pool, and behind the bar was a long buffet heaped with delights flown in for the occasion from opposite coasts. Lantern-lit tables flanked the pool and filled the space to the garden walls. At the other end of the pool, a stage was set up for a jazz quartet. I recognized the piano player, Casey, from the night before; he played along with drums, a bass, and a guitar. Lines of "This Is a Lovely Way to Spend an Evening" slipped between cracks in the din.

Well, maybe lovely for some. I felt lost. I think Carol felt out of place too, from the way she gripped my hand, but she didn't complain. It was too noisy for us to talk to each other anyway without yelling.

"Guy!" someone yelled. "Guy and Carol! Over here!"

We looked, and there we saw a table with friends. Friends? Well, people we knew anyway, and we rushed to their safe company, threading our way among tables filled with strangers.

As luck would have it, we got to the table at the same time our host, Charles Levin, arrived, holding hands with the guest of honor, Linda Sonora. He looked elegant in his white jacket and black tie. She looked dazzling in a sparkling midnight blue evening gown cut low so that a long necklace of garnet beads could fall into and be warmed by her cleavage. Charles shook my hand and Linda kissed the air beside my cheek.

"So, Charles," Beatrice Knight shouted over the din, loud enough for the people at our table to hear, "you're here to check on how many two-bit Californians crashed your party?"

Charles smiled graciously. "You're not two-bit, Beatrice. None of you Californians are two-bit. And you're all welcome."

"I'm not a Californian," Taylor Bingham said, knocking over his drink.

Beatrice held up a cocktail glass and said, "To Guy Mallon, the last honest publisher in America!"

"Hear, hear!" Mitzi Milkin cried.

"Har, har," Carol muttered, loud enough for me.

"Well I like that!" Charles fumed with a mock scowl, or at least a scowl that quickly turned to laughter.

"Charlie, my boy," Linda said, "it's time for another trip to the bar."

With that the two of them flashed more glamorous teeth at us and proceeded to the next table, and Carol and I sat down among friends. Around the table: Mitzi Milkin, Arthur Summers, Beatrice Knight, Maxwell Black, Carol on my right, and on my left Taylor Bingham, who was already clearly stewed, his eyelids at half mast and his tie in a puddle of kung pao chicken.

"We're missing someone," Carol remarked. "So where is she?"

"Who's that, dear?" Mitzi asked. Mitzi was overdressed as usual, wearing both a diamond pin and pearls. Her stiff lacquered hair looked as if it had been manufactured in New Jersey. You had to hand it to Mitzi, though. Over the hill, maybe, but still a dish. Statuesque as a showgirl, with a smile like an obscene phone call.

"You know who she means," Beatrice snapped. "Has anybody seen her?"

"I doubt if she was invited," Arthur said. "But then Max is here, so—"

"Max is with me," Beatrice said. She adjusted the yellow bandanna at his throat.

"Max?" I asked. "Where's your fair lady?"

"Ol' Heidi?" he said, brushing Beatrice's hand away. "She said she'd be here, told me to meet her here. Said she had somewhere to go first, and me, I don't ask questions."

"Max is here with me tonight," Beatrice repeated, covering his hand with hers. "He's my new star client."

"That's not official yet," Max said, to all of us because all of us were staring at him.

"How's Heidi going to take that?" Mitzi asked.

"In stride, let's hope," Arthur Summers commented.

"I'm not a Californian," Taylor insisted. "I'm a two-bit Massachusian. A Massachu-settsian."

"Come on, Guy," Carol said. "Let's go stand in line for some food."

"I'll join you," Arthur said. "I'm starved."

I wondered how long it would take for him to show up. I'm sure he wasn't properly invited to the party, but like a lot of people, he had scored an invitation somehow and here he was, snaking his way through the crowd to where we stood in the food line. He looked different, perhaps because he had shed the mustard-stained linen jacket and was wearing a blue blazer and a regimental striped tie.

He barely acknowledged Carol and me, just nodded and said, "Carol, Guy." Then went straight to work: "Mr. Summers, I'm so glad to see you, because I wanted to congratulate you in person."

Art smiled down on the obsequious collector and said, "Thanks, Lawrence. Nothing special, my number just came up, that's all."

"Oh nonsense," Lawrence replied, with adoring eyes. "Poet Laureate? That *is* something very special indeed, and you deserve it."

"Lawrence, are you butting in line here?" Carol asked. "You'd be welcome to join us, but I'm afraid our table's full."

"No no no no no," Lawrence replied. "I must be rushing off. I just wanted to pay my respects. Oh, but before I go, Mr. Summers, could I impose on you?" He pulled a book out of his Penguin tote bag, then fished out a pen. "Could you do me the honors?"

Art chuckled graciously and took the book and pen from Lawrence. He signed with as much flourish and grace as a person could manage standing in a crowded line, then closed the book.

"Hold on," I said, taking the book out of his hand. "This is an advance reading copy. From our booth, right? Where did you get this, Lawrence?"

"Well, I acquired it," Lawrence sputtered. "I am a book collector, after all."

"Right," Carol answered. "You lifted it off our display table yesterday afternoon, before the show even opened."

"Well, freebies are freebies, right?"

"Right, but that wasn't a freebie. It's a display copy to show, not give away. We only brought five copies."

"My mistake," Lawrence said, smiling boyishly. "But now that it's signed to me, I guess there's not much to be done about it." He snatched the advance reading copy out of my hand, deposited the book in his tote bag, and turned to go.

"Just a minute," Carol said. He stopped and turned. "You forgot something, Lawrence."

"What? I really have to be going."

Carol took the pen out of Art Summers' hand. "Here. Your pen."

"Thanks." Lawrence snatched the pen, turned again, and vanished.

Art laughed. "What a character. Same old Lawrence Holgerson."

"Not quite," Carol said. "This one's the new and improved Lawrence Holgerson."

"The blazer?" I asked.

"No, the goatee. He shaved it off."

Somebody behind me in line gave me a gentle shove that almost demonstrated the domino theory and said, "Could you move forward, please?"

"Oh, I forgot," Carol said. "Las Vegas is on New York time."

I never did get back to our table with my food. Halfway there, I heard, "Guy, come here a second, wouldja? You gotta do me a favor."

I parted company with Carol and Art and weaved over toward the VIP table, where I could see that Taylor Bingham had plopped himself down next to Linda Sonora and was treating her to an earful. Charles Levin rose from the table and rushed to meet me halfway. "I want you to get that drunk piece of shit out of here," he said. "Now."

I looked up at his furious face and said, "Charles, do you think I'm big enough to be a bouncer?"

"He seems to respect you, for some reason," Levin answered. "Come on, you owe me one."

"I do?"

"You're having a good time, right? Good food? Free drinks?"

"You're right," I said. "I owe you at least one. Thanks for the invitation. Who invited Taylor, by the way? Was that you?"

"Hell no. Now get him out of here, please, Guy. Put him on one of those shuttle buses."

"Are they running now?"

"They're supposed to be running all evening. Maybe you'll have to wait because it's so early they're only using one or two of them. I don't care, just get him out of this house. He's spoiling it for Linda. She's going to be making a speech in a few minutes, and Bingham is spooking her. Just take him for a walk, is all I'm asking. Push him in a ditch. Hail a cab, I don't give a fuck, just get him out of my party before…oh no."

"What?"

"Oh *fuck.*"

"What?"

"Look over there." He nodded across the terrace to the table where the Californians were sitting, and there she was, the rival of honor, moving about the table bestowing kisses.

"Don't ask me to get rid of Heidi too," I said. "I know I'm not that big."

"Excuse me?" *Flash!* Marjorie Richmond stood before us with a grin and a camera. She wore striped stretch pants and a slithery silver top. "Again?" she said. "Smile, publishers!" *Flash!*

Levin said, "Who are you?"

"*Publishers Weekly,*" Marjorie told him. "Hi, Guy. Great shot of you two. Heidi Yamada's publishers, right?"

"Once upon a time," Levin admitted. "Now if you'll excuse us, miss—"

"Don't mind me," Marjorie said. "Listen, I'll try to get Mitzi Milkin over here. Maybe I could get a shot of all three of you together, like all of Heidi's publishers? Maybe with Heidi in it too?"

"You don't want to do that, Marjorie," I said. "Bad combo."

"We're busy right now," Levin said. "If you don't mind."

Marjorie said, "One more." *Flash.* "Great! Bye." With that she was off, hauling her cameras and flashing the literati along the way.

So I followed Charles Levin back to his table, gave gorgeous Linda another peck on the cheek, and tapped Taylor Bingham on the shoulder. "Taylor, could I talk to you for a few minutes?"

Taylor stumbled up from his chair. His eyelids weakly defying gravity, he nodded at me, then at Charles Levin, then at Linda Sonora. "Remember, Linda," he pontificated. "There *were* times. I just don't want you to forget that there were *times.*"

"Right, Taylor."

"Times."

"Times, Taylor. Of course there were. Thanks, Guy. You two have a good talk."

"Have a good walk," Charles added.

"Come on, Taylor," I said. I set down my plate of food, which was getting cold anyway, and led the book critic away from the table toward the door to the main part of the house.

Inside Elvis' parlor, we sat on a white leather couch and Taylor began to weep. "You should have known Linda, Guy," he bubbled. "She was such a sweet person once. She was the light of my fucking life."

I never know what to say when somebody does stuff like this. "Yeah, well."

"See? You know what I mean," he went on. "People used to listen to what I had to say. You remember. I was an important critic then."

"You were sober, too," I commented.

"Not all the time."

"But some of the time."

"Quit busting my balls," he said. "You know, I'd still be an important critic if it weren't for that bitch."

"Linda?"

"No, not Linda. God. Yamada."

"Taylor, Charles Levin kind of wishes you'd go home now. Should we call you a cab?"

"Home? I don't live in Las Stupid Vegas." He put his feet on the marble coffee table before him. With that his eyelids gave up the fight. He fell back into the white leather cushions and hiccupped, then sobbed, then snored.

Well, I hadn't gotten Taylor onto a shuttle or out of the house, but I was pretty confident that he wouldn't be wrecking Linda's speech, so I got up from the couch and walked back out onto the terrace. I was hungry. My plate of food was on Charles' and Linda's table, but I didn't want to go back there, so I returned to the buffet table. They had run out of food and were cleaning out their hot trays. So I picked up another drink at the bar and a handful of cocktail olives and started a meandering stroll back to the California riffraff table, hoping to find that Heidi had already moved on and that Carol had not yet eaten all her food. The band had stopped, and all I could hear was loud, literary laughter all around me.

◇◇◇

When I got to the table, Heidi was hard at work putting everyone on the spot. "Guy Mallon," she cried as I sat down next to Carol. "The shortest, sweetest man I ever got, you know, like, published by."

"Howdy, Heidi." I turned to Carol and said, "Do you have any food left? Where's Arthur?"

"He never made it back to the table," she said. "Said something about seeing someone from the NEA he had to talk to."

"He saw me coming and went off like a jackrabbit," Heidi said. "Typical. Beatrice, what are you doing with your hand on my boyfriend's knee?"

Beatrice brought both of her hands above the table and showed them. "My hands are clean, sweetie."

"Looked like they were in the cookie jar."

Beatrice flashed a pleasant, businesslike smile and put one hand back into her lap, then brought it up again, her fingers folded around a bright yellow bandanna. "Look what I found!" she said. "Ta-dah!"

Heidi gasped. "You bitch! You give that back."

"It's mine now," Beatrice purred. She stuffed the bandanna into her bosom.

"God damn it, Beatrice Knight!"

"Heidi, honey, lower your voice. Have a couple of glasses of champagne and mellow out. You're going to embarrass yourself."

"You may not have noticed this, Beatrice, but I never embarrass myself," Heidi answered. "I only embarrass other people."

"I have noticed," Beatrice said. "You're good at that."

"Beatrice, I'm going to give you five seconds to leave this table. If you don't scram I'm going to scream your name out loud. I'm going to scream bloody murder."

Beatrice laughed. "Much as I love your singing voice, dearie, I do have to find the ladies' room." With that, she rose, ran her fingers through Max's hair, nodded to the rest of us, and walked away from the table.

Flash! Marjorie Richmond arrived at our table just in time to photograph Beatrice's exit. She sat down and grinned at us all. "So. How's everyone doing?"

Max's face was bright red. "Heidi, darlin'—"

"Go on, Maxwell," she spat. "Just go on. Go sniffing after your new girlfriend."

"Aw now Heidi—"

"Better hurry," she said. "Don't let her get away. You've already lost one girlfriend tonight."

Maxwell Black bunched up his napkin and threw it into the middle of the round table. "Screw it," he muttered. He rose to his feet and strode off.

Flash! Marjorie caught that exit as well.

Only a skeleton crew remained at our table. Heidi and her publisher, Mitzi; Carol and myself. The last of the California low-lifes, lost in a New York wonderland.

"LADIES AND GENTLEMEN, IF I COULD HAVE YOUR ATTENTION FOR A MOMENT…" Speaking of New York wonderland, Charles Levin was speaking through a microphone on the stage at the foot of the swimming pool. "IN A FEW MINUTES OUR GUEST OF HONOR, THE LOVELY AND TALENTED LINDA SONORA, WILL ADDRESS US AND TELL US THE SECRET OF HER SUCCESS. BEFORE SHE DOES, I WILL INTRODUCE HER, AND AT THAT TIME I'M GOING TO PROPOSE A TOAST. SO, MAKE SURE YOU HAVE A GLASS TO RAISE. THE BAR'S STILL OPEN. MEANWHILE, THANK YOU ALL FOR COMING, AND I HOPE EVERYONE GOT PLENTY TO EAT."

The applause was loud, and when it died down, a blond waitress was at our table, holding a silver tray toward Heidi Yamada. Heidi took one of the three champagne flutes on the tray. *Flash!*

Mitzi reached across the table, in front of Heidi's face, and snatched another of the glasses before the waitress could pull the tray away. The waitress stood there with a perplexed look on her face.

"Hey," Heidi said. "You already have a drink."

"I could use another," Mitzi said.

"So could I, then," Heidi said. She grabbed the last glass of champagne from the tray. *Flash!* The waitress opened her mouth, then closed it and rushed off.

"What's her problem?" Heidi wondered. "I'm sure there's plenty to go around." She drained her champagne, one glass after the other. "You don't mind, do you Guy, Carol?"

Carol shrugged. "I don't like champagne," she said. "Doesn't mix with gin."

"I don't like to drink champagne on an empty stomach," I said. "So Carol, what happened to your dinner?"

"I ate it. While you were brown-nosing Random House and getting your picture taken."

Marjorie said, "Isn't this great? Isn't this a great party?" *Flash!* That one left Carol and me blinking our eyes, seeing red spots, ready to break cameras. Marjorie turned to Heidi and said, "Move over next to Mitzi, Heidi. Let's have a picture of you and your publisher."

"Publisher my ass," Heidi mumbled. She turned to Mitzi and said, "This ABA sucks. You know why? You could have had some books bound, you know. A few books bound. You know. This is making me look dumb. You too. Dumb. Fuck."

"I'll send the sheets to the bindery after you sign them," Mitzi answered. "Not before. We've discussed this. I've already lost a lot of money on this project. God."

Flash!

"Oh put. That thing. Away," Heidi said. She sounded like she had two tongues in her mouth.

"Before I ram it up your ass," Mitzi continued. She yawned.

Heidi stood up and spread her arms, then let them drop. "I have to go pee. I have to find Max. I have to get out of here." She shuffled away.

I put my hand on Carol's and said, "Some party, huh?"

Flash!

"Oh for Christ's sake, Marjorie," Carol said wearily. "Give it a rest."

"Marjorie's just doing her job," I said.

"Brilliant," Carol said. "Keep it up, Guy. Maybe you'll get your picture in *Publishers Weekly,* and then you can retire."

"Looks like Mitzi Milkin has already retired," I said. On the other side of the table, the publisher of Ongepotchket Press had slumped forward with her shiny, scuptured head on the tablecloth. "This is some party," I said.

Flash!

Carol stood up. "I'm going to go to the bar," she said. "Then I'm going to try to find Arthur. He promised to dance with me after Linda makes her dumb speech."

"What about me?" I asked.

"Talk about a dumb speech," she said.

"Well?"

"You can dance with Marjorie," Carol said. "If she can put down her camera for five minutes. See you later."

So Marjorie Richmond and I were the only people still awake at the table. "Well?" she said.

"I don't dance," I told her. "And there's no music anyway. And I don't want to sit here and listen to a speech by Linda Sonora. And this party sucks. How about you?"

"Let's go for a walk," she said. "Let's look around the house. Maybe we can find Elvis. I want to shoot Elvis."

"He's already dead."

"Maybe."

We did not find Elvis. Apparently he had left the building. The same could also be said of Taylor Bingham, apparently. At least he wasn't still sacked out on the white leather couch in the parlor. As we passed through the front hall, we were nearly run down by Lawrence Holgerson, who was on his way out, his blazer over one arm and his Penguin tote bag over the other shoulder.

"Good night, Lawrence," I said. "Have a good time? Get some good autographs?"

"Yeah," Lawrence said. "Bye." He ran through the door to catch a shuttle bus that we could see revving up in the circular driveway.

"He's out of here," Marjorie observed. "That's what we folks from the right side of the Hudson call a New York minute." We watched the bus leave the drive and disappear beyond huge hedges into the Nevada night.

We walked back into the house and strolled its overdone rooms till we found a long hallway to parts dimly lit and off limits; it was roped off with a thick velvet cord. Marjorie took my hand. "Let's see what's back there," she said.

"Oh? I don't think—"

"Come on." She squeezed my hand. "I have to change the film in my camera." She ducked under the red velvet cord and stood up again on the other side. "Come on."

Okay, so I did. We walked softly to the end of the carpeted hall, turned a corner, and found a door that was slightly ajar. It was a huge bedroom, and although no lights were on, the full moon shone through the skylight and lit part of the room enough so that Marjorie could fish in her camera bag and open her camera.

"You really are going to change your film?"

"It'll only take a sec. Here," she said. "Hold this." She handed me the roll of exposed film, which I slipped into my jacket pocket. "Oh shit. My unexposed film's in my other bag. Oh well, whatever. Wanna kiss me, big Guy?"

"No," I said. "I'm not a big guy, and besides, I'm married."

"No you're not."

"Well, practically."

"Too bad." The moonlight danced on her slivery blouse, but that didn't change anything. I was still practically married to Carol Murphy, who was out there dancing with Arthur Summers, who *was* a big guy. Even *that* didn't change anything. I was still practically married.

"Do you suppose this was Elvis' bedroom?" Marjorie asked.

"Well, the bed is king size."

"Not even one little kiss?"

"We have to get back to that party," I said.

"Aw damn."

"Carol's pissed off at me enough as it is."

"Yeah. And I have pictures to take," she said. "Why is your wife mad at you?"

"She's not my wife. She's just mad."

"Why?"

"Because I'm with you."

"But we're not—"

"Let's go," I said. "It's been lovely."

I found Carol standing by herself at the side of what was now a poolside dance floor. The crowd had thinned out some and many of the tables had been folded up and rolled away, making room for publishers, booksellers, and celebrity authors to twist and shout. The jazz quartet was sending out music classier than this crowd deserved, but they had turned up their volume and they stuck to up-tempo tunes with insistent rhythm, and everyone on the dance floor seemed to be having a good time.

Carol did not. "There you are," she said when I touched her elbow. "Where have you been? You missed Linda's speech. What have you been up to, Guy? You and Miss Priss?"

"Looking around the mansion," I answered. "It's pretty cool."

"Smooching the little phony, too. I bet that's pretty cool."

I shook my head in disbelief. "'Little' is a relative term, Carol," I scolded. "And I still don't know why you think Marjorie Richmond's a phony. And what makes you think we were smooching?"

Carol put her drink in my hand and then put her hands on my shoulders. "I apologize for the word 'little.' That was insensitive and stupid of me. As for the smooching, it's written all over your face, in guilt."

"Is not."

"Is too. And of course she's a phony." She retrieved her drink from my hand.

"Is not," I said.

"Is too."

"Where's Arthur Summers? I thought you were going to dance with him?"

"Bathroom break," she said. "We've been dancing."

"What's it like dancing with someone so tall?"

"'Tall' is a relative term, Guy Mallon," she said. "Here comes Arthur now." She waved at the approaching poet, giving him a much bigger, much happier smile than the one I got when I joined her a few minutes earlier.

"I suppose you want me to leave you two alone?" I asked her. "It's written all over your face."

Arthur showed up with a scowl that spelled distress. Was he upset that I had returned? Was I a crowd? He nodded at each of us, then pulled a pipe out of his jacket pocket.

"Arthur, are you okay?" Carol asked.

"Yeah." He pulled his tobacco pouch out of another pocket.

"Don't start smoking, Art," Carol said. "I want you to dance with me."

Summers looked at me as if for permission, and I smiled and waved both hands in a gesture that signified chopped liver, and the two of them took to the dance floor, the world-famous poet lothario and my business partner, and I felt icy green.

I looked around, taking stock. It was a smaller and mellower party now. The band was a little louder, but the guests were much quieter. Maxwell Black was out there on the tiles, dancing with Linda Sonora, cheek to cheek in spite of the salsa beat. Beatrice Knight was seated at a table with Charles Levin, and they seemed curiously relaxed with each other and perhaps even happy. At another table, the table where I'd first sat down, Mitzi was still out cold, and Marjorie was there too, loading her camera. And I was standing on the outskirts of fun, all by myself.

I looked out across the dance floor and saw Carol plant a kiss on Arthur Summers' chin. The icy green got colder, greener. It was time to take a walk and see if I could learn to breathe again.

I went out into the front hall, and I could see through the front door that shuttle buses were out there waiting to take me away from this scene. Yes, I was tempted. Tempted to make a big statement by going back to the Landmark by myself. Wouldn't that be something. And who would take care of Carole, escort her home? Forget it. I sat down on a chair in the front hall and looked at the fists clenched at the ends of my wrists.

"Hey, there you are."

I looked up. Marjorie again. "Hey."

"Come on. Let's take a walk," she said. "We're not done exploring this place."

"I don't feel much like exploring," I said.

"Aw come on, Guy. Don't make me do this alone."

"Do what?"

"Sneak into Elvis' bedroom again."

"What do you want to do that for?" I asked.

"Well duh? Elvis Presley's bedroom?" She patted her camera case. "I'm a photographer, remember? Celebrity bedroom? Come on."

She offered me her hand but I kept my fists in my pockets. I didn't want her to know how cold my hands were. For a minute I thought about what Carol would say about all this, but I refused to feel guilty for something I had no interest in doing.

So Marjorie and I ducked under the velvet cord and walked side by side, not touching, down the forbidden hallway and back to the master bedroom. We walked in. The moon was still shining through the skylight. Marjorie closed the door and said, "Turn on the lights, will you?"

I found the light switch and flipped it up.

The ceiling light came on. Marjorie gasped. I turned. There was a body lying sideways on the bed. She was on her back. Her mouth was open, and so were her eyes.

"Holy shit!" I said. "That's Heidi."

"What's she doing here?" Marjorie asked.

I walked slowly over to the bed and looked down into her lovely face. Her hair was spread out and cascading down the side of the bed behind her head. Her arms rested beside her body, and her legs stretched out together. Her shoes were still on, and her clothes were modestly in place. I felt her throat and couldn't find a pulse. She looked comfortable on that king-sized, King-sized bed.

Comfortable and dead.

"Jesus Christ," I whispered. "Oh sweet Jesus Christ. Is there a phone in this room? We've got to call somebody. Heidi's dead, Marjorie. We've got to go out and tell somebody."

"Just a second," Marjorie said. "We'll do all that, but give me a minute." She already had her camera out of the bag, and now she started walking around the room, focusing and flashing, focusing and flashing.

"Marjorie, for God's sake—"

"Right," she agreed. "But this won't do any harm and she's not getting any better or any worse, so give me just a minute or two." *Flash!* "Good." *Flash! Flash!*

There was a loud knock, and then the door opened and a very tall man in a very black suit walked in. "Excuse me," he said, "but this room is off…" His expression went from businesslike to astounded as he took in the sights. Then back to businesslike again.

"We were just leaving," I said.

"I don't think so," he answered. He pulled a gadget off of his belt and held it to his mouth. "Mike? I'm in the master bedroom. Take a look, over."

The gadget spoke back. "Still can't see a damn thing, Steve. Check out the camera, over."

Steve turned and looked up to the corner of the room high above the door, and we followed his gaze. A yellow bandanna was hanging there, draped over what I gathered was a surveillance camera. Then he closed the door and walked over to the bed and took a long look at the body.

"Who is this?"

"We were just leaving," I tried again.

Marjorie had her camera bag open and was stuffing her camera into it.

"Give me the camera," Steve said. He held out his hand.

"But—"

"Give me the camera."

"Who the hell are you, anyway?" Marjorie thundered. "Why should I give you my camera?"

"I am security."

"So? You can't just take my stuff."

Security paused a beat and then said, "Believe me, lady, I can. Give me the camera."

Marjorie did as she was told.

"What's in the bag?"

"It's my purse," Marjorie told him. "Just my purse."

"Let me see."

"We were just leaving," I said.

"Will you shut up?" Steve told me. He got on his walkie-talkie and said, "Mike, we have a situation here. I need backup. Send a couple of boys, and call the police right away. Tell them to go to the back entrance, and then bring them to the master bedroom. Keep them away from the party. Get me backup right away." He hung the walkie-talkie on his belt and turned to Marjorie and snapped his fingers. "Bag."

"You can't—"

"Bag."

She handed him the camera bag and he looked inside. He took out Marjorie's other camera and put both cameras on the King's dresser. Then he fished out a handful of film cannisters and lined them up on the dresser. He closed the bag and set it on the dresser too.

"I need that film, you know," Marjorie complained.

"You'll get it back."

"When?" Marjorie demanded.

Steve crossed his arms and shook his head. "I have no idea, ma'am."

The door opened and two young men walked in. They were as tall as Steve, but not so dressed up. They wore tee shirts from Circus Circus and jeans from hell. They were grinning. "Hey, Steve," one of them said. "What's up?"

"Take these two nice people to the office," Steve told them. "Stay with them till the police show up."

"Who's the chick?" one of them asked, pointing at Heidi.

"She like dead?" said the other.

"Come on, move it," Steve said. "Take these people to the office. Stay with them. If they want some coffee or something, get it for them. Go on, now."

So we were ushered out of the master bedroom by big guys with big muscles, and we were led down a hallway to a stairway and up the stairway to another hallway and down that hallway to an anteroom and through the anteroom to what looked like the waiting room of a dentist's office. The walls were decorated with gold records. Marjorie and I sat next to each other against one wall; the strapping lads sat opposite us. "You guys want coffee?" one of them asked.

Marjorie said, "No."

I said, "No thanks."

"Cool," said one kid. He stood up and fished a box of Marlboros out of his jeans pocket, pulled out two cigarettes and gave one to his buddy, who fished a Bic out of his jeans pocket. They sat side by side, sucking on cigarettes, their knees bobbing.

Nobody talked for what felt like about fifteen minutes. Marjorie and I occasionally exchanged looks. I tried a smile once, and that earned me a mighty scowl, so I decided not to try another. A bit later she looked at me and shook her head in disbelief, as if what we were going through were bad management on my part. I shrugged.

"So," I said, when the silence was finally too loud, "what's up here? How long is this going to go on like this?"

One of the boys checked his wrist where he wasn't wearing a watch and then shrugged. The other one said, "No idea, dude."

"What if I have to go to the bathroom?" Marjorie asked.

"Do you?"

"No. Not now. But what if?"

"Rest room's through that door," the boy said, pointing to the back corner of the outer office.

"Thank you."

"Hey, no problem."

So much for conversation. We waited through several more cigarettes, and the room was smoky and hot by the time the door finally opened and Steve ushered in a couple of gents in light linen suits. One was blond and beefy and middle-aged; he reminded me of a jovial biology teacher I had in high school. The younger fellow looked like a palace guard: dark, handsome, good posture, and no expression whatsoever.

"I'm Detective Dan Plumley, with the Las Vegas Police Department," the blond man said. "And this is Detective Perry

Stone. We'd like to ask you folks a few questions." The two
police investigators opened their wallets together to reveal their
badges, then flipped them shut and pocketed them.

"Come on, guys," Steve told the young men.

The brawn patrol shuffled to their feet and followed Steve out
the door, and we were left alone with the detectives, who pulled
chairs away from the wall and sat down close to us, facing us.

"Stuffy in here," Dan Plumley said. "I wonder if there's a
window we can open. Have a look, will you, Perry?"

Detective Stone got up and wandered through the door in
back of the outer office.

"Now then. Could I have your names?" Plumley pulled a note
pad and pen out of his jacket pocket. "Starting with you, ma'am."

"Why are we being held?" Marjorie answered. "We don't
know anything about all this. And I need my purse back."

He smiled. "Your name, please?"

"Marjorie Richmond."

"Thank you. You, sir?"

"Guy Mallon," I said. I spelled the last name for him, and
he wrote it down.

Perry Stone returned to the outer office and said, "Those
windows don't open."

"Too bad," Plumley said, smiling. He handed his partner the
notebook with our names and the pen. "Really smoky in here.
Well, I guess we'd better make this brief, then. If that's okay with
you folks?" He winked.

"Where's my purse?" Marjorie said.

"It's downstairs," Detective Plumley answered. "I'll give it to
you when we're done here."

"And the stuff in it? My wallet, my cameras, my film?"

"We may have to hold onto the film for a day or two," Plumley said. "Make sure it doesn't have any photographs that shed
light on this case, things of that nature. I'm sure you understand.
You can have the wallet back, of course. And the cameras."

"I want those rolls of film returned to me as soon as possible.
I need them."

"Are you a photographer, Ms. Richmond?" Detective Stone asked. It was the first time he'd spoken to us, and Marjorie responded with a dropped jaw.

"Duh," she said.

Dan Plumley chuckled. "How about you, Mr. Mallon? What do you do?"

"I'm a publisher," I said. "Book publisher."

"Lot of you folks in town this weekend. Having a good time?"

"Sure," I said. "Up until about an hour ago."

"And how did things change an hour ago?" Perry Stone asked. This guy needed some lessons in the art of interviewing.

"I saw my first dead body," I said. Detective Stone dutifully wrote that down.

"That can be pretty upsetting," Dan Plumley said. "Let me ask you a few questions about that, so that we can get on with our lives. We're really in the dark here, and I'm hoping you folks can get us started on the right foot. Okay. First. Can you tell us the name of the deceased?"

"Heidi Yamada," I said. I spelled it for him.

"And what was she doing here at this party? Was she a publisher too?" He turned to Marjorie. "A photographer?"

"She was a poet."

Perry Stone was writing this all down. It seemed to take him half a page to write the word "poet."

"And how well did you folks know Ms. Yamada? Ms. Richmond, how about you? Did you know the deceased well?"

"Me? I hardly knew her at all. I had a photo shoot with her yesterday afternoon, that's all. I really don't know much about her. Listen, do we really have to answer all these questions? Aren't you supposed to be reading us our rights or something?"

"Miss Richmond, at this point we're not investigating a crime and you're not suspected of anything. If we were investigating a crime and we thought you were suspects, you'd be down at the station and we'd be talking to you separately. But that's not what's going on here. A woman is dead, probably because she took too many of the wrong kind of pills, and we're trying to find out something about her so we can put this matter to rest, and since you were there when the body was discovered and since you knew the unfortunate woman, we're hoping you can shed some light on this situation. Okay? Now then. Are you working for a newspaper, Ms. Richmond? I just wonder, because we like to keep the press informed but there are times—"

"Freelance," Marjorie snapped.

"Mr. Mallon? How did you know Heidi Yamada?"

"I've known Heidi for ten years," I said. "I was her first publisher."

"And what was the nature of your relationship? I'm sorry for being so nosy, but that's my job," Plumley said. "By the way, I'm not trying to grill you here, and I repeat: you're not under suspicion at this time. Okay?"

"What does 'at this time' mean?"

"Would you folks mind standing up?" Plumley asked. "Just for a second?"

We did as we were told, and I said "What?" with my hands.

"So what do you think, Perry?" Plumley asked.

"Not under suspicion at this time," Detective Stone confirmed. "You may sit down."

"Now then, Mr. Mallon. The nature of your relationship?"

"It changed," I said. "We used to be quite close."

"And now?"

"Now she's dead, right?"

"Before now. Recently, I mean." Plumley chuckled. "I can be pretty persistent. I think you can appreciate that. Wisecracks are fun. They're part of the job. But they take up time, and we're eager to get this over with. I think Ms. Richmond agrees, right?"

Marjorie nodded.

"Mr. Mallon? The nature of your relationship with Heidi Yamada?"

"We were lovers once, but that was almost ten years ago. We remained friends, but not good friends. Heidi had a way of ending close friendships."

"Sounds like quite a story there," Detective Plumley said. "Were there other people here at this party tonight that had been intimate with the deceased?"

"Quite a few."

"Lovers?"

"Lovers, or close friends. Like that."

"Can you tell me a little bit about them?" he asked.

"All of them?"

"Oh boy. We're in for the long haul, huh?" Dan Plumley scratched his cheek.

"Just a minute," Marjorie said. "Is there any way you could deal with me first and let me go? I'm supposed to be meeting somebody after this party, and the party may be almost over."

"We're sorry about the inconvenience, ma'am," Detective Stone said. "But somebody died, and it is imperative that we gather as much information as possible. I'm also sorry to tell you the party was pretty much over by the time we arrived. The caterers were cleaning up, and the last shuttle buses had left. We'll be driving you to your hotels after we're done here."

"The band has left?"

"Yes ma'am."

"Shit."

"You said we're not under suspicion at this time," I said. "What does that mean, 'at this time'?"

Plumley nodded. "We're looking for somebody pretty tall," he said. "Show them, Perry."

Detective Stone pulled a yellow bandanna out of his pocket. "Do you know what this is?" he asked.

"A yellow bandanna?" I guessed.

"Have you ever seen it before?"

"I've seen lots of them in my day," I answered.

"You see," Detective Plumley explained, "that bandanna was carefully draped over the surveillance camera in the room where Heidi Yamada died. Or at least the room where she was dead. It appears from the marks on the plush carpet that the person who covered that camera was standing on tiptoes, which makes sense, because that camera is very high on the wall. I'm afraid neither of you two would have been able to do that without a chair or something, and there's no indication that a chair was used. So for now (and that means until we get some other kind of information), Detective Stone and I are guessing that you two people just happened upon the body by accident, and that she was dead when you got there. Am I right about that?"

"Bingo," Marjorie said.

"And what were you two doing in that bedroom?" Stone asked. "It was off limits to the guests, so how come you were there?"

"I needed a dark room to change my film," Marjorie answered.

"Is that the way you remember it, Mr. Mallon?"

"Yeah," I said. "Pretty much."

"I was under the impression that you don't need a dark room for that kind of procedure anymore," Stone persisted. "And why did it take two of you to change one roll of film?"

"Okay," Plumley said. "I think we can let that go for now. Let's hear about Heidi Yamada, the poet, and all her close friends. Sounds like there's a lot to tell. Perry, you ready to take notes? Oh. Before we start, is anybody hungry?"

"I'm starved," I said. "I never got dinner."

"Maybe there's some food left in the kitchen," Dan Plumley said. "Perry, would you mind—"

"I really want to get this over with," Marjorie said.

"Okay," I said. "I can do this. I'll be brief."

"That's fine, Mr. Mallon. Take your time. Be brief. I think you know what we're looking for here."

It took me about twenty minutes to spill all the beans I could think of.

So we got to ride in the back seat of a police car. When I was a kid that would have thrilled me. At this point, I wasn't thrilled. I was hungry and tired, nervous and mad. Marjorie sat next to me, hugging her camera bag. They had given everything back to her except for the film. The car was clean and comfortable enough, although it was spooky to be confined like this: a wire mesh separated us from the front seat, and there were no inside handles on our doors.

Detective Stone drove, and Detective Plumley kept up a reassuring patter, pointing out the sights. Actually there weren't many sights in Elvis' old neighborhood, just empty streets and handsome houses. But when we got back to the Strip there were sights aplenty. "Sands," the detective said. "Dunes. Flamingo. A lot of history around here. You folks been to Las Vegas before?"

"Never," Marjorie said.

"I used to drive through back in the sixties," I said.

"It's changed a lot," Dan Plumley said. "I've lived here all my life. This part of the Strip used to be pretty much open country. A few of the big casinos were out here, you know, Frontier, Stardust, these ones we're coming to right now, but in between was just desert. Now look."

It was hard not to. The Strip was a jumble of franchise clones and strip mall staples—Thrifty Drugs, Arby's, Fast Foto, Adult BooXXX & Novelties, all still open for business—cramming all the space between the casinos, and the sidewalks were swarming with people gaily dressed for hot weather, even though it was nearly midnight. The lighting was as bright as day and twice as colorful.

"Saturday night in Las Vegas," Detective Perry Stone commented. "Nothing like it."

"Actually there is one thing just like it," Dan Plumley said. "And that's Las Vegas on any other night of the week. Here we are. Landmark Hotel and Casino."

Detective Stone pulled in front of the entrance and stopped. Detective Plumley turned around in his seat and addressed us. "Before I let you out, I have to repeat what I told you earlier. We can't have you mention any of what happened tonight. Not to anyone. Not until we give the story to the media. You two understand that? You agree to that?"

"Yes," I said.

"Ms. Richmond?"

"Yes."

"Good. Because if you want to see your film again, you will have to cooperate. We don't know what happened to Miss Yamada yet, and I don't want any speculation before we find the answers."

"But if I ask around and try to find out—"

"Don't do that, Mr. Mallon. I warn you: do not do that. That would be a big mistake, and you would not like what might happen."

"You make it sound—"

"Take my word for it. The people who run this town, and I'm talking about the tourist industry, but you know who I'm talking about, right? They do not appreciate a lot of idle talk about things like this. We do not have murders in this part of town. My guess is Miss Yamada died of an accidental overdose. It happens all the time. But until we know more, we know nothing. So you say nothing. Because if the word gets out that there's an investigation going on, you two are going to find yourselves behind bars, for your own protection. You will also be considered material witnesses and prime suspects. Let's don't let it come to that."

His shoulders were climbing up to his ears and the smile on his face had turned upside down. I was done being annoyed for the moment. I was frightened.

The car radio crackled and a voice said, "Danny? You there?"

Plumley took a mouthpiece off the dash and answered, "Here I am, pal. What's up?"

"We picked up a prowler in the neighborhood of that party you were investigating. We're holding him down here."

Plumley sighed. "Looks like it's going to be a long night. Okay, I'll be there in about fifteen." He turned back to us and said. "Okay? We have an understanding?"

"But the word's got to get out sometime," I said. "People are going to wonder. A lot of people spend a lot of time talking about Heidi Yamada."

"Let them wonder and let them talk," he said. "But you keep your mouth shut. Keep your eye on the paper. Miss Yamada's death will be reported, of course, probably in a couple of days. But only when we know what happened. When we've established for certain that it was an accidental overdose, is my guess. Once the news breaks, Ms. Richmond, I'll give you back your film and you two can go on your merry way."

He got out of the car and opened our doors. He handed each of us a business card. "In case you want to get in touch with me," he said. "Good-bye now. You all get a good night's sleep and enjoy the rest of your stay in Las Vegas." He smiled and got back into the police car.

As we watched the car disappear into traffic, I said, "Marjorie, I've got a couple of questions for you."

"I've got a question for you, too," she said.

"Do you suppose the hotel coffee shop's open?"

"Probably not," she said. "If it is, it probably sucks."

"How about across the street?" I pointed to the Paddlewheel, whose giant marquee read THREE-EGG BREAKFAST 99¢ 24 HRS A DAY!!!

"Okay, big spender," she said. She smiled, the first smile I'd seen since the last time she saw a dead body, and we walked across the street and into the insistent noise and glare of the casino.

The hostess at the restaurant wanted to take our names and have us wait among the slot machines, but I told her we were down to our last ninety-nine cents. She gave me the fish eye. "Look," I said. "You have a roomful of empty tables, and we're ready to drop. Have pity?"

"I'm diabetic," Marjorie added.

"Right this way."

A waitress took our order and while we waited for food, Marjorie said, "What did you want to know?"

"Is it true you were planning to meet somebody after the party tonight?" I asked her. "That's what you told the detective. That was true?"

"Yup."

"That piano player, right? Casey? The guy with the bad shirts?"

"His shirts aren't so bad. Why? What?"

"I didn't know you were going to be meeting somebody later is all. You never told me that."

Marjorie's look reminded me that I was still a short teenager among men. "Oh," she said. "So you're saying you weren't planning to meet up with Carol after the party?"

"Yeah, well."

"Yeah, well. So we both had plans for later. Does that mean I can't have a little fun while I'm waiting around for the band to quit?"

"And that's what I was? A little fun?" I asked.

"Yes, Guy. Yes. A little fun. How does that make you feel?"

I thought about that a minute, then felt a grin growing on my face. "Pretty good, actually. Pretty damn big."

"So quit being so touchy. It's not like we were going to do anything anyway. You made that clear. Good, here comes breakfast."

We ate without talking: greasy hash browns, runny fried eggs, toast medium rare. It was delicious. I enjoyed being across the table from Marjorie, with whom I'd experienced death firsthand, even if she didn't want to talk about it. She wasn't pretty anymore, or at least she looked a lot more tired than pretty, but I felt closer to her now. A little honesty is a great relaxer.

"So," she said when we were finished eating. "That's all you wanted to ask me?"

"No, that just popped into my mind. No, I want to know who you think did it. Killed Heidi."

She shrugged. "No idea. I don't want to know. Let's don't talk about it."

"But we can't talk to anybody else about it," I said.

"Fine. Don't talk to me about it either."

"Aren't you curious? Why don't you want to know?"

"What are you getting at, Guy? What's the difference? I'm here on assignment, I don't have time to play detective. There are real detectives on this case, let them do it."

"That's another thing," I said. "You're here on assignment? Why did you tell Detective Plumley that you were freelance? Why didn't you tell him you work for *Publishers Weekly?*"

"It was none of his business."

"Oh come on."

"Because I don't want to get fired, okay? Also, those shots I took of the body? I own those. If the cops turn them over to *PW,* they'll never be printed and I'll never get credit."

"So that's all those shots mean to you?"

"Hey. I'm a photographer, remember? She's a celebrity, remember? That was the Elvis Presley Memorial Mansion she died in, okay? Hello? Now let's don't talk about this anymore."

"Okay."

"And another thing," she said. "How come you told that cop about all those people hating Heidi? You're going to be the next one killed, you keep talking like that. Which may be okay with you, but I don't want any part of that. What made you say all those things?"

"I just wanted to be helpful," I said. "Maybe I did talk too much. But I want to know who killed her. Or if it was accidental, I want to know that too."

"Why?"

Why? Why did I care how Heidi Yamada died?

Because I could still remember how she made me feel when she first walked into my shop ten years ago, when she spread her arms and snapped her fingers and whirled her black satin hair in my face. Because she was my lover once, and I've never entirely gotten over that. And all of a sudden, right there in the restaurant of the Paddlewheel, I started to weep into my folded hands.

Marjorie Richmond cleared her throat. "Pay the bill," she said. "Let's go back to the hotel. It's been a long day."

I let myself into the room as quietly as I could. I needn't have been so careful. The bathroom light was on and the bathroom door was open, and I could see Carol in bed. She was snoring the way she does when she's had far too much to drink. Her clothes were scattered all over the room.

I went into the bathroom and closed the door. There was a note on the counter:

Guy—

If you come back and see this note, don't wake me up.
Please sleep in the other bed. Don't wake me up in
the morning, either. You're on your own at the show
tomorrow. I'm taking the day off.

C

I washed my face, brushed my teeth, and peed. I went back
out into the bedroom and emptied my pockets and put all my
stuff on the table by the window: my keys, my wallet, my comb,
my handkerchief, my pen, my watch-calculator, my ABA badge,
the party invite, assorted business cards I'd acquired that day,
and the roll of film from my jacket pocket, which I discovered
I was still carrying for Marjorie. I set it down carefully as if it
might break. I undressed and hung my clothes in the closet by
the light coming out of the bathroom. Then I picked up Carol's
clothes and folded them and put them on the dresser: her skirt,
her blouse, her jacket, her underpants, her bra. And another item
I couldn't see clearly in the shadow, so I took it to the bathroom
to find out what it was.

A yellow bandanna. I folded it carefully and left it on the
bathroom counter.

I went back out into the room and slipped the roll of film
back into the pocket of my jacket.

Taylor Bingham

Out on a Limb

First let me say what a pleasure, what an honor *it is to be among all of you again. My old drinking buddies. I have always valued my place in literary circles, and I have treasured the friendships I have made in this crazy business of literature. It's a brotherhood, or should I say a siblinghood, that is both very welcoming and very selective. As a prominent critic, which need I remind you, I was, I have been part of the welcoming committee. As a book reviewer I also wielded much power in the gate-slamming department. And I too know what it's like to be welcome, and I treasure my back-scratching, back-slapping, hand-shaking memories of better times. I also know how it feels to have a door slammed on my nose. In a word, ow. Like Richard Nixon and Frank Sinatra, I know what it's like to win, and I know what it's like to lose. I like winning better, but I know how important it is to lose if the reason you lose is courage.*

Anyway, thank you for inviting me to speak today. I didn't prepare a speech, so I'm sort of winging it here. I know you didn't ask me to speak about myself, but I had to say those few words about the experience of earning, enjoying, losing, and missing the admiration of my peers, because I feel that gives me an insight into what made Heidi Yamada the poet she was, and what made her lose the support of her closest supporters, and how she coped with failure, got stronger, and came back unafraid to tell the damn truth.

Heidi wrote because she had to write. She wrote what *she had to write. She didn't write to sell, and she didn't write to give comfort to the sentimental. She wrote from her brain and her heart and her gut and some other places I dare not mention. Heidi Yamada wrote what only Heidi Yamada could, and she wrote only what Heidi Yamada could write. It was as simple, and as strong as that.*

That's what I saw when I wrote the review of her work that earned me such scorn. If I learned anything from Heidi Yamada, it is that the pen is only mighty when it blazes a trail of truth. If that means going out on a limb, so be it. If the limb breaks, the cradle will fall, the cookie will crumble, the ball will bounce, and no one will salute.

I went out on a limb for Heidi Yamada because she went out on a limb for me. She dared to be experimental beyond anything that had ever been called poetry before, and I dared applaud. I went out on a limb, and I'm still out there. It's cold out here. But I'd rather be out here in the cold than basking in the warm, self-satisfied candelabra of a snotnose literary clique that's afraid to notice the genius of artists like Jackson Pollock, John Cage, Lenny Bruce, and Heidi Yamada.

That's another thing I learned from Heidi Yamada. Yeah.

Well, Heidi's here with us today, and so am I. Heidi's dead and much admired and remembered with love. Perhaps the same can be said of me already. Perhaps not. Maybe that posthumous recognition will come when I'm even deader, and perhaps not. Fact is, I don't care all that much.

I think I'll close by saying that there's a lot more I could say in defense of this woman, this poet, this star we've all started, too late, to appreciate. Remember, I appreciated her a long time ago, and I did so out loud. I still think the world of her.

By the way, after the service, if anybody would like to buy me a drink, I'll share with them some of the juicier things Heidi told me about Linda Sonora. Joke. Sorry.

Thank you very much.

Okay, so here it is, the review that changed Taylor Bingham's life and severed his connection with *Newsweek* and the rest of the New York literary establishment:

> With Jump Start, *the most innovative collection of poetry to be published in New York in the past many years, young and brash Heidi Yamada has reinvented the color wheel of the English language.*
>
> *One gets the feeling that Yamada, who rises from the ocean of small press publishing to surf the waves of the Literary Establishment, sees life not through a microscope or a telescope, but through a kaleidoscope. She is a poet for whom impressionism is carried to the extreme: the impressions are not created by images. Rather, the images are created by impressions, the clash of juxtaposition. The technique may not be easily explained, but it is helpful to know that what Jackson Pollock gave us with his paint and John Cage gave us in his music, Heidi Yamada dares us to accept in her poems.*
>
> *Vibrant splashes of color. Driving meters, unrepeating but insistent, a whirlpool of words you've never heard used together before. Even more striking are Yamada's references to a shared, pan-national human culture that mixes Greeks with Orientals, the Renaissance with the Old Testament, the art of Egypt with the paintings of Impressionism.*
>
> *But what is truly ground-breaking is Yamada's highly developed wordplay, a creative association of concepts that, by its very audacity, differentiates itself not only by*

quantity but in quality: Yamada has invented a new style of poetry all her own. This poetry knows its own vocabulary, works in its own grammar, has its own idea of syntax.

In fact, it is not too much to say that Heidi Yamada has invented a new poetic language. The purpose of this language is to explore new frontiers of understanding, by hyphenating odd couples of beauty, combining sensual visual images with concepts and interpolating references to antiquity from all ages and all human cultures, putting layer upon layer of thought and feeling, juxtaposing nature with art, music with base nouns.

The challenge is there. Read not to understand but to be understood. And whatever you get from the work of this marvelous new poet, whatever you glean from her coined words, you won't escape reeling in response to the inventive use of linguistic skyrockets by this young mistress of romantic imagery.

—*Taylor Bingham,* Newsweek, *May 17, 1982*

That was the review that gave a goose to Heidi Yamada's career and laid a goose egg on Taylor's. If anybody can tell me what it means, I'll give them a free copy of *And Vice Versa.*

I know what you're thinking: that Taylor was sleeping with Heidi, so he owed her one. But that wasn't the case. At that time Heidi was still Charles Levin's personal exercise machine, and as for Taylor, he was totally snowed under by Linda Sonora, a Hispanic intern from San Diego who had come to New York to screw her way to the top of the literary mountain.

Oh stop it.

Well, it's true.

And the reason Taylor Bingham gave Heidi Yamada's book a rave review (if that's what it was, I'm still not quite sure) had nothing to do with either Heidi or the book. He was doing favors. A favor to Charles Levin, so that Levin would publish Linda's short story collection, *Desert Nights,* and a favor to Heidi Yamada, so that Heidi would give Linda's book a glowing blurb for the back cover. Not to mention a favor to Linda, so that she would suck his toes on Sunday mornings, he was that far gone.

Well, Charles Levin returned the favor in the fall of 1982 and took Linda into his stable. And for all I know Linda sucked Taylor's toes clean off as long as their affair lasted, which wasn't long, I'm afraid.

But Heidi did not take kindly to the idea of another exotic young Californian under the Charles Levin imprint of Random House, and she did not pay Taylor back with a blurb for Linda.

Instead, after the rivalry had attracted public attention in the fall of 1983, she reviewed *Desert Nights* for the *New York Review of Books.* Which was ironic, because before the distinguished critic Taylor Bingham came out in support of Heidi Yamada, the *NYRB* would never have considered having her review for them.

It was a lulu.

It nearly nipped Linda's literary career in the bud. It finished off an already dying affair between Heidi and her editor, and it effectively ended the affair between Bingham and Sonora. Sonora took up with Levin where Yamada left off.

Time reported the scandal with glee, reprinting Taylor's review of *Jump Start* and Heidi's review of *Desert Nights* side by side.

They dubbed Bingham "The Empress' New Taylor."

Within a year, Taylor Bingham had left *Newsweek* and had taken a job writing unsigned Forecast reviews for *Publishers Weekly.* That gig did not last long either. Now he's a stringer for *Metropolitan Book Review.* He still attends the ABA each year as a member of the press, but each year fewer people remember his face or his name.

I wonder, and perhaps Taylor does too, whether the spectacle he made of himself at Charles Levin's party would make people remember him or forget him forever. I know that by the next morning there were far more interesting people bouncing around in my mind than that one hapless has-been.

When Saturday night finally ended, exhaustion won out over grief, fear, and jealousy. I slept soundly through a bunch of bad dreams and woke up at eight-thirty. Carol was still snoring peacefully in the other bed. I tiptoed into the bathroom and showered, then dressed quickly. If I moved fast and skipped breakfast I'd be smiling in my booth by nine o'clock, drinking convention hall coffee and pretending things were normal.

I was out of the room by eight-fifty, and I was halfway down the hall to the elevator when I heard, "Hey, Guy, wait up."

I turned back, and there was Marjorie, yawning and padding toward me barefoot, wearing a terry cloth bathrobe, no makeup on her face for a change and her red hair every which way. When she reached me she took my hand and squeezed it. "Can you come in my room for a sec?" she asked.

"I'm late for the show," I told her. "I'm on my own today."

"I need to talk to you," she said.

"About what?"

"What do you think?"

"Maybe you could come to my booth when you get over there? I really have to be running—"

"Come on, Guy," she pleaded, tugging on my little finger. "Come back to my room. I won't bite. I'll just throw on some clothes and we can walk over there together. We can talk while we walk, how's that?"

"Marjorie—"

But it was too late. I was walking into her hotel room. I knew better, but what was I to do? And if she had something to say about Heidi, I was ready to listen.

One of the beds appeared to be torn up by a restless night. A suitcase was open on the other bed, and her clothes surrounded it in piles. On the table by the window was a cluster of film canisters. Marjorie told me to sit down, grabbed a few articles of clothing from the mess on the bed, and carried them to the bathroom. "I won't be long," she told me. "Give me five minutes." She shut the bathroom door.

I lined the film canisters up in rows and columns and then rearranged them into columns and rows. Stonehenge. A snake. A pyramid. I yawned, checked my watch, stood up and paced. I opened the drawer of the table between the two beds and found a Gideon Bible, a *Book of Mormon,* and a copy of *Great Dates: A*

Directory of Escort Services in Clark County, Nevada. I returned to my chair and stared across the Landmark parking lot, Paradise Road, and the convention center parking lot. People were swarming in, and I wasn't there to greet them.

"Sorry." Marjorie came out of the bathroom looking great. Slacks and a floral-print blouse, flashy but businesslike. She slipped into some flats, clicked her heels, shrugged her camera bag over her shoulder, and said, "Giddy-up. Let's go. Wait." She picked up her plastic key from the dresser and slipped it into her camera bag. "There."

We didn't talk in the elevator. She smiled at me several times, but kept her mouth shut. We walked quickly through the lobby and out into the Nevada morning. Hot already. Blazing hot. We marched across the asphalt parking lot without talking. We waited at the light, but we couldn't talk because we were surrounded by people, chattering booksellers going back for more goodies.

As we crossed the convention center parking lot I said, "What did you want to talk to me about, Marjorie?"

"It's too hot out here," she answered. "Let's go inside."

When we got inside the building we went to a bench against a side wall. "You want to sit down?" I asked. While I waited for her answer, I took my ABA badge out of my jacket pocket and pinned it to my lapel.

Her eyes widened. "Oh shit!"

"What?"

"I forgot my badge," she cried.

"Where is it?"

"It's on the counter, next to the sink in my bathroom. I was in such a hurry I forgot to put it on when I…Christ, now I'm really in trouble!"

"Well, it's a short walk. You could go back for it. Now what did you—"

"No way," she said. "I have to go in there right now. Mr. Levin told me to be there at ten. Shit, it's almost ten now. They won't let me in without a badge. Fuck!"

"Mr. Levin?"

"He said he'd introduce me to Toni Morrison. We're going to set up a shoot. Guy, honey, would you do me a big favor?"

"You want me to go talk to Toni Morrison, stall her off till you get back?"

Marjorie reached for my lapel. "Could I borrow your badge for just a minute? Please? They'll let me in, I'll go to the Random House booth, Charles will loan me his badge or get a badge for me from somebody, I'll come get you, and we'll go in together, and you'll have your badge back. Please, Guy? It'll only take me five minutes. Please?"

"The last five minutes lasted fifteen," I said.

"Aw, come on, Guy. We've been through a lot together."

"Shit," I said.

"Yeah, Guy, but I need this break. Toni Morrison! I'd do it for you. Give me your badge. Loan me, I mean."

"Give me your camera case," I said.

"My camera case?"

"Loan me, I mean."

"Aw, come on, Guy."

"Come on, Marjorie. A swap till you get back." I took off my badge and held it in my left hand. I held out my right hand, palm up.

Marjorie quit smiling. "You don't trust me?"

I didn't answer.

"Shit," she said, shrugging the camera case off her shoulder. "Fuck. Here."

We swapped, she split, and I sat down. I wondered if I'd ever get to my booth that day.

◇◇◇

Five minutes turned to fifteen of course, and fifteen to thirty, then forty-five. Call me a snoop, but the truth is I was just bored. People were going in and out of the exhibition hall, and I was just sitting there. I didn't even have anything to read. So yes, I looked in her camera bag, her purse.

Guess what. No camera. No film, either. There was a change of underpants, the room key, a comb and some lipstick, two tampons, and a wallet with a couple of hundred dollars in twenties, several credit cards, a driver's license (she was five foot two), and some business cards, including the one she got the night before from Dan Plumley of the LVPD plus a bunch of her own cards from *PW*. An address book and an engagement calendar; I didn't recognize any names in the address book, and the calendar was blank. And no camera. No film.

Marjorie may have come to the convention center to meet Charles Levin and Toni Morrison, but she wasn't there for a shoot. Meanwhile, she was standing me up, and I was tired of it. I decided to go back to her room and get her badge. Maybe she'd come out into the lobby and find me gone. Tough.

So I went back out into the morning, which was baking, and I returned to the famous Landmark Hotel, former home of the richest man in Las Vegas. I rode the grinding elevator to the twelfth floor and strode to room 1224, fished the key out of Marjorie's bag, and let myself in.

Fortunately, the room had not been cleaned, so the badge would still be on the counter, next to the sink. I put the camera bag on the table next to the pyramid of film canisters, then walked into the bathroom. My plan was to take Marjorie's ABA badge, go back to the show and in through the door with her badge on my lapel, find her at the Random House booth, hand over her room key and camera bag, swap badges, and be done with it. Unless of course she wasn't at the Random House booth, in which case I'd just wear Marjorie's badge the rest of the day. Unless of course the badge wasn't on the bathroom counter where it was supposed to be.

Guess what. There were three cameras on the counter. No badge.

I put the room key in my pocket and left the room, leaving her camera bag on the table with the pyramid of canisters. If I never saw Marjorie Richmond again, it would be soon enough, and she could get another key from the front desk.

I went next door to room 1226 and let myself in quietly. Carol was up. I heard her in the bathroom, with the shower running, so I sat down in the chair to wait. I checked my pockets, maybe to see if Marjorie had stolen anything else from me while I wasn't looking, but all was in order, including the canister of exposed film she had handed to me the night before.

When Carol came out of the bathroom and saw me sitting across the room she raised her eyebrows. "Hello," she said. "Why aren't you taking care of business at the booth?"

"Why aren't you?" I asked.

"Because I don't feel like it. I have other plans."

"How are you, Carol?" She looked beautiful, standing there naked, her skin rubbed pink from a hot shower. I was one lucky man, or had been until I blew it.

"Hung over and pissed off," she answered. "But otherwise just dandy. How are you? How's Marjorie?"

"Marjorie is a phony," I said.

"You don't say." Carol briskly donned her underpants and bra, then went to the closet and yanked a blouse off a hanger.

"How did you know she was a phony?" I asked her. "Woman's intuition or what? I want to know what I missed."

"Her business card," Carol said. "She doesn't really work for *Publishers Weekly.* That business card is bogus. There's no apostrophe in *Publishers Weekly.* Besides, she's a phony just because she's a phony, and if you didn't pick up on that you were spending too much time picking up on her instead. You were being stupid, Guy. Sorry. So why do *you* think she's a phony?"

"She used me to get into the show this morning. She took my badge. She doesn't have a badge of her own. She was in the show yesterday, but come to think of it, she wasn't wearing a badge then either, so she must have borrowed somebody's yesterday too."

"Wait a minute," Carol said. "She took your badge? Why did you give it to her?"

"That's the part about me being stupid."

"Now what?" she asked.

"I want to borrow your badge for today," I said. "If you won't be using it. I have to get back into the show."

Carol laughed out loud. "Oh, Guy, stand up. I want to kiss you."

I stood up. "So you'll lend me your badge?"

"Call me stupid," she said. She picked her badge up from the dresser and pinned it on my lapel and kissed my forehead, then my upturned lips.

The phone rang. I picked it up.

"Mr. Mallon?"

"Yes."

"This is Dan Plumley, from the Las Vegas Police Department?"

Oh, Jesus. "What are you doing working on Sunday?" I asked.

"Do you know a man named Taylor Bingham?" he answered.

"I do."

"He says he's a friend of yours."

"I guess that's sort of true."

"I'll have a car for you out in front of the Landmark in five minutes. I need to have you come down to the station."

"Is Taylor in trouble?"

"We're not sure. I'll explain when you get here. Now I have another call I have to take. I'll see you shortly." He hung up.

Carol said, "Guy, what's wrong?"

"Carol, I think I need to tell you something about last night."

She put a finger on my lips. "Don't," she said. "I won't ask. It's okay, whatever happened. ABAs are weird, Guy, we both know that. We'll get through this thing. Okay?"

I nodded. "I guess I'd better go," I said. "So what are your plans for today?"

"I'm playing golf," she told me. "Arthur asked me to play golf with him. He said there was something important he wants to talk to me about."

"Arthur Summers?"

"You didn't know he played golf?"

"I didn't know *you* played golf," I said. "Funny the things you don't know about people. Have a good time with Arthur, I guess."

"Don't pout, Guy."

"Shut up, Carol. I have more on my mind than you can possibly imagine."

I slammed out of there, caught the elevator, left the Landmark, and hopped into a black and white car.

A uniformed woman from the front desk showed me into Detective Plumley's office in the back of the Las Vegas police station. He waved me in and pointed to a chair while he finished up a telephone conversation, which appeared to be about his son's high school graduation.

He hung up the phone and smiled at me. "Thanks for coming down, Mr. Mallon."

"Did I have a choice?"

He chuckled. "Doesn't mean I don't appreciate it."

"What can I do for you?" I said.

"How well do you know this man Taylor Bingham?" Plumley asked.

"Not too well. He used to be a prominent book critic, but he's kind of slid downhill."

"You're telling me. We had him in the tank all night, and for a while there he was screaming like a banshee. DTs, I guess. Anyway, he seems to like you. He says you're the only honest man in the publishing industry and he says you'll vouch for his character. Is that so?"

"Which part?"

Plumley opened up a file on his desk. "I had my notes typed up from last night. I've read them over, and you didn't mention Mr. Bingham when you told me what you could remember about what happened at that party. Can you tell me if he really was at the party, Mr. Mallon?"

"Yes, he was, as a matter of fact. That slipped my mind. Taylor isn't a really memorable person, and I guess I just forgot about him. The last I saw of him he was passed out on a parlor sofa."

"Well, one of our fellows found him passed out on a lawn three blocks from the Presley Mansion. They brought him to the station, but when he told them he'd been at that party, they called me down to have a talk with him."

"And? What did he have to say for himself?"

"Nothing. He was out cold, and I didn't get to talk with him until this morning. He remembers going to the party in a shuttle bus from the Hilton Hotel. From that point on, he claims amnesia. Frankly, I believe it. Blackouts happen, or so I'm told. That man is a basket case. What I'm anxious to know is if he's also dangerous."

"Do you suspect him of foul play?" I asked. "Is that why you're holding him?"

Plumley laughed. "'Foul play'? Did you pick that up in some old copy of *Police Gazette*? Cops don't really talk that way, you know. No, the only thing we're holding him on is public drunkenness. We could get him on trespassing, too, if we wanted to bother the owner of the lawn where he spent the night and the palm tree he urinated on. But we won't. He doesn't contest the public drunkenness, but in this town we don't press a lot of those charges. So really, if you're willing to vouch for his character, we're ready to let Taylor Bingham walk out of here with a red face and a warning."

"Well, I don't think Taylor has much character left," I said, "but what there is of it is clean as far as I know."

"That's fine then. Oh. There's one more thing. Does Mr. Bingham have any unusual sexual behavior patterns that you're aware of?"

"What?"

"Is he a transvestite, by any chance?"

"That would be news to me," I answered. "And a total surprise. I don't believe it for a minute. Not that I care, but it doesn't sound like the Taylor Bingham I know slightly."

"Nicely put. Well, he denies it, of course. But he can't deny that we found him sleeping with his head on this pillow." Detective Plumley reached down beside his desk and lifted a tote bag and plopped it on the desk. "Do you know what this is, Mr. Mallon?"

"A Penguin bag," I answered. "That's the hottest giveaway at the show this year. Everybody has one. Everybody who got to the Penguin booth early, that is. They went fast."

"That's what Mr. Bingham told me. But he says this isn't his."

"So you're saying that Taylor stole somebody's Penguin bag?"

"Probably didn't steal, at least not intentionally. Maybe it's his and maybe it isn't. He admits he had a tote bag of this description, but he says this one isn't his."

"They're all the same. What difference does it make?"

"Think, Mr. Mallon." Plumley sounded cross for the first time. "Come on, I'm trying to sort this out. It's not the bag that matters, it's the contents. That's what Bingham doesn't want anything to do with."

"What was in the bag? Looks empty to me."

"It's empty now. The contents are being held in the lab. Bingham saw the contents and claims they're not his and he never saw them and has no interest in ever seeing them again. Mr. Mallon, do you think he was telling the truth?"

"Okay, Detective Plumley—"

"You can call me Dan. You're Guy."

"Okay. Dan, this time, *you* think. How would I know if he's telling the truth? I don't even know what contents you're talking about. Are you going to tell me that, or do I have to guess? I want to cooperate. Help me cooperate."

"Good point. Okay the bag contained a number of items. Several books—"

"Natch. Freebies from the show. Could be anybody's. What books, by the way?"

"I can get you a list of the titles."

"That might be helpful. But most people are pretty indiscriminate when they pick up freebies. Anything else in that bag?"

"Yes, Guy. A bra stuffed with falsies and a blond wig."

"Oh."

"Oh? 'Oh' as in 'Oh that makes sense'? Or 'Oh' as in 'Oh that's Taylor Bingham for you'?"

"No. 'Oh' as in 'Oh shit.' And it's certainly not Bingham."

"Does it remind you of anybody else? Anyone you can think of?"

"Detective, as far as I'm aware, I don't know any cross-dressers."

"Another question. Did Mister Bingham ever mention rohypnol to you?"

"No. I've never heard of it. What is it?"

"A very strong sedative. It's a dangerous drug. It's also illegal in the United States."

"I don't think Taylor Bingham needed a sedative last night."

"No," Dan said. "And there was no rohypnol in his bloodstream. However, there was plenty of rohypnol in the bloodstream of Heidi Yamada. See the connection I'm getting at?"

"How much is plenty?" I asked.

"That's why she's dead," Dan said.

"Oh dear," I said.

"Yeah. So although it's still possible we're dealing with an accidental drug overdose, and that's the way it will probably be reported in the newspaper, it's more likely we're dealing with what you call foul play."

"Oh."

"Now I want you to know something. I want you to know that you don't know what I just told you. Do you understand? I am speaking frankly with you because you're not a suspect, yet, and you seem to know a lot about the deceased and about many of the people who were at that party last night. I think you could be very helpful, and I want that help. Now. Well, Mr. Bingham is ready to leave here if you'll vouch for his character."

"Sure. If Taylor says those aren't his things, I'm sure they're not. And I assure you I don't know whose they are. But there are a lot of people carrying around tote bags from Penguin Books, and it would have been easy for Taylor to have grabbed the wrong one when he left the party, especially considering the shape he was in."

"Okay," Dan Plumley said. "I'd like you to sign this paper, and then I'll have a car take you and him back to your hotels. Oh, one more thing. Have you mentioned this unpleasantness to anybody? Anybody at all?"

"Not a soul," I said.

"As you can imagine, now it's even more imperative that you keep all this to yourself. We may be dealing with a murder here. How about your girlfriend?"

"Girlfriend?"

"Miss Richmond? Has she discussed—"

"She's not my girlfriend," I told him. "I doubt if she's talked to anybody about what happened last night. She wouldn't even talk to me about it."

"Good. When you see her, don't mention this conversation, okay?"

"If I ever see her again, I won't."

Taylor was staying in a cheap motel, the Somerset House, just up the street from the Landmark, so we both got out there and thanked the cop who had given us a ride. As we stood on the hot sidewalk outside the Somerset, Taylor said, "There's a fairly quiet bar in that strip mall on the next block. Want to join me for a drink?"

"I'm tempted," I said, "but I have to get to the show. My booth's been empty all day."

"Oh."

"Why? Was there something you wanted to talk to me about?"

Taylor gave me a shameful grin. "Nothing special. I could tell you what it smells like in the drunk tank. Thought maybe you'd like to buy me a drink. Just kidding. I'll buy the first round. Sure you won't join me?"

"Rain check," I said.

"No problem, Guy. I should take a shower first anyway. I'll see you around." With that, Taylor turned toward his motel and walked slowly away from me, his shoulders slumped and his hands hanging on the ends of his arms like weights.

I hadn't eaten anything since last night's midnight breakfast at the Paddlewheel, and the noon sun was frying me. The booth could wait another twenty minutes. I ducked into the Landmark and went to the coffee shop and had a tuna sandwich, which was served to me on top of a flashing game of video poker. The sandwich had not been made that day, of that I was sure, but it was delicious, and I washed it down with two tall glasses of iced coffee. The casino sounds drowned out my thoughts, and that was fine with me too.

Why was I here in Las Vegas? Remind me next year: ABAs are for the strong and the insane.

I paid my bill, left the loud, and went back out into the hot. Once again I crossed Paradise and the convention center parking lot, and then, with Carol's badge pinned to my lapel, I crossed through into the other world.

I walked as quickly as I could, not reading anybody's name tag, not looking at posters or freebies, till I got to the Guy Mallon Books booth, expecting to see a mess, with our display in disarray from nosy browsers and freebie poachers.

But the booth looked immaculate and cheerful, with stacks of books all neatly arranged. And behind the booth, a man smiling pleasantly, a clipboard in one hand, the other hand outstretched to shake mine.

"Lawrence," I said. "What are you doing here?"

"I've been taking orders for you, Guy. I hope you don't mind." He passed me the clipboard, and sure enough there were four book orders tucked behind the blank order forms.

"Thanks," I said. "I appreciate that."

"Glad to cover for you," he said. "After all, we're fellow collectors."

"I'm not sure how I can return the favor," I told him. "I've already promised you the Heidi Yamada poster, but not till after we knock down on Tuesday morning."

"I don't want to be paid. I just want to help out."

"You sure?"

"Well, I wouldn't mind having the other poster too, the Arthur Summers?"

"Fine," I said. "You can have it now, for all I care."

"You sure?" he asked.

I looked around the booth. It did look tidy and he must have
dusted while he straightened up. But. "I see another advance
reading copy of the Summers is gone," I said.

"I gave it to the poetry editor from *ZYZZYVA*. I think you'll
get some mileage from that."

"You're on the ball, Lawrence."

"Guy, I just want to help out. Some party last night, huh?"

"Was that last night? Seems like weeks ago by now. Yeah, that
was a bash all right."

"Have you seen Taylor Bingham today?" he asked me.

"Why?"

"He looked pretty trashed last night. I just hope he got back
to his hotel all right."

"As far as I know, he did," I said. "Mitzi got pretty wasted
too. Did she make it back all right?"

"Who knows? She didn't come to the show today, but I wasn't
really expecting her. She should have done something with that
booth; she paid for it. Where's Carol?"

"I'm not sure. Lawrence, are you in love with Heidi Yamada?"

He blushed. "I'm a collector," he said. "I'm not a lover."

"No?"

"Well, that's a different story. I'm a homosexual, Guy. You
know that."

"No, I didn't know. So this Heidi Yamada thing of yours, it's
like star worship?"

"Let's don't talk about this," Lawrence said. "Really, Guy."

"I apologize, Lawrence. None of my business."

"No offense taken," he said. "Don't tell anybody I said this,
but it's Maxwell Black I have the hots for. Him and that yellow
bandanna?"

"What do you mean? What are you talking about?"

"Just joking. You don't know about yellow bandannas? Get
real, Guy Mallon."

"Lawrence, are you a cross-dresser?"

His blush turned into a florid scowl. "Absolutely not. I don't
care if you don't like me, Guy, and if you want me to leave you
alone, fine. Keep your fucking posters."

"No, no. Those posters are for you. You can have them when we knock down on Tuesday morning. I want you to have them, really. Thanks for helping out today, Lawrence," I said. "I mean that."

"You're welcome. I'll be running along." He picked up his Penguin bag and nodded.

"One more thing," I said.

"Yes?"

"There is no poetry reviewer at *ZYZZYVA*. They don't review poetry."

"Well, I know that, of course. I meant the general book review guy. He said they'd make an exception in this case."

"Lawrence, come on. *ZYZZYVA* doesn't have a book review guy. They don't review books, period."

"What are you saying?" he asked.

"I'm saying you're welcome to keep that second advance reading copy of the Summers. Thanks again for covering for me at the booth."

I had the next couple of hours pretty much to myself. I stood in the booth, a plastic smile on my face, my mind a maelstrom. I kept thinking to myself, wouldn't Heidi get a kick out of all this trouble she's causing? And I'd have to remind myself that Heidi wouldn't be getting any more kicks, and that thought brought me close to tears, over and over.

Why did Lawrence want to know if I'd seen Taylor? Did he grab Taylor's Penguin bag last night by accident? Does that mean Taylor walked off with Lawrence's tote bag? If so, so what? Even if he exchanged bags on purpose, so what? Lawrence had nothing against Heidi. He might not admit it, but he was in love with Heidi, in his own way. Besides, I thought, Lawrence's not especially tall, and right now we're thinking tall man, right? Or a tall woman? As tall as Carol, for example, but of course it wasn't Carol.

Speaking of whom, where was Carol? And then I came close to tears again. She's spending time with a tall man. Golf? I don't think so.

And where did she get that yellow bandanna? And what does a yellow bandanna really mean? Why am I such a clueless shrimp? Why is Heidi dead? Why did I get into this stupid business? What business does a rinkydink California small-press poetry publisher have exhibiting at the ABA? What time is it anyway?

Questions like that. Fuck.

It was four o'clock when Max Black walked up to the booth looking a little like how I felt. Another bandanna-packer, another tall man. But obviously not a Heidi-killer. And for a change he wasn't wearing a yellow bandanna, or any other cowboy clothes either, just chinos and an Oxford-cloth blue button-down shirt.

"Hey, Guy."

"Hey, Max."

"You seen old Heidi?"

"Not today," I said. "Why?"

"She didn't come back to the hotel room last night. Least I don't think she did anyway."

"Don't think she did?"

"Yeah, well I didn't go back to the hotel after the party either is the point. I went over there this morning to face the music, and looks like nobody spent the night there. So I was wondering if you knew where she was. Stupid bitch. Pardon my Japanese."

"You're pretty mad at her, huh Max?" I said.

"Well, I had it coming, I guess," he admitted. "We haven't been getting along so good lately. It's like she hasn't been getting along so good with anybody, and try living with someone like that."

"Do you still love her, Max?" I asked.

"Heidi? I don't know if I ever did. Yeah, I guess I did, and yeah I guess I still do, but maybe it's time to mosey on."

"Mosey?"

"You know, Guy, I don't really talk cowboy like that. That was her idea. I was born in Milwaukee, for God's sake. And I'm done wearing those stupid bandannas. I told Beatrice."

"Beatrice?"

"She bought a gross of yellow bandannas and she's been passing them out, like a publicity stunt. Trying to get me some kind of book deal. I don't much like this being an author for a living. I was happier tending bar. Well, thanks for letting me bend your ear. If you see Heidi, tell her I was looking around for her."

"I'll do that," I said.

"You know," he added, "if I really was a cowboy like she wants me to be, I'd rope her and brand her and mostly de-horn her. Ball-buster. Hey, you and Carol going to the Ingram party tonight?"

"Sure," I said. "I'm going. I don't know about Carol, but I'll be there. I don't want to miss the Rock Bottom Remainders."

"Then you'll get to see me wear my bandanna for the last time," Max said.

"Oh?"

"Yeah. Steve King said I had to wear rodeo clothes."

"Are you part of the band?" I asked. "Wow!"

"Just for one number. Ridley Pearson and Dave Barry made a song out of one of my poems, and I get to perform it. I'll be doing the vocal."

"I didn't know you could sing," I said.

"I can't," he answered. "I'm tone deaf. It's a rap song."

Five-thirty finally got there. The kindly uncle's voice boomed out over the public address system, *"Well, people, we've come to the end of another day at the American Booksellers Association Convention. Thank you for coming to our show, and thanks to the exhibitors for putting on such a delightful display. Have a wonderful time this evening in this fabulous city, and we'll see you tomorrow, bright and early. Good-bye for now."*

I let the plastic smile dissolve and walked slowly from the exhibit hall and back out among the crowds crossing Paradise Road. Still hot. I had three and a half hours to kill before the Ingram party was scheduled to begin. I was both worn out and wound up tight, so I decided to have a nap when I got back to my air-conditioned room in the Landmark. Unless Carol was there, of course. If Carol was in the room, I had no idea what would happen, and I was nervous about finding out.

I needn't have worried. No Carol, no message.

So I took off my jacket and hung it up and took off my slacks and shoes and stretched out on the bed. I lay there for twenty minutes not sleeping. The ceiling looked like fine desert sand just after a brief rain, and Heidi was still dead, and Carol was still gone. Golf. Yeah right.

I decided to take a long bath. If Carol came in and wanted to step into a cool shower after her hot day out on the golf course, she'd have to wait. Tough. Probably showered at Art's hotel room after her hot day not out on the golf course.

The bath did relax me a bit. Enough to let the tears roll down my face, mingle with my sweat, and plop into the bathwater. I didn't cry out loud. I wasn't ready for that one yet. I wondered how bad this mess was going to get. I had a tantrum inside me eager to come out, but I wanted to wait until I really needed it.

After my bath I dressed and went down to the coffee shop where I ordered a cheeseburger and a beer. After I ate, I asked my waitress for a roll of quarters, and I slid them one by one into the video poker game on the surface of my table. I went up six dollars, then down nine, then up two, then went broke.

It was eight-thirty. I left the coffee shop and took the elevator back up to my room. Carol wasn't there. No message.

My fault. This wouldn't have happened if I hadn't gone off to play golf with Marjorie.

But Heidi would still be dead.

I was done crying, but God damn it, I wanted someone to talk to.

So I went next door and knocked. No answer. I let myself in.

The room had been made up. Marjorie's clothes were still still in piles around her suitcase on the bed; it looked as if she hadn't been back at all that day. Her cameras were still on the bathroom counter, next to the sink. Her film canisters were still on the table by the window, in the pyramid that I had built. Her camera bag was next to the pyramid, where I'd set it that morning.

I took the scratch pad from the bedside table and carried it to the table and wrote, "Thought maybe you'd want a ride to the Ingram party. Thought maybe…"

I wadded up the note and left the room.

Linda Sonora

Heidi at the Vanguard

Ethnic women writers owe a lot to Heidi Yamada. If it weren't for her there might not be an Amy Tan, a Sandy Cisneros. She was one of the brave ones who said, out loud, Hey. I've got ovaries, an attitude, and *color.*

People can say what they like about her writing. Some liked it a lot, and so for a while it sold very well. Some didn't understand it, and so after a while she was dropped like a stone by the New York Literary Establishment. But whether you liked the poetry of Heidi Yamada or not, whether it spoke to you or not, what did speak to many, including myself, was the courage it took to become a celebrity and a success in a world dominated by white males.

I am grateful.

We should all be grateful. She led the way.

Heidi and I were not always the best of friends. I think everyone knows that. I'm not ashamed to say we didn't see eye to eye, and I'm proud to wear this battle-stained dress; I wear it as proudly as Hester Prynne wore her A.

In fact, that's the point. We didn't have to love each other to be sisters in the fight for racial and gender equality in the field of contemporary literature. We were at odds, and frankly I still would like to stick her pigtails in the inkwell sometimes; but listen up: she's dead, she's a martyr, and she's a hero. She's my hero. I know that her success paved the way for me, so that I could go as far as she did and even farther. And I think she'd be the first to say I surpassed her on the road to the Pulitzer Palace, and she would wish me well.

I certainly wish her well. And all other struggling young women writers of Asian, Hispanic, Arab, or African descent should send flowers to her grave.

And let me say this. We traveled together, we talked with each other, and even though we often disagreed, we bonded. You know? We understood each other and, even if we put on a Punch-and-Judy show sometimes, we loved each other. Loved.

So send flowers, women of color. Let flowers smother that brave dead woman.

Roses. Chrysanthemums. Lilies. I'll add a cactus flower.

Thank you, Heidi. Viva la Raza.

Well, of course Linda Sonora is a writer of fiction, and it is the business of fiction writers to arrive at the truth by telling a pack of lies. I don't know what truth Linda was trying to reach by telling that whopper about the bonding experience she and Heidi had on the road together.

The truth is, those two glamorous ladies of literature hated each other on sight, and their mutual loathing grew over the course of a month of companionship on a twenty-city book tour. Hotel rooms together, shared bathroom counters, adjacent airplane seats, joint interviews, readings, and signings. I expect they began their odyssey competing to see who could appear most cordial and accommodating, but the relationship soon began to fester, and by the end of the trip it was a tempest of snarling, public insults.

I had the good fortune to catch their act at Dutton's Books in Los Angeles. It was a beautiful fall afternoon, and Doug Dutton had set up a table for the two of them out in the courtyard. Heidi was on the right, dressed in indigo and scarlet silk in a raku pattern, her painted face beaming out between stacks of *Second Helpings,* her second book for Random House, the one that had spent several weeks on the *New York Times* bestseller list.

On Heidi's right (our left) sat bronze-skinned Linda Sonora, dressed in an embroidered sunflower yellow folkloric dress that must have cost her half her advance. Her eyes flashed, her teeth shone, her throaty laughter chuckled like a springtime stream. Before her were stacks of her first book, *Desert Nights,* the collection that Random House and Charles Levin had such high hopes for.

You have to give Random House credit for their promotion efforts. *PW* ran a big story about the tour, with a joint interview by Lisa See, in which Linda and Heidi expressed their mutual admiration and support for one another. Charles Champlin of the *Los Angeles Times* wrote a feature about them that appeared two days before the Dutton's signing, calling them fresh newcomers who demonstrated the rich cultural diversity of Southern California. The photos in the View section of the *Times* showed two dazzling glamorpusses smiling at each other, on the verge of bursting into laughter over the sheer joy of each other's company. Their pictures were also on posters all over West L.A., on the sides of buses and kiosks, and on the postcard invitations that Pamela Hentzel, Random's West Coast publicist, sent to everyone in the L.A. literary scene.

In any case, the courtyard was packed with wine-drinking, cheese-eating, book-buying shmoozers. They were lined up all around the courtyard and out onto a full block of San Vicente Avenue.

I stood in place, inching forward patiently, waiting for my chance to say hello to my old friend and buy a copy of her new book. There was one line for both authors, which pretty much forced each customer to choose and thereby insult one of the ladies or to spring for both books, which is what most of us seemed to be doing. They took their time signing and chatting up their public, charmingly contradicting one another. Linda used a fountain pen. Heidi, however, was wielding a small Japanese calligraphy brush, dipping it into a cloisonné goblet full of violet ink.

I finally made it to the front of the line. I picked up a copy of *Second Helpings,* the cover of which proudly displayed her gorgeous buttocks in full dorsal nudity, and plopped it in front of her. "Hello, Heidi," I said.

She looked up into my face and her slender eyes widened to circles. "Guy," she whispered. "Guy, it's you!"

"Last I checked," I said. "So, Heidi, how's the fast lane?"

"Sucks," she said, rolling her eyes to her right. "Too much traffic."

"Pardon me, are you Guy Mallon?" This from Linda Sonora, who gave me a large, carnivorous grin. She held her hand out across the table, and as we shook she squeezed hard and whispered, "Heidi's told me so much about you." She turned to Heidi and said, "You're wrong, honey. This man is good looking. And he's not *that* short."

Heidi ignored her. "How you been, Guy baby? I hear you've got some more poetry books coming out."

"I try to keep busy," I said. "How are sales? You two are quite a media event."

Heidi shrugged. "So far I've sold twice as many as Linda here." She smiled sweetly at the señorita and the señorita smiled back.

"Well," I said, "I'll buy one of each. I picked up a copy of *Desert Nights* and turned it over. The book that Heidi Yamada had refused to blurb had favorable comments by Alice Walker, Anne Tyler, and Bobbie Ann Mason. The front cover sported a full moon hanging over a stark dark jade horizon. "Nice cover."

Linda said, "Heidi and I are both into moons."

"Oh shut up and sign his fucking book," Heidi muttered. "That joke is so old by now. Shit."

Linda gave me a smile that said more than I understood, then opened her book to the bastard title page and wrote, "To Guy Mallon, a much better-looking, much nicer person than I was led to believe. Someday you'll have to explain to me your taste in poetry. Abrazos. Linda Sonora."

"*Muchas gracias, amigo,*" she said. She shook my hand. "*Hasta luego.*"

"Let go of his hand," Heidi said. "He's got another book to buy." She slapped open a copy of *Second Helpings* and dipped her brush and made a few quick strokes on the flyleaf.

"What does that say?" I asked her.

"It says '*Muchas gracias,*" Heidi said.

"Why don't you write something in Japanese?" Linda asked.

"Because I don't speak Japanese any better than you speak Spanish."

Linda laughed gently. "I would never guess that you weren't right off the boat. You have such delicate manners." She picked up Heidi's inkpot and sniffed it.

"Give me that," Heidi said.

"This?"

"That."

Linda held the goblet out and wiggled it. Heidi snatched it and flung the contents at Linda's chest. Purple ink covered her left breast and splattered the rest of the front of that bright yellow dress.

Linda shrieked.

Heidi groaned. "Oops. *Ay Chihuahua.*"

I took my two books and scooted to the register, paid up, and left the store. I got into my car and hit the freeway back to Santa Barbara.

Los Angeles is too violent a town for a mild-mannered publisher like me.

After that incident, Heidi quit the tour and flew back to New York alone. She had a brief meeting with Charles Levin, who informed her that they were no longer a couple. He told her he would not return her phone calls, and she said, "What phone calls?"

The next day Heidi wrote "The Pencil-Dick Blue-Pencil Blues" and sold it to *The New Yorker.* Then she wrote the review in the *New York Review of Books* that said, among other things, "People ask me why I won't read stories by Linda Sonora, and I tell them I don't have patience for things I don't like. They ask me how I know I don't like the stories of Linda Sonora if I won't read them. I tell them, 'Sweetie pie, I've had to listen to those stories read aloud, over and over, on our book tour, and I know them by heavy heart, and believe me, it's sleepy out there on the desert at night, and the more I heard the drone of her prose, the more it echoed in me: *sonora, señorita, snore snore, snore....* "

Charles Levin called me and asked to buy the reprint rights to *And Vice Versa,* and I turned him down. Then he called Heidi to discuss the status of their three-book contract, and she informed him that she would never publish another book with Random House or Charles Levin Editions. He happily drew up a letter of agreement cancelling their obligations to one another, and as soon as it was signed, he remaindered *Jump Start* and *Second Helpings*.

Heidi Yamada was out of print and dead in New York. Levin put out the word to all of his colleagues that publishing Heidi Yamada had been a big mistake for him, and if any of his colleagues were to make the same mistake, they would be making a big mistake.

Linda Sonora got the most mileage out of the whole affair. Levin obviously took her side in the feud, because he and she were seen side-by-side for the following season. And thereafter, whenever possible, at readings and signings and cocktail parties, Linda wore her sun-yellow folkloric hand-stitched dress, complete with its violent violet stain.

It was not her trademark performance outfit, the purple-stained yellow folkloric dress, that Linda Sonora wore Sunday evening in Las Vegas at the Ingram Party as the new headliner for the Rock Bottom Remainders. Hardly.

"Ladies and gentlemen," snarled Stephen King into the microphone he was choking to death, "I'm commanding you to give a monster welcome to the Chicana Chicklet, the Border Bunny, the Hispanic Hysteria, Miss Linda (eat your heart out, Ronstadt) Sonora!"

The crowd cheered and whistled, and here she came strutting, sporting sequined denim, fringe, and her own toffee-colored flesh, her smile the brightest spot in the room. She snatched the mike from King, whirled around and thrust her fist in the direction of Barbara Kingsolver on keyboards. Kingsolver hit a loud collection of notes, which was echoed by King and Dave Barry, who wailed on their guitars. Ridley Pearson rumbled in on bass, and the intro built to a thunder of drums and cymbals from Michael Dorris.

Then, flanked by backup vocalists Matt Groening and Amy Tan, Linda rocked into a loud, driving "La Bamba," which lasted a full ten minutes, growing in pace and volume, while pulsing lights played all over the stage and made her look like a giant. Her breasts and belly glistened with sweat, and she never lost the dazzling smile. She covered the stage, right, left, up, and down, and the energy in the room was enough to light Las Vegas, till the song ended and the room went silent and black for a split second.

"Whoo!" she shouted, and the audience—booksellers and publishers with their jackets off and their hair down—screamed for more.

She gave them more. She gave them "That'll Be the Day." She gave them "You're No Good." "It Don't Matter Any More." "When Will I Be Loved?"

Then she got quiet. "Hey," she said. "I want to thank Steve King for inviting me to stand up here tonight."

The crowed whistled, and she held up a hand for more quiet.

"You know, last night Random House threw a party in my honor, and I want to thank them too." More whistles, more silence. "Well, now I'd like to sing a song for someone very special to me, someone who was at that party last night and behaved as if it were her party, not mine. Heidi, babe, this is going out to you."

Then in a sweet, clear voice she sang, unaccompanied, "Nobody knows where my Johnny has gone, but Judy left the same time…" Ridley came in with the bass, Steve hit the chords, and soon the whole band was backing her up as she crowed, "It's my party, and I'll cry if I want to—"

"Holy shit," Beatrice Wright muttered, standing next to me. "She's declaring war, isn't she?"

"I have a feeling she's going to regret this," I said.

"Oh? Why's that?"

"Can't say." I wasn't trying to be cryptic. Or maybe I was, but there was too much noise in the joint for a real conversation.

"Where is Heidi, anyway?" Beatrice said. "I haven't seen her all day."

Charles Levin said, "Who cares? Heidi Yamada is history." Levin stood on the other side of Beatrice, with his arm across her shoulders.

You have no idea, I thought. Or maybe you do. I looked at Beatrice's face to see how she reacted to that pronouncement, but she gave me no clue. She took Charles Levin's hand, and they grinned into each other's faces. What is this, I wondered. Auld lang syne? They were both sporting yellow bandannas.

Then, after the song ended, the Critic's Chorus and the Remainderettes began a rhythmic series of arpeggios: "Bm bm bm bm bm bm bm bm, boom boom boom boom boom, bm bm bum…" and Linda came in, sweetly singing, "Mister Sandman, bring me a dream…" which she kept rocking sweetly till the final "Please, please, please, Mister Sandman, bring me a dream."

And that's when Maxwell Black came strolling out on stage, looking very much like a dreamboat, wearing a big bandanna and a bigger grin. He took Linda's hand, and they leaned across her microphone for a kiss. The mike caught the kiss and Dorris followed it with a rim shot and the crowd cheered.

"Amazing," Beatrice crowed. "That boy has got talent, Charles."

"I can see that. Okay, let's sign him up."

"You mean that?"

"Come to the booth tomorrow morning. We'll sign him up, right on the ABA floor."

Beatrice threw her arms around Charles, then turned to me, bent down, and kissed me too. "See," she shouted in my ear, "that's how it's done."

"I thought that anthology was Gibbs Smith's idea," I said. "Isn't he publishing it?"

"The breaks, honey. Random is where the money is." She turned back to Levin and said, "Let's have a drink or two."

"You'll excuse us?" Charles asked me.

"Gladly," I answered.

Up on the stage, Linda Sonora stepped back to join the Remainderettes, leaving Max holding the mike and grinning out into the bright lights. The entire band made nothing but rhythm with their voices and instruments—bunkachoochoo, bunkachoochoo, bunkachoochoo bomb—and Max shuffled and struggled into his rap song, which was lifted and twisted from *Gol Dern It:*

> Boy Howdy, Heidi Ho
> Hi Heidi Howdy do
> Catch a poet by the toe
> If she hollers, holler too
> If she hollers dirty words
> Tells you that she's for the birds
> Maybe then it's time to fly
> Howdy, Heidi, and good-bye…

The number, which lasted through a dozen stanzas, went over like lima beans. When it ended, finally, Max Black was ushered off the stage to mild and polite applause. Stephen King grabbed the mike and took the audience back into his claws while the band started making louder and better noise at once, notching the energy level back up to severe. Good recovery.

I was alone in a crowd, with nobody to talk to, nobody to wonder with: Was Max deliberately trying to hurt Heidi's feelings? Did he think she was out on the crowded dance floor with tears in her eyes? Or did he know perfectly well that she wasn't in the room, and that she'd never cry again?

In spite of the noise and in spite of the crowd, or perhaps because of both, I felt like a scared kid in a new school. It hit me again, as it had every few minutes, how much I needed Carol right then, and how lost I'd be without her, but I didn't have time to think about that. I felt a tap on my shoulder and turned to face a tall good-looking man dressed in a green plaid smoking jacket with black velvet lapels. He must have bought that one from a garage sale at Liberace's house. The smoking jacket was unbuttoned, revealing a Minnie Mouse tee shirt, and he wore a white bowler hat.

"Casey, right?" I said. "The piano player?" I had to shout because the band was playing "Knock on Wood," sounding like thunder and lightning.

He nodded and yelled into my ear, "You Guy?" When I nodded he said, "There's a lady who wants to talk to you outside."

"Who?"

"She told me to give you this." Casey handed me an ABA exhibitor's badge. My badge. I put it in my pocket.

"Marjorie?"

"She's waiting to speak with you. She told me to come find you and bring you out there."

"Why doesn't she come in and see me? It's an open party. She doesn't need an invitation."

"She doesn't want to get out of the cab," Casey told me. "She's been hurt. Listen, it's really loud here. Would you just come with me? Please?"

I stood my ground. "Well, she kind of hurt me, too, you know."

"I'm not talking about her feelings, asshole. I'm talking about her lip. Let's go."

He turned and strode for the door, and I followed him, racing to keep up. Just getting out of the ballroom and into the jingling casino made a lot of difference, and in the relative quiet, as we weaved our way through the slots toward the outer doors, I asked Casey, "How did you know how to find me?"

"Marjorie described you pretty well," he said.

"She told you I'd be the shortest man in the room, right?"

"Don't get your feelings hurt again, big guy," he said. He stopped and tipped his hat at me. "I don't mind being pegged as 'the guy with the bad shirts.'"

"We're even," I said. "Let's go."

We left the building, crossed the parking lot, and walked into a parking garage. "Over there," Casey said, pointing to a Yellow cab that was parked against a far wall; the logo on the side of the cab said LV-VIP CABS. "She's in the back seat. I'll wait here and give you two some privacy."

I crossed the garage and tapped on the back window of the cab. Marjorie unlocked the door and I slid inside. She was dressed just as I had last seen her, but the split, swollen lip made all the difference.

"Marjorie, who did this?" I asked. "What happened?"

She shook her head. "I don't want to answer any questions, Guy. I just want to keep my mouth shut and get out of town, okay?"

"Well—"

"I need you to do me a favor, okay?" she asked. She put her hand on mine. It was icy. "Will you do me a favor?"

"Of course," I said.

"I'm sorry I left you stranded today," she said. "I can't say any more, but I am sorry, okay?"

"Don't worry about it," I said. "What do you want me to do?"

"Do you still have my camera bag?"

"Not with me," I said. "We could ride over to the Landmark and I'd get it for you."

"I can't," she said. "I have to leave town right now. Here's what I need you to do. The key to my room is in that bag. So's my wallet."

"The bag's in your room," I told her. "So's your wallet. But the key's in my pocket."

"Okay, fine. Go into my room and get all my exposed film, okay? It's on the table by the window. And get my wallet."

"What about your clothes, your cameras?" I asked.

"I don't need anything but the film and my wallet. Just get those things and hold onto them till you hear from me. Please, Guy. You've got to do this for me."

"Okay, sure," I said. "How will I get them to you? Where will you be?"

"I'll call you. I'll phone you in Santa Barbara when this is all over. They can do whatever they want with my cameras, just make sure the film is safe. And my wallet."

"When what's all over, Marjorie? Who's they? Come on, I need to know."

"No you don't."

"Where are you going?"

She sighed and said, "Leave me alone, Guy. Casey and I are taking this cab to his hotel and then we're getting in his car and we're going I don't know where, just away. Okay? Guy, I really appreciate this."

"I wish I could kiss you good-bye," I said.

She smiled, then winced. "That would hurt too much, Guy. I wish we'd kissed when we had a chance. Go now." She put a cold, trembling hand on my face, then turned the other way.

I got out of the cab and walked across the garage to where Casey was waiting by a Dumpster, smoking a joint. "She's all yours," I said. "Take good care of her."

Casey flipped the roach into the Dumpster and buttoned his smoking jacket, but even before he could start walking toward the cab, it was in motion. As it sped past us I could see the panic on Marjorie's face, her fist pounding on the window. I also got a quick look at the cabbie's knit cap and pig-nosed face, a profile of a man who meant business. It was a memorable face, one I was sure I'd seen before, but I'd seen a lot of faces over the past couple of days, and I hadn't taken any taxis. There wasn't time to take a longer look. The tires squealed and the cab tore out into the parking lot, then across the lot and onto the Strip, where it disappeared in heavy traffic.

I looked up into Casey's sad, handsome face. "What just happened?" I asked him. "What's going on?"

"I don't know."

"You must know something," I said. "And whatever it is, you're going to tell it to me."

"What makes you think—"

"Shut up and talk," I said.

"I really don't know much," Casey said. "I was playing over at Caesar's tonight. One of the publishers was hosting what they called a Bad Taste Party, and I was hired to play cocktail piano. I should have been insulted, but I need the money. You publishers are a weird bunch, my friend. Anyway, I was right in the middle of 'Moonlight Becomes You' when this cabbie comes in and says I have to talk with a lady waiting outside in his cab. I needed a break anyway, and it was time for my eleven-o'clock smoke, so I finished the song and followed him out, and there was Marjorie looking beat up. I met Marjorie Friday night—you remember, that party? Well, so that's how well I know the lady: a one-night stand is all, but I guess that means I owe her a favor. She begged me to walk out on my gig at that stupid party and take her to Los Angeles, like tonight, like right away. I don't know why, but I said I'd do it. I'm tired of Las Vegas, I guess, and those drunk publishers were giving me a pain in the ass. So I said yes. But first she wanted to come over here, because she knew you'd be here. Whatever, man, and that's it. Now she's gone, and I'm back to plan A. That's all I know, and to be honest with you, I don't want to know any more. I've got to hail a cab and get back to my gig or I'll have a fat lip too. Either that or get out of town fast."

"There's a lot more to know," I said. "We've got to help her out. She knows something she shouldn't know, and she's in danger. Are you going to help me help her?"

Casey shook his head. "I am a piano player, dude. Just a piano player. For a few minutes there I thought I was going to be a hero, like rescue some damsel, but the look on that cabbie's face just now set me straight. Let me tell you something. Free advice: you come to Las Vegas for fun, you came to the right place. You come here for any other reason, you're in way over your head. That includes meddling in other people's business or solving crimes."

He adjusted the white bowler and walked away from me toward the parking lot.

"But I need help," I called after him.

Casey called back, "You can say that again. Don't we all?"

I walked all the way back to the Landmark. I don't know how far that was, but it took me the better part of an hour. The hike gave me a chance to think and work off my nervous energy, but by the time I let myself into the room, I hadn't come to any conclusions, nor had my nervous energy abated one bit.

Carol was sitting in an armchair, waiting for me. I was so glad to see her I raced across the room. She stood up, and we hugged.

Then we pulled apart and stared tentatively into each other's faces.

"How are you?" she asked.

"Fine. No, shitty. How are you?"

"About the same."

"How was your golf game?" I asked. "Did you play a round?"

"We didn't play golf, Guy. That wasn't why Art wanted to see me today."

"Doesn't surprise me." I felt some smartass remark coming up about a hole in one, but I kept my mouth shut for once.

After a delay of maybe thirty seconds, she said, "Arthur and I spent all afternoon at the police station. Guy, I have some bad news. No, stop. Listen, sweetie. Heidi's dead. She died last night at the party."

"I know," I said.

"You know?"

"I found her."

"No you didn't," Carol said. "Arthur found her. Found her body, I mean. He went to the men's bathroom, but it was locked, so he went looking for another bathroom. He got lost in the back of the mansion, found a bathroom, and there she was, on the floor. Dead."

"She was on a bed when I found her," I said. "In Elvis' bedroom."

"Art put her there. He carried her into the room and laid her on the bed. When he turned on the light he realized there was a surveillance camera in the room, so he turned the light off right away and covered the camera with his bandanna."

"Why? Why did he do that?"

"That's what the detective wanted to know. Art said it was to give Heidi some privacy. It doesn't make sense, and he knows it, but the detective seemed to understand."

"Was it Dan Plumley? The detective?"

"That's right. Detective Daniel Plumley. We were with him all afternoon."

"Did Dan tell you he'd talked with me and Marjorie? We were the ones who found her on the bed."

Carol shook her head. "What were you doing in there, or shouldn't I ask?"

I shook my head.

"It's okay, Guy," she said. "Now what?"

"Well, for one thing, I understand we're supposed to keep this quiet. At least that's what Dan told Marjorie and me. He told you the same thing, right?"

"No, it's not a secret. He had a reporter there from the *Review-Journal.* We'll be reading the story tomorrow in the morning papers. So will everybody else."

I sat down hard on the bed and let out a long sigh. I covered my face with my hands and rubbed.

"Are you okay, Guy? I'm sorry, sweetie. I know what she meant to you."

I dropped my hands. "Does Plumley have an idea of who did it?"

"Did it?"

"Killed Heidi," I said.

"She killed herself, Guy. It was either suicide or an accident. Probably an accident. It wasn't a murder."

"You're sure of that?"

"Detective Plumley seemed certain of it."

"And I'm certain he's wrong." I stood up and headed for the door.

"Where are you going?" Carol asked.

"Next door."

"I see."

"It's not what you think," I said.

"Then why are you going to Marjorie's room?"

"Because Marjorie asked me to. I'll be back in a few minutes."

"Take your time," Carol said. "She must be very important to you."

I let myself into Marjorie's room and flipped on the light.

The place was a wreck. Her suitcase had been dumped and the clothes were scattered all over the bed. The drawers of the dresser and the bedside table were open. The clothes in the closet were on the floor.

The cameras were still in the bathroom. They were open.

There were no film canisters on the table by the window. Whoever had taken them probably stuffed them into Marjorie's camera bag, because that was gone too, and so was her wallet.

Maxwell Black

She Smiled at Me That Way

Even now I can't forget
The night she smiled at me that way
That was the evening that we met
And had so much to say

We talked of Lord knows what and when
We knew we'd talked the night away
We said goodnight and once again
She smiled at me that way

I shook her hand and shyly said
I'll call tomorrow, if I may
She told me, darlin' go ahead
I'll be around all day

And so for years it seemed so right
We were together every day
I'm pleased to say, and every night
She smiled at me that way

That lady taught me how to write
The words to use and what to say
I'd work until I got it right
To please her night and day

She was the muse who gave me art
She taught me work was full of play
And when I opened up my heart
She smiled at me that way

But now she's gone. She's gone out west
For every lady has her day
To leave, to lie in heaven's breast
But she's not far away

For even though I've lost my love
I think about her every day
And know that still, from up above
She smiles at me that way

When she realized she was washed up in New York, Heidi sold her house in Connecticut and moved back to Santa Barbara. I suppose she thought she could still make a big splash in her small West Coast pond. She called me up the day she got back to town. Carol answered the phone.

Wait. Back up.

Meanwhile, Guy Mallon Books had grown. I got out of the used book business and sold what was left of the front-room stock to Eric Kelly of the Book Den. He didn't pay me a lot for the books, but he was fair, and it was enough to finance another Arthur Summers collection, the one that got short-listed for the National Book Critics Circle Award. I still had my postwar poets in the back room, but I didn't do much trading in that area anymore. No, it was publishing for me from then on. What was formerly Guy Mallon Books, a bookstore, became "Guy Mallon Books, Publishers." I bought shades for the storefront windows and painted "By Appointment Only" on the front door.

Back up some more. In the four short years since Heidi Yamada walked into my shop and turned my life upside down, I had brought out over a dozen books. I started by publishing a few local poets, including Arthur Summers of course, and then began signing up poets from farther afield, poets I had read and collected, met and liked: Charles Gullans, Janet Lewis, Kingsley Tufts, Hildegarde Flanner, Judson Jerome. I became what Lin Rolens in the Santa Barbara *News-Press* called "a cross between an oxymoron and a dinosaur—a successful small-press publisher." And this without the help of the National Endowment for the

Arts. The secret was that I was filling a niche: good poetry, by good poets, published by a serious publisher and sold to a subscriber list of enthusiastic customers, a list that grew with each new poet. I published in small print runs for the trade, but for each title I also brought out a limited, signed, numbered edition of a hundred copies, and they all sold right away. In fact there was a waiting list of collectors who wanted to get onto that list whenever a subscriber died. I always kept copy number one, and the author always got copy number two, and of course number three went to Lawrence Holgerson. He offered to pay double for a number one, and I told him I'd think about it, but of course I never will.

As the business grew, I needed help, and once again I hired a woman. Carol Murphy, a tall, brainy blonde five years older and half a foot taller than I, was the third and final and greatest discovery of my life among books. She had owned a small bookshop in Dallas, Texas, and I first hired her to mind the front room when I still had used books for sale. But she was quick to encourage me to sell the stock to the Book Den and concentrate on my newfound passion. She then took on the role of business manager for Guy Mallon Books, and sales manager too. We became partners with a handshake. It's a move I've never regretted.

A few months later I realized I was eager to get to work each morning for the sake of work but more for the sake of spending another day with Carol. I took the biggest risk of my life so far and declared my love over a glass of wine at the Paradise Cafe.

"You damn fool," she responded from her lofty height on the other side of the table. "What took you so long?"

We dated, if that's what you call it, for a couple of weeks, then I moved my few possessions out of the Schooner Inn and into Carol's bungalow on the east side of town, where we've been ever since. It's crowded, and that suits me. I think it suits her, too. So for the past seven years, we've worked together and slept together, and the lines between work and play and love have all but disappeared.

◇◇◇

So that's how it was when I got the call in late spring, 1984. Actually, it was Carol who answered the phone, and when she told me to pick it up, she said, "It's her."

"Herself?"

"Her Highness."

I picked up the receiver and said, "Hello, Heidi."

"Guy, honey, you gotta rescue me from this place I'm in."

"What kind of place is that?" I asked.

"It's a place without love. A place without you. I've come home, Guy. Take me back."

"Uh Heidi..."

"I'll be good to you, Guy baby. You don't know the things I've learned. I'm going to make you feel like a hundred bucks. Oh, Guy, I need you. I want your arms around my thighs. I want your nose in my nest."

"Stop," I said.

"Huh?"

"Heidi, there's another woman in my life now."

"Better than me?"

"Different," I said.

"Different how?" she asked.

"Better," I answered.

"That woman who answered the phone?"

"That's right."

"I thought so. I knew it. I could tell by the way she answered the phone."

"Sorry, Heidi, but...."

"It's okay, Guy. These things happen. Will you publish my new book?"

"No," I said.

"I'm calling it *Random Thoughts.*"

"No."

"Or we could call it *Out of My Face.* I've got a great cover idea for that one."

"Good-bye, Heidi."

"God damn it, Guy, after all I've done for you?"

"Someone else is doing that now," I said.

"You are such an asshole, you know that, Guy?"

"Good-bye, Heidi."

So she left Santa Barbara. Next I heard she was a presenter at the Yellow Lake Writers' Conference in Great Falls that summer. She was still somewhat of a celebrity, and since nobody really knows what a poet really is, she could pass herself off as one wherever people were willing to let her perform in public. That's where she met Maxwell Black.

Most of what we've heard about Max Black is probably true. Born in Milwaukee and became a westerner by going to the University of Montana at Missoula. Dropped out of college to be a ski bum in Sun Valley, then farmed a small marijuana plantation in Colorado for a while, then ended up a bartender in Great Falls. Poured generous daquiris for a famous poet one night and it changed his life. The poet stayed till the bar closed, took him back with her to the Holiday Inn where she was staying, and made a writer out of him.

A cowboy poet.

I can just imagine it:

"Max, honey, I want you to write me a poem."

"Shit, I can't write."

"Sure you can, baby. If you write me a poem, I'll do that for you again."

"Aw, Heidi…"

"I want you to write lots of poems. I'm going to make you a famous poet."

"I don't know how."

"How difficult could it be? Look at me."

"What would I write about?"

"Write about what you know. That's what they all say."

"Bartending?"

"No. The cowboy life. Nights under the stars. Camping out. Herding cattle. Stuff like that."

"I hate camping out. I hate cows."

"What difference does that make? Do you have a good-looking hat?"

I just made that up of course, but I bet it's mostly true. In any case, Max Black, poet, got himself a sponsor, and Heidi Yamada, celebrity, got herself an ornamental poet. She moved him back to Santa Barbara with her.

They became regulars at the Wednesday lunches at the Miramar, and the Santa Barbara writers took kindly to Max. He was a bit of a cartoon, the way Heidi had him dressed: polished boots and pressed jeans and starched chambray workshirts with a floppy yellow bandanna always tied around his neck. None of the other writers took him seriously as a poet, any more than they had taken Heidi seriously as a poet, but they liked Max as a beer-drinking, slow-talking, wisecracking fellow, and they put up with Heidi mainly for his sake.

It was clear that he adored her, and it was clear that she had big plans for him.

Perhaps he was more of a poet than we thought, or perhaps Heidi still had more influence than she deserved, but anyway, Max started getting published. He was a vanguard in the cowboy poetry movement, and his first book from Gibbs Smith was a hit. *The Yellow Bandanna* didn't make any bestseller lists, but it was kindly reviewed by *PW* and *Kirkus* and of course *Library Journal*. They noted his competent rhymes, his narrative gift, and most of all his sincerity, which *Library Journal* assumed must have come from his working knowledge of rodeos and bordellos and the backside of the Sawtooth Mountains.

Heidi, meanwhile, praise the Lord, had stopped writing. She devoted herself full time to managing Max's career, and she was brilliant. She got him hired on as a regular faculty member of the Squaw Valley Community of Writers, where she made sure he chatted up the right editors and publishers. The next book, *Howdy, Mr. President,* was published by Chronicle Books in San Francisco; it was a gift book full of sunset photos and hokey couplets, but it sold well. Some of the images and couplets were bought to sell Toyotas on television, and Max started selling song lyrics to Garth Brooks and George Strait. HarperCollins brought out *Gol Dern It*. Bestseller, Costco, Bantam trade paperback, the works.

Through it all, Max remained a quiet, self-effacing fellow with a bottle of beer in his hand and a yellow bandanna around his neck. The shit-kicking cowboy image was phony, but he was genuinely pleasant and witty, and he always let Heidi be the one to brag about him. He seemed to enjoy the life of a poet, never let fame go to his head, and never took his eyes off his beautiful patroness. As for Heidi, she was through writing poems. She had her hands full managing Max's career and dressing him in prefaded jeans from top designers.

Beatrice Knight offered to take Maxwell Black on and be his agent, and Heidi told Beatrice to get real, give her a break, take a hike, and piss up a rope.

They had a good thing going, Heidi and Max, until Mitzi Milkin came along and wrecked it all by tempting Heidi to start writing again. At that point Max found himself back in the backseat again, which he didn't really mind until people like Beatrice Knight, Charles Levin, and Linda Sonora began to convince him that his talent was more important than Heidi's ego.

Carol went to our booth early on Monday morning because I told her I needed an extra hour of sleep. As soon as she had left the room, I placed a call to Detective Dan Plumley. The receptionist asked my name, then put me right through.

He didn't say hello, he said, "It's all over, Guy. It was an accidental death, a great shame, but these things happen. You're free to come and go as you wish. I want to thank you for your cooperation while this matter was being resolved."

"Resolved?" I responded. "You think it's resolved?"

"Yes sir," he said. "Heidi Yamada took an overdose of sedatives. Whether or not she did it intentionally is moot now, and out of respect for her family—"

"She has no family."

"—we're calling it an accident. Damn shame. Again, Mr. Mallon, many thanks for your cooperation."

"Hold on," I said. "Don't hang up."

"Mr. Mallon—"

"Do you know where Marjorie Richmond is?" I asked him. "Have you heard anything?"

"No, I haven't spoken to Miss Richmond since we said good-night on Saturday. Of course she's free to go, too."

"I have a feeling she is gone," I said. "I also have a feeling she's not free."

"I don't know what you're talking about."

"Do you care what I'm talking about?"

"Mr. Mallon," Detective Plumley said, "I am relieved that this case is closed. I have a lot of other stuff on my plate right now. What happens to you and Miss Richmond is now entirely up to you. Again, I appreciate your help in bringing this matter to a close. I advise you to respect that, and to understand that a closed case is a good case. I have another call waiting. You enjoy the rest of your stay in Las Vegas, okay?"

"Okay," I told the dial tone.

Shit, I thought. Shit shit shit shit shit shit shit shit shit shit shit shit shit shit shit shit shit shit shit shit shit shit shit shit shit shit shit shit shit shit shit shit shit shit shit shit shit shit shit shit shit shit shit shit shit shit shit shit shit shit shit shit shit shit shit shit shit shit shit shit shit shit shit.

I finished dressing and went downstairs to the front desk. I rested my elbows on the counter, which was at the level of my shoulders, dinged the call bell, and waited. The desk clerk emerged slowly from behind the scenes, a pimply teenager in a black suit who had the eyes of a basset hound. "Yes, sir? May I help you?"

"I'm concerned about the woman in the room next to mine," I told him. "Marjorie Richmond? Room twelve-twenty-four? She was supposed to meet me this morning, and she didn't show up and there's no response when I knock on her door."

"I'm afraid that's between she and you, sir. The hotel can't, like—"

"Hold on," I said. "Okay, listen. I have her room key, okay? I went into her room when she didn't respond. It's a mess in there. I mean the place is in shambles. Something's going on, and I think you should investigate. Looks like violence, okay?"

The desk clerk danced his fingers on the keyboard of his computer, frowned, and then went through an upright file on the counter. He looked at me and said, "Miss Richmond checked out yesterday, sir. One p.m. It says here."

"I don't believe that," I said.

"Says here, sir." He tapped his monitor. He pulled a page out of his file, looked at it closely, then put it back without showing it to me.

"It may say that," I said, "but that's not what happened. What happened is that your guest was kidnapped and robbed, and if you don't investigate this, I'll make a big noise about it." I reached into my wallet and pulled out Dan Plumley's business card. "I'm working with the Las Vegas police on something pretty important, and they've asked me to keep them informed."

"Well, sir, there's not much I can do."

"Is there anybody else I can talk to? Your supervisor? Who's in charge here?"

"I am, sir." He yawned and tilted his head back, and I had the pleasure of looking up his nostrils.

"Then you're the person elected to come with me to room twelve-twenty-four, right now, so I can show you the problem. Believe me, you have a problem on your hands. What's your name?"

"Robert, sir."

"Come with me, Robert."

Robert looked at his watch, lifted the phone, and told some-body, "I need you to cover me on front desk. I'll be back in about five minutes."

"It may take longer, Robert," I said.

"I doubt it, sir." He opened a drawer and pulled out a key.

"That won't be necessary," I told him. I jingled Marjorie's key.

He put a key in his pocket anyway and came out from behind the counter. "Let's go, sir," he said, and we walked together to the elevator.

The gears of the elevator ground especially loudly as we rose. I said, "You really ought to do something about that noise. Just some WD40 or something, so your guests won't think the building's falling down."

"I'm not in charge of maintenance, sir," Robert said. He was one of those teenagers who look taller than they will ever look as adults. His shiny suit didn't quite fit him, and his tie was knotted limply. He didn't look at me once during the ride, which was just fine with me.

The elevator stopped within a few inches of the twelfth floor, the door opened, and we stepped up and walked down the hall to Marjorie's room. He got there first, so he used his key and entered the room without waiting for me. I followed him in.

The room was immaculate. It showed no signs of having been occupied recently, let alone torn apart by violence. The beds were made, the drawers were all closed, the counters and tables dusted. It was a freshly cleaned, vacant room, waiting for its next occupant.

Robert finally looked at me, his eyebrows high on his forehead.

"What's going on?" I said.

"Sir?"

"This room was a mess last time I saw it. I want to know who cleaned it up, and why."

"Like I told you, sir, Miss Richmond checked out yesterday in the early afternoon. The maids cleaned it up after she left. It's a vacant room."

"I'm telling you, Robert, that this room was a disaster zone at midnight last night. I saw it myself, so don't tell me it wasn't."

"I thought you said you were inside the room this morning," Robert said.

"Well, it was after midnight, actually. That's morning."

"Sir, all I know is what I see, and what I see is a vacant room, ready for occupancy. You tell me you were in this room, but I have no proof of that."

"What about this key?" I countered. "Why else would I have this key?" I held the key up in front of his face.

Robert snatched the key from my hand and said, "That's hotel property. Thank you sir. Now, Mr. Mallon, I have to get back to the front desk."

"How do you know my name?"

"You told me you were in the room next to this one. I checked on the computer. Let's go."

"Robert—"

"Let's go." He took my arm and led me out into the corridor, then turned and locked the door to 1224 behind him.

On the elevator going down, I said, "I'd like to speak with who-ever was on the desk when Marjorie Richmond checked out."

"They're not here today, sir. That was the weekend shift. They won't be back until Saturday."

"You guys really have this whole thing covered, don't you?" I said.

Robert said, "Sir?"

"Never mind."

I left the Landmark and walked away from the convention center until I reached the Strip. I went into Fast Foto and gave the clerk the roll of exposed film that I'd been carrying around for what felt like days. In fact that film was less than thirty-six hours old, but I was glad to have the weight out of my pocket. The clerk assured me the prints would be ready by noon and I thanked her and asked her to change a dollar into quarters for me.

Outside, on the sidewalk of the Strip, I fed fifty cents each into two newspaper boxes and got two copies of the *Las Vegas Review-Journal.* I tucked them under my arm and went into the nearest eating establishment for some breakfast. It happened to be an Arby's. I was the only customer, which was fine with me.

Even in Las Vegas they don't sell a whole lot of ersatz roast beef sandwiches for breakfast. And coffee.

The story of Heidi's death was not on the front page of the paper. It was not in Part I either. The story showed up on page 4 of Part III, and it commanded less than three inches of ink.

> *Poetess Heidi Yamada died Saturday night of an apparent drug overdose. Her death occurred at a party held in the Elvis Presley Mansion on Strong Drive. The party was hosted by Random House, a New York publishing company. Yamada was the author of three books of poetry in the early 1980s. She was well known among poets at that time but went into semi-retirement in the mid-1980s. "She had her 15 minutes of flame," said Carol Maloney, the business manager of a small publishing company that had done business with Yamada. Maloney said that Yamada appeared heavily sedated on the evening of the party. "She had been battling depression for quite some time," Maloney added.*

It didn't bother me much that Guy Mallon Books wasn't mentioned by name. It didn't bother me that they got Carol's last name wrong. It didn't really bother me that the newspaper was joining the police force and some other force in covering up a murder by calling it an accident and implying that it was a suicide. I didn't even care that they used the word "poetess," which usually sends me into fits.

I guess what disturbed me, so much that I couldn't even finish my breakfast, was that Heidi had died such a has-been. Not just because she was my first poet, not just because she was my friend, not because her poetry was any good, but just because the world doesn't care about poets. So she had her "fifteen minutes of flame"—did Carol really say that? I doubt it—and appeared on Johnny Carson. The truth is, nobody remembered her anymore.

Going through the paper backwards, I learned that George
Gobel was in the hospital in Palm Springs, David Nelson gave
a speech to a PTA in Pennsylvania, and Freddy Cannon had
canceled a performance in Laughlin, Nevada. They all got bigger
stories than Heidi Yamada. That's Las Vegas for you.

That's the world for you.

◇◇◇

When I got to the booth I found Carol standing there, not even
trying to smile for the public. I plopped the newspapers down
on our display table, opened one of them up and spread it out,
pointed to the article about Heidi, and said, "Take a look."

Carol picked the paper up and read it, then folded it and put
it back on the table. She looked at me with white fury in her
eyes. "This is horrible," she said. "I feel violated."

"They got your name wrong," I agreed.

"Oh who cares? I could give a shit about that," she said. "Guy,
I never said those things."

"No?"

"I didn't say she appeared heavily sedated. I said she appeared
highly agitated. And I never said she'd been battling depression,
either. What a crock of shit."

"Well," I said, "Heidi had been pretty upset lately."

"I never called her depressed," Carol insisted. "I don't say
things like that about people. That reporter wasn't listening to
me at all."

I shrugged and shook my head.

"This is horrible," Carol said again. "You know what I think?
I think that interview was just a sham. The police gave the paper
that story, and they printed it. This looks like a cover-up to me,
Guy. You know what I think? I think maybe Heidi Yamada was
murdered."

"Carol, I love you," I said.

She frowned at me. "I love you too, Guy, but what does that
have to do with this?"

"Nothing," I agreed. "I'm just so glad to have somebody agree
with me for a change."

"Tell you what," she said. "Let's don't go straight home to Santa Barbara after this show is over. I want to spend twenty-four hours in the desert, temporarily forgetting everything that's happened."

"I'm for that."

"Good. I'll make a reservation at the Nipton Hotel." It was our favorite getaway spot in the East Mojave Desert.

I folded up both newspapers, with the story about Heidi on the outside, and put them under our table, hidden by the drop-cloth. When I straightened up I saw that she was smiling, so I walked into her arms and we kissed.

"Did you really say 'fifteen minutes of flame'?" I asked her.

"Yeah, they got that right. Clever, huh?"

"Andy Saint Vincent Millay," I said. "Not bad."

I can't remember how long our second kiss lasted, but it was interrupted by the cheerful voice of the most powerful agent on the West Coast. "My oh my," she chirped. "Look at the lovebirds!"

There she was, standing in front of our booth with Maxwell Black by her side. They were both wearing purple bandannas around their necks, and they were both smiling. "You've heard the news, I suppose?" Beatrice said.

"You two don't look that upset by it," I observed.

"Well, so they skipped out on a meeting. He still wants to do the book."

"What the hell are you talking about?" Carol asked.

"Charles Levin and Linda Sonora," Beatrice said. "Tell them, Max."

Max grinned and shook his head. "They got married last night, after the Ingram party. Shit fire, talk about a surprise. Linda made an announcement from the stage, after the Remainders quit and packed their axes. There weren't a whole lot of guests left, but her and Levin invited us all over to the Midnight at the Oasis Wedding Chapel to watch them tie the knot."

"Ye gods," I said. "So where are they now, the newlyweds?"

"They've left for Maui," Beatrice said. "Honeymooners."

"How convenient for them," Carol remarked.

"How's that?"

"Max, I thought you and Linda were becoming an item," I said. "That's the way it looked last night, anyway."

"Aw that was just a publicity stunt. I guess I was getting back at old Heidi for being such a bitch lately. Naw, the item's still me and Heidi. We'll make up. We always do. I'll go back to being her dumb cowboy, if she'll ever come back to our hotel room, which she will when she gets tired of bustin' my balls."

Oh God.

"Max. Beatrice. There's something I have to tell you both," I stammered. I turned helplessly to Carol, and Carol knelt down to retrieve the Las Vegas newspapers from under the table. She stood up and handed one paper to Max and the other to Beatrice.

I've never seen a face change the way Max's did as he read that article. It went from cocky and strong and easy-going to shocked, then to pained red, then to terrified white in thirty seconds. Suddenly Maxwell Black looked like a little boy and an old man, lashed together by electric barbed wire. He dropped the paper to the floor and brought his shaking clenched fists to his chin. Carol took him by the arm and led him to the metal chair in the back of our booth, where he collapsed and gasped for breath. "Oh fuck!" he wheezed, loud enough to be heard out in the aisle. *"I killed her!"*

"No you didn't," Beatrice said. She handed her newspaper to me. "I knew she'd self-destruct. It was only a matter of time." She bent down to pick up the other paper.

"Max, what do you mean?" I asked. "You killed her? How?"

"I was the reason she was so depressed," he sobbed. Tears streamed down his cheeks. "I was always giving her shit. I'm such an asshole! Aw, *Heidi!*"

"Max, I don't believe Heidi killed herself," Carol said to him. She rubbed his shoulders. "It was an accident, honey. You're not to blame."

Max shook his head. "She was always taking tranks. I wasn't any good for her. I was stingy with my love. She, she, she wanted me to, aw fuck, oh Christ that poor girl, I made her feel like shit and she took all those pills and they don't mix with alcohol and she drank too much too and now she's, aw Heidi, aw Heidi, I'm so fuckin'…" Now his hands were all over his face, rubbing away the tears, scrubbing at the grief-torn terrain. Carol handed him a box of Kleenex, which he squashed and threw across the booth.

Beatrice knelt before him and put her hands on his knees. "Max, stop it," she said. "I want you to stand up and walk with me out of this building. I'm going to take you back to your hotel room."

He looked at her in horror. "I can't go to that room!"

"No, of course," she said. "You're right. I'm going to take you to *my* room and leave you there till you cry all this guilty crap out of your system. But no more crying till we get out of the convention center. Okay?"

Max ripped the purple bandanna from his throat and blew his nose and wiped his face. "Okay." He stood up.

Beatrice stood up with him. She looked at me and said, "Poets. You gotta love 'em." She grabbed Max's arm and said, "Okay, cowboy. Let's go."

The agent and the cowboy left our booth and walked down the aisle and turned the corner.

The news spread. You could hear the hush and feel the chill as people streamed to our booth, slowed down, looked at the poster of the dead poet on our display wall, then moved on, shaking their heads and whispering to each other.

Carol and I stood, hand in hand, prepared to answer questions if anybody asked them, but nobody did. Not till a reporter showed up and handed me her card. "Mr. Mallon?" she said. "I'm from *Publishers Weekly.* Could I ask you a few questions?"

My chance to be in *Publishers Weekly.* How little it mattered now.

I answered questions.

"I've lost a dear friend," I said. "The world has lost one of the most innovative poets of the twentieth century."

"No, as far as I know, everyone loved and admired her," I said.

"I'm afraid I don't know any more than what I read in the newspaper this morning," I said. "I gather it was an accidental overdose."

"High-strung?" I said. "Well, maybe a bit. She was an artist after all."

"Suicidal?" I said. "No way."

"A great shame," I said. "A great shame."

"Thank you, Mr. Mallon," the reporter said. "I really appreciate this. You don't have a picture of Miss Yamada, do you?"

I handed her a copy of *And Vice Versa*. "Feel free to use that cover shot," I said. "Heidi was proud of it. What issue of *PW* will this appear in?"

"Tomorrow," she answered. "It's for the *PW ABA Daily.* Thanks again."

So much for my words showing up in *Publishers Weekly.* It was a relief, frankly.

◇◇◇

Lawrence Holgerson showed up at the booth about eleven o'clock. His rumpled linen jacket looked as if he'd just used it to wash a Greyhound bus. He had a twitch that jerked his left eye around and he was chewing gum furiously. "You've heard?" he asked us.

"We've heard," Carol answered. "How are you, Lawrence?"

"Heartbroken." He pulled a bent Salem out of his shirt pocket and stuck it in his mouth, then pulled it out of his mouth and put it back in the pack and put the pack back in his shirt pocket. He pulled a tissue out of another pocket and got rid of his gum. "This is the worst thing that's ever happened to me."

"To you?" I asked. "You?"

"Well, to us all. To Heidi of course, yes, naturally. But what will the rest of us do without her?"

"She meant a lot to you, didn't she, Lawrence?" Carol said.

Twitch. "The focus of my collection." His face began to crumble.

Carol put her arms around him as his body began to shake. "I loved her," he cried. "I have every edition of every book of hers. Signed. Letters, pictures, and now…" He let his words be swallowed in sobs.

I straightened books on the display tables. It was something to do while Carol was rubbing the back of Lawrence's head. Finally he pulled himself together and let go of Carol. He sniffed, twitched, and gave us both a shaky smile. "Thanks, you two," he said. "You're the best."

"You'll be all right?" I asked.

He nodded. "By the way, you haven't seen Taylor Bingham today have you?"

"Nope. You asked me that yesterday. What's up with you and Taylor?"

"Nothing. I mean nothing like that. Thanks, Carol. You two are wonderful." Then he turned to me and said, "Do I still get the poster after the show?"

"Sure," I told him. "Come to the booth tomorrow morning while we're knocking down."

As he walked away, down the aisle and into the swim, I asked Carol, "Did you know Lawrence's gay?"

"Of course. Why?"

"How did you know?" I asked.

"It's no secret, is it? I thought everyone knew. I don't think he tries to hide it, and if he does, it's not working."

"So how do you know stuff like this? You were able to see that Marjorie Richmond was a phony, you know Lawrence's homosexual. Are you some kind of mind reader?"

"Guy, what's going on? Why do you care if Lawrence's gay? What does that have to do with anything at all? Are you going phobic on me?"

"No," I said. "It's not that he's gay. Okay, let me ask you this. Do you think Lawrence's a cross-dresser?"

Carol shook her head.

"No?"

"I'm shaking my head in disbelief, Guy."

"You don't believe he's a cross-dresser?"

"I don't believe this is you talking. Maybe he is, I don't know. But why does it matter to you?"

"It doesn't. But he keeps asking if I've seen Taylor Bingham, that's all."

"And Taylor's a cross-dresser? I wasn't aware."

"No, he's not," I said. "Or maybe he is, but that's not the point."

"I don't get it, Guy. What is the point? I don't know what you're talking about."

"I don't either," I said.

◇◇◇

Beatrice came back to our booth and said, "Max is sleeping off a Valium, poor boy. How are things going here? Are people paying homage?" She nodded at the poster.

"A few," I said. "Beatrice, tell me something. All those yellow bandannas. You were giving them away at the Random House party, right?"

She laughed. "What a mistake that was," she said. "I wanted everyone to pay attention to Max. It was a way of announcing that I had this hot new client. Then Lawrence Holgerson told Max the yellow bandanna had something to do with urine, and Max told me he was done with them forever, but I said he had to wear one for the Rock Bottom Remainder show, so he—"

"Fine," I said.

"So now we decided purple. It's a brand-name imaging type thing, honey. Whatever works."

"Fine," I repeated. "Now tell me about the invitations."

"What invitations?"

"Were you the one passing out all the invitations to the Random House party?"

"Lord, no."

"Where did you get yours?" I asked.

Beatrice gave me a get-serious look. "Charles gave me an invitation. I want to remind you, Guy, that I am a major player in this industry. I go to the best parties every year. You know that, or you would if you were at the right parties."

"Fine," I said. "So you don't know who was passing out all those invitations? I mean to all the California riffraff?"

"Absolutely no idea. Carol, honey, I have to be running along. I just wanted to let you know Max will be all right. What a shame about Heidi! Bye-bye, you two. I'll catch you later. Are you going to the small press party tonight?"

"Probably," I said.

Carol said, "I doubt it."

Arby's sandwiches are like Chinese food: you don't eat them for breakfast, and if you do, you're hungry again an hour later. By the time two o'clock came around I was starved, so I offered to go stand in line and get hot dogs, potato chips, and beer for both of us.

It was one of those snaky lines that goes back and forth around posts and between heavy red cloth ribbons. Just like at Disneyland: you move forward slowly, and sometimes it seems like you're moving backwards because you're seeing the faces of people ahead of you in line, and then you're looking at their backs again. I saw, a couple of bends in the road ahead, Mitzi Milkin. She was overdressed as usual, in a gold lamé blouse and navy slacks, with globs of garnet jewelry hanging on her wrists, her ears, and her chest. If she had heard the news about Heidi, it didn't show on her face, which was cheerfully animated as she talked to her companion, a bald, brawny fellow in a rugby shirt who sported a bushy Stalinesque moustache. I had seen that man before, but I couldn't remember when.

Just my luck. When I was finally rounding the last bend and in the home stretch for hot dogs, the Kindly Uncle spoke over the PA system. *"Mr. Guy Mallon,"* he intoned. *"Will Mr. Guy Mallon please come immediately to the ABA office on the second floor. Mr. Guy Mallon, please come to the ABA office. We have an urgent message for you. Thank you. I hope you folks are enjoying the show."*

So I left the line and found the nearest escalator, then negotiated the long mezzanine and followed signs down hallways to the ABA office. There were at least a dozen people in the office, all of them munching hot dogs and sipping coffee and beer. The far side of the office was a bank of windows overlooking the convention floor. The cafeteria was directly below, and the display halls stretched out right and left from there. I looked down and spotted Mitzi and her companion having lunch. That face...

A young woman asked if she could help me and I told her my name.

"Oh yes," she said. She went to a desk and picked up a piece of paper and handed it to me. "You need to call this number right away. Sunrise Hospital. They said it's urgent."

"May I use your phone?"

"Of course. Dial nine."

I called the number and asked for the extension. I was put through, and after a number of buzzes, a tired voice answered. "Nurses' station."

"My name is Guy Mallon," I said. "I was told to call this number."

"Right. Mr. Mallon. Do you know a Taylor Bingham?"

"Yes," I said. "Now what?"

"Mr. Bingham was brought in here an hour ago. He came to emergency, and he's been transferred to our ward. We need you to come in and sign a few papers."

"What's wrong?" I asked. "What happened?"

"We just need your signature, sir. The patient can't sign because he's too heavily sedated, and we're not allowed to provide care unless we have some proof of insurance or the signature of somebody who will—"

"Okay, I'll be right over, but—"

"Otherwise we have to send him over to County. Not a good option."

"I said I'd come."

"Nurse's station, third floor."

"Can you tell me what's wrong? What happened? How is he? What happened?"

"Injuries to the neck, sir. It looks as if the patient tried to hang himself."

"Oh my god."

"So if we could just have you sign a few papers—"

"I'm curious," I said. "How did you get my name?"

"He wrote you a note," the nurse told me. "The ambulance driver found it on the desk in his motel room. It was addressed to your booth number at the convention center."

I rushed back to our booth empty-handed. "Carol, honey, I have to go," I said. "Taylor Bingham tried to kill himself."

"Oh my lord!"

"I'm sorry I didn't bring you a hot dog, but—"

"It's okay. I heard you being paged. I wondered what that was about. So tell me."

"I don't know much. Tried to hang himself. I have to sign papers for him. I hope he has medical insurance. If not we may have to sell the company."

"Wouldn't that be lovely," she said. "Poor Taylor!"

"By the way," I added. "Lawrence's not a cross dresser. Just thought you'd like to know."

"Oh? Did you ask him?"

"Well, yes, but that's not how I know. I know because until two days ago, Lawrence wore a beard. You can't have a beard and pretend to be a woman."

"That makes sense. Very observant of you, Watson."

"Yeah, and another thing. I saw Mitzi Milkin having lunch with a man."

"My, that *is* news."

"Listen. This guy she was with had this huge bushy mustache, you know, like in a barbershop quartet?"

"And that's what made you think of Lawrence's beard?"

"Well, yes, but that's not the point. The point is, I've seen that man before. I just figured it out. He was the sous-chef for Julia Child in the Knopf booth on Saturday morning."

"Amazing," Carol said, shaking her head. "Guy—"

"No. It *is* amazing. He was the one who smashed a cream pie into Charles Levin's face. I got to go. See you. Bye."

Taylor Bingham looked like shit. He was strapped into the hospital bed, tubes stretching from his arms to two separate IVs, oxygen lines stretching from his nostrils to a tank behind the bed, wires coming out from under his hospital smock and extending to a box with a screen full of wavy lines. His face was white, but his neck and chin were purple. His mouth was wide open, and his eyes half shut.

"Guy," he said in a hoarse whisper.

"Taylor, what the fuck," I answered.

"I'm sorry."

"What the fuck?" I said again, this time a question.

"Did you get my note?" he asked. His words were slow and sloppy.

I held the note in my hand and read aloud, "'Tell *Metropolitan Book Review.* Tell *Publishers Weekly.* Tell *Newsweek.* Remind them who I was. Thanks. Taylor Bingham.' You call that a note?"

"I wasn't feeling chatty." Monotone.

"How do you feel?" I asked.

"How do I look?"

"Probably better than you feel. Taylor, what's going on? Why did you do this?"

"I didn't. Better luck next time." His voice was barely audible.

"Was it because of Heidi?"

"Isn't everything about Heidi?" he droned. "Little JAP."

"You can't use that word, Taylor."

"What? I'm calling her a Japanese American Princess, and that's what she is."

"Was," I said.

"What?"

"Taylor, did you kill Heidi?"

"Hell you talking about?" he mumbled.

"Are you aware that Heidi died Saturday night?"

Taylor's eyes opened up. "Bullshit." His voice grew louder with each syllable.

"It's true," I said. "I'm sorry. I assumed you knew."

"It's bullshit. You're nothing. You're a nightmare. Get the fuck out of here." His voice was soft and dreamy again. "You're a hemorrhoid, Guy Mallon. Go away."

He closed his eyes, and I did as I was told.

"You'll be happy to hear that people have been staying away from our booth in droves," Carol said when I got back to the convention center. "I feel like the plague."

"So you've had an easy afternoon?" I said.

"Easy? Standing on my feet smiling at nobody all afternoon, wondering if you're okay, wondering if Taylor's okay, wondering if Lawrence's okay, wondering what has happened to the gentle world I thought I knew, and talking to nobody? That's not easy, and I'm dead tired, although the word 'dead' has already been claimed by somebody else dear to your heart. No, I'm cranky and tired, and I really, really, really do not want to go to the small press party tonight."

"Me neither," I said.

"You mean that?" she asked. "I thought you were addicted to parties."

"Things have changed," I said. "Let's skip it. How about we quit early, find a restaurant someplace far from the Strip, someplace that serves gin and Thai food, and have a quiet dinner, then go back to our room and watch TV."

She put her hand on my cheek. "You're so good to me," she said. "I want you to know how much I appreciate that."

"Shucks."

"No, I mean it. And another thing," she added. "I didn't mean it when I said it would be lovely if we had to sell the company."

"No?"

"No. I love our company."

"Well, we won't have to worry about that anyway. Taylor probably has health insurance, and if he doesn't we'll let Heidi pay his hospital bills."

"Heidi?"

"She gave me the advance from Ongepotchket Press for *Out of My Face*. Ten grand. That'll cover Taylor, I'm sure."

"She gave you ten thousand dollars?" Carol asked. "What for?"

"I promised not to tell," I said. "But Heidi's dead, and the book's probably dead too. Heidi paid me to ghostwrite the poems in her last book. She had dried up."

Mitzi Milkin

Packaging Panache

Heidi Yamada used the simplest ingredients an artist can use. She used words. Not fancy words, not long and foreign words, not words you have to use a dictionary to understand. Just words.

But what magic that poet performed with words! It was a different magic from anything any poet had done before. That is why her work needed to be published differently from the work of any other poet, living or dead. Packaged uniquely, produced exquisitely, published with fanfare.

Heidi Yamada and I were made for each other, because at the time I met her I had decided to be a one-of-a-kind publisher, the publisher with the most panache, éclat, élan, and pizzazz of any publisher in the history of the written word. I was well on the way to achieving that goal, but I needed the perfect poet to fulfill my dream.

I'll never forget the moment I met Heidi Yamada. It was a literary luncheon, and I saw her across the crowded dining room, her merry laughter rising from the table like a flight of larks, floating above the idle literary chitchat. She was wearing orange and pink, with purple ribbons. Her hair was an inky waterfall. I asked the man sitting next to me, "Who is that woman?"

When I learned who it was, I was doubly delighted, for I had already read the poetry of Heidi Yamada, and it was the first poetry in years that had moved me to tears.

It took all the bravery in my soul, but I stood up from my chair and walked across the dining room and knelt at her side. "Miss Yamada," I said, "I want an autographed copy of your book."

"Which book is that?" Heidi answered. "I've written more than one, you know."

"I'm talking about your next book," I told her. "The one we're going to make together, you and I. The best book ever made."

I had never knelt before any other human being, but I knelt for her, and she granted my wish. She put her hand on my shoulder, and I was dubbed for glory.

Mitzi Milkin is of course the proprietor of Ongepotchket Press, the publisher of the other edition of this anthology of elegies, the one minus the gossip and commentary, the one supposedly endowed with previously unpublished poems by the great lady herself, the one that will cost $800 apiece (plus shipping and handling) because she knows she can presell at least seventy-five copies to collectors who will be more than glad (finally, finally) to complete their collections of the works of Heidi Yamada, not to mention the eccentric millionaires and overendowed institutional special-collections librarians who buy every Ongepotchket book printed. Yes, it will be printed by letterpress, with handset type, on handmade paper, handsewn into uncut quarto signatures of eight. There will be deckle edges, handtooled half-morocco covers, and marbled endsheets. It will be printed in a numbered edition, the size of which will be determined by the number of presold books but in any case limited to one hundred copies. None of the labor will cost her a dime, because she uses student interns from the College of Creative Studies at UCSB. The materials are provided by the University also, courtesy of a gift from the National Endowment for the Humanities and the California Arts Council, with matching grants from the Ford Foundation and Lord and Lady Ridley-Tree of Santa Barbara. The book will be finished in two or three years. Last I heard there are still a few copies unclaimed, so if you aren't satisfied with the trade edition, the one you're holding in your hands, you can get your order in.

My edition of *The Poet's Funeral* doesn't have any of those ruffles and flourishes, partly because I couldn't afford them, and partly because I don't think that's what publishing is all about. The books I publish don't require a glass case to display them in, and unless you've been gardening or changing the points and plugs in your car you don't need to wash your hands every time you touch my books.

Mitzi Milkin began her career by designing outrageous costumes for second-rate T&A shows in Las Vegas back in the seventies. Rumor has it she also starred in the shows, parading around nearly naked even if she was overdressed, making the most of what she had the most of. I don't know if those rumors are true. Anyway, she quit show biz and left Vegas so she could do something more dignified. She came to book publishing after she was fired by Neiman-Marcus, where she had been developing giftwrap design concepts until they determined that she was "overly creative." She decided it was time to go back to school—a brave move for a woman in her forties who wore too much makeup and jewelry—and so she searched for college programs that would nourish her strongest asset, overcreativeness. She chose the University of California at Santa Barbara because of its College of Creative Studies, and came to this town in the early 1980s and enrolled in Harry Reese's course on the book arts.

She learned from Harry how to set type, make paper, mix ink, construct boxes, sew signatures, operate a platen press, and dozens of other arts and chores involved with hand-making books. I have to admire her: she got her fingers stained with ink for a solid academic year. At the end of that year, Harry told her there was nothing more that he could teach her, which was perhaps his polite way of saying, "Mitzi, please, please, please don't take my course again."

She asked him, "Is my work any good at all?"

"At all?" he asked.

"The truth," she urged. "Tell me what you think of my book designs."

"Ongepotchket," he answered.

She laughed. "That's what they told me at Neiman's."

"Run with it," he advised.

So she did. She quit the university and rented space in the Upper Village of Montecito where she established Ongepotchket Press, a nonprofit corporation. She hired two employees, a bookkeeper/office manager and a grant proposal writer; she herself was president, publisher, designer, and marketing director. Then she set about worming her way into Santa Barbara and Montecito society, and she quickly discovered the magic words: *I am a publisher.*

"Oooh really? What sort of books do you publish?"

She would smile and reply, "What sort of books do you write?"

Then she started selling shares of expensive stock in the company to the writing wannabes of Montecito: rich widows and movie stars mainly, most of whom became authors of elegant Ongepotchket chapbooks. The authors praised her lavishly and paid her handsomely for her talents.

It was just a matter of time before she met Heidi Yamada, who was to the written word what Mitzi was to the printed word. It was at one of Barnaby's Miramar lunches, and Mitzi made the mistake of telling Heidi that she loved her poetry.

"You've actually read it?" Wilson asked. By then Heidi had formally given up writing and was used to being kidded about her work.

"Every word," Mitzi said.

"Do you understand it?" Betsy asked.

"Of course."

"Then you haven't read it carefully enough," Mickey said.

"What are you writing nowadays, dear?" Mitzi asked Heidi.

"Nothing at the moment," Heidi answered. "I'm concentrating on promoting Max's career." She snuggled up to her lover's shoulder. Max grinned and took a pull on his Budweiser.

Mitzi persisted. "Maybe we could put together a collection of some of your finest work from the past? I'm thinking velvet slipcase-type thing."

"Oooh," Heidi said. "I like it."

So Heidi was off on a new roll, with a new publisher, and a new book to put together, *Love From My Velvet Slipcase.* She let Max fend for himself while she turned all her attention to her favorite poet, herself. She showed up in my office the following week, hiked up her skirt, sat on my desk, and crossed her legs.

"Guy, honey, I want to use some of the poems from *And Vice Versa* in my new book. You got a problem with that?"

I scratched my chin. "I'd rather you didn't, Heidi."

"Why?" I stopped scratching my chin because she was taking over and scratching it for me, very gently, with her paisley nails. "Huh? How come I can't use my own poems in my own book, stingy-pants?"

"Oh okay," I said. "But don't put my name in the acknowledgments."

She brushed the forelock off my forehead and said, "Thanks, baby. And another thing?"

"What?"

"What do you mean, 'what'? Don't be so unfriendly, Guy-baby."

"Yeah," said Carol, who had appeared at the door, wearing an expression that mingled amusement with murder. "Give the poet what she wants, Guybaby. But save some for me, of course."

Heidi spun around on her butt and slipped her feet to the floor. She brushed her hair back and gave Carol a giant empty smile. "Guy's helping me out with my new book," she explained.

"He doesn't seem in that great a hurry to help you out the door," Carol observed.

"What is it you want, Heidi?" I asked.

"I want the names and addresses of all the people who bought *And Vice Versa*," she said. "Mitzi's going to do a direct-mail promotion to my collectors."

Oy.

It made me feel a bit creepy, and Carol thought it was gross and crass, but I printed out the customer base and sent it to

Ongepotchket Press. What harm could it do me? People who bought poetry because they liked poetry would not buy another book by Heidi Yamada; they'd been stung by that blurb from Arthur Summers but wouldn't fall again. Collectors like Lawrence Holgerson would no doubt buy this new fancy-ass book of hers, but they deserved to lose their money anyway.

Love From My Velvet Slipcase was limited to two hundred copies, of which ten were kept by Mitzi and Heidi. The other hunded and ninety sold, and sold out, at two hundred dollars apiece. Limited, numbered, and signed by the author, the books sold to Heidi's loyal collectors and to Mitzi's shareholders. On the title page of every copy, Heidi planted a fuchsia lipstick kiss.

Mitzi Milkin, the big spender, paid Heidi Yamada a thousand bucks for the one-time use of her recycled poems. Heidi didn't need the money, but it pleased her to be back in the spotlight. She made the cover of *Santa Barbara Magazine.* She lunched with Bo Derek. She played golf with Bob Mitchum. She wore dark glasses everywhere. She even started to write again, or so she claimed.

The new collection was to be called *Out of My Face,* and Mitzi started the buzz early. These were to be verses of gossipy memoirs, naming names from Heidi's decade-long literary career. Arthur Summers. Beatrice Knight. Charles Levin. Taylor Bingham. Linda Sonora. Max Black. They'd all be there, parading in the nude, Mitzi intimated. Plus the bit players, like Wilson Williams and Paul Shelley and Mickey Raskin and Ray Bradbury. Mitzi started selling subscriptions to this one early: eight hundred dollars apiece for a numbered and signed limited edition of three hundred copies. This was going to be a blockbuster, and Heidi even started hearing from her old friends at *People* magazine again.

Now all Heidi had to do was write the poems. Mitzi was already ordering materials. Paper would be made from Max's old jeans. Ink would be made from ground mussel shells from Japan. The boards would be...boards, mahogany. Mitzi was writing checks, getting a loan to cover the expenses. Receiving advance orders. Lawrence Holgerson paid an extra three hundred dollars to get the lowest number available for sale.

Mitzi reserved and paid for a full booth at the American Booksellers Association convention in Las Vegas, which was coming up in June 1990. And a full-page ad in *Antiquarian Bookman.*

And it was time, past time, for Heidi to write those poems.

That's when Heidi discovered for the first time the shoals, the doldrums, the disease known to every writer, with the possible exception of Sue Grafton.

Writer's block.

She called me up. "I can't think of anything to say, Guy!"

"When did that ever stop you?" I asked.

She hung up.

Mitzi called me up. "Heidi's being difficult," she told me. "She said you're the only person who ever gave her any real encouragement, and now you're acting pissy."

"All she has to do is write a bunch of poems," I said. "How difficult can that be?"

Mitzi hung up.

Arthur Summers called me. "Have you heard from Ms. Yamada?" he asked.

"Poor Heidi," I said.

He chuckled and agreed. "Poor Heidi."

When I told all this to Carol, she said I was being cruel. She said I should get Heidi some drugs.

"I don't know how to score drugs anymore," I said. "What drugs did you have in mind?"

"They say cyanide's nice," Carol said. "On the other hand, maybe you ought to write the poems for her."

"I'm not a poet," I said.

"Neither is she."

"I can't do it. I won't do it. Don't bring it up again. Jesus."

So I had a meeting with Heidi and Mitzi and we worked out a deal. I would write the poems, Heidi would pay me the ten thousand dollars that Mitzi paid her, and I would keep my mouth shut. I wouldn't even tell Carol. Mitzi would spare no expense designwise, and Heidi would promote like a movie star. The only actual writing she had to do was to sign her name on the bastard title of three hundred copies. That's all the writing she had to do. Two words.

I wrote the god damn poems. Heidi and Mitzi both liked them, even if I thought they were somewhere between parody and gibberish. I agreed with Heidi and Mitzi: I wouldn't tell if they wouldn't tell. Mitzi wrote me a check, which I cashed and put into a new bank account that even Carol didn't know about.

So sue me. I wrote a bunch of poems and made a bunch of money. Wouldn't most poets like to say the same thing? I listened to Heidi babble about her past and then wrote the poems. It took me about fifteen minutes apiece and a lot of my stomach. Yes, I wrote them. And now you know where I got a lot of the inside gossip that has filled the rest of this book.

It doesn't matter anyway, because for some reason Mitzi didn't get the book ready for ABA, which was to be its big debut, and now that Heidi's dead it looks as if the book may never come out, in which case Mitzi lost a lot of change.

I'm glad I cashed my check.

After I finally told Carol the truth about my contribution to *Out of My Face,* on Monday afternoon at the ABA, we left the convention hall and walked over to the Landmark to freshen up. We were almost out the door to an early dinner when the phone rang.

"Don't answer it," Carol said.

She can do that; I can't. When a phone rings, I have to answer. "Hello?"

"Guy, darling, this is Mitzi. Where in the world are you?"

"Well, guess, Mitzi. Where did you just call?"

She gave me a false tinkle of laughter. "But Guy, darling, the show isn't over yet. It's only five o'clock. You're supposed to stay till five-thirty, aren't you?"

"It's been a long day, Mitzi."

"Tell me about it. You got a minute?"

"Actually, no," I said. "Carol and I were just on our way out the door."

"There's a lot of money at stake here, Guy. A lot of money. It would be worth your while to just sit down and chat with me over a drink or two. May I come over to the Landmark and buy you a glass of wine?"

I thought about a lot of money, and then I thought about Carol standing in the doorway wearing her face of amused disgust, and I said, "Mitzi, it will have to wait. If it's a lot of money, it will still be here tomorrow morning."

"We have to get this project going, Guy. Like yesterday."

"What project?" Wrong. Should not have said that.

"I'll be right over. We can discuss it. Meet me in the lobby and we'll go into the cocktail lounge there. I'll see you in five minutes. Bye!"

I hung up. "Carol," I said, "there's been a change of plans."

"Oh?"

"Yes. I don't really feel like Thai food. How about Italian?"

"Sounds good."

"Let's go."

◇◇◇

We got into our station wagon and drove out Charleston Boulevard for several miles till we found an Italian restaurant called Fellini's in a strip mall. It turned out to be a pleasant place, with a carpet on the floor and red Naugahyde booths, checkered tablecloths, and Chianti bottles smothered in candlewax. The waiter wore a stained tuxedo and a clip-on bow tie, and he handed us huge leather-bound menus. We ordered martinis, and he bowed.

When he was out of earshot I said, "These menus look like something Mitzi Milkin might have designed."

"You know what I'd like?" Carol said. "I'd like it if we didn't talk about business during dinner."

"Fine with me," I answered.

"That includes this year's ABA and all its parties. That includes Heidi Yamada and how she died. That includes anybody we've spent any time with over the past few days. Okay?"

"That sounds wonderful. Here come our drinks."

The martinis were tasty. Carol had ordered Bombay, as she always did, and I had asked for Boodles, which I usually do. We traded tastes and then talked briefly about the difference between Boodles and Bombay.

When that conversation fizzled, we spent some time looking at the menu and discussing the relative merits of penne and ziti. When the waiter returned to our table Carol ordered ziti and I ordered penne, plus salads. We asked for refills on our martinis and reminded him who had the Bombay and who had the Boodles.

We smiled at each other across the candlelit table and didn't say another word until the waiter brought us our second drinks, and then I asked Carol if she liked baseball.

"No," she said. "I mean there's nothing wrong with baseball, but I just never got interested. How about you?"

"No. I've never been to a ball game, why?"

"Well? You asked me."

"I have a cousin in Vermont who's into baseball," I said. "He writes for *Baseball Digest.*'"

"Really?" Carol said. "What's his name?"

"Guy. Guy Mallon, just like me."

"Oh."

That conversation was enough for a while. During the salad course, Carol asked me who my favorite book illustrator was. "Arthur Rackham," I said. "Yours?"

"Barry Moser. Rackham's wonderful, of course."

"So's Moser."

We had to wait a while for the pasta to arrive. It was quiet in the restaurant. Monday night.

"So," I said. "How do you like California so far?"

"I've been in California over seven years," she said. "In fact, as you know, I was born and raised in Pasadena. I was only in Texas for a decade. I'm glad to be back."

"You like California better than Texas, then?"

"Much better."

"Me too."

"I thought you'd never been to Texas?"

"I haven't. Here's dinner."

We both poked at our pasta, and it seemed to take half an hour to eat half a plate of food. There was so much not to say. Finally, Carol set down her fork, leaned toward me, and said in a low voice, "Guy, who do you think killed Heidi Yamada?"

Suddenly the meal got delicious. The conversation revved up as we shoveled pasta into our mouths and talked with our mouths full, holding hands across the table.

"For a while there I thought it had something to do with yellow bandannas," I said, "and I was ready to pin it on Arthur Summers. I'm pissed off at him anyway, hitting on you that way."

"He wasn't hitting on me. I was hitting on him," Carol said. "But only because you were hitting on Marjorie."

"I wasn't hitting on Marjorie."

"You toured the mansion with her."

"Because I was jealous of you and Summers."

She smiled. "Aren't we both a little old to be playing this game?"

"Damn right," I agreed. "At our age we could get injured."

"Anyway, at some point during the party Art got quiet and weird. That was after he came back from the bathroom. Now we know why. At the end of the evening he asked me if I'd meet him for breakfast the next morning. I said okay, but what for and it would have to be after nine, because I didn't want any flak from you about it. He said okay and I asked him again what for, and he told me he had to go to the police, but I didn't find out why until we got there yesterday morning. Guy, honey, we didn't play golf."

"I knew that."

"Or anything else. I promise you. And I know Arthur Summers didn't kill Heidi Yamada. He was terribly shaken up and eager to help the cops, who didn't seem to want his help at all.

They gave him back his bandanna and told him to be on his way. They kept me there for a while so I could give that bogus interview to the newspapers. So who do you think did it? It wasn't Arthur."

"Beatrice? All those bandannas were her idea."

"Forget it. Yellow bandannas are a red herring."

"Thank you, Dame Agatha. But you'll have to admit she wasn't all that broken up to hear the news today."

"That says to me that she has nothing to hide."

"You're right. She's a first-class phonus balonus, and if she killed Heidi she'd have put on an Oscar performance about how shocked she was."

"So who, then? Max? I doubt it. Taylor Bingham? Poor Lawrence?"

"I'm leaning towards Levin," I said. "I never did like that man."

"There are a lot of men not to like," Carol answered. "And a lot of women. What about Linda? She hated Heidi's guts."

"I kind of like Linda," I said.

"You like her cleavage."

"What makes you think that?"

"Because you're a man."

"Then you're a sexist," I countered.

"Is that what you like so much about Marjorie?"

"Poor Marjorie. I wonder what happened to her."

"What do you mean?" Carol asked.

So I told Carol about Marjorie in the taxicab. The look on her face, the mean grin on that pig-nosed cabbie as he tore out of the lot. And about Marjorie's room being trashed.

"My God, do you think she's all right? Shouldn't you call the cops, that detective, Plumley?"

"I did. He hung up on me. He's tired of this case."

"Well I am too," Carol said. "But you can't just let people kill people."

"Okay, here's another question," I said. "Who stole the invitations and got everyone invited to the Random House party?"

"Does it matter?"

"The next question is: why? All I know is somebody at that party slipped Heidi a mickey."

"I love it when you talk tough. Cliché me, big boy."

"Which reminds me: the man who put a pie in Levin's face, or vice versa, was eating hot dogs with Mitzi Milkin this afternoon, and Mitzi now wants to talk to me."

"So?"

"So maybe Mitzi swiped the invitations while Levin was wiping custard off his mug."

"But she didn't."

"Why not?"

"Because she was at our booth most of the time you were off hobnobbing with Random House. She wanted to talk to you then, too. Besides," Carol said, "there's no way Mitzi slipped Heidi a roofie."

"Roofie?"

"A mickey for the nineties. And Mitzi wasn't guilty."

"No?"

"No. Remember? Mitzi got drugged too."

That's when I remembered the champagne that was passed around. I remembered Levin urging everyone to grab a glass of champagne. It was only a few minutes after that that Heidi wandered off to dreamland and Mitzi went kerplop on the table. And then I remembered....

"I have photographs!" I announced.

There was no place to park in front of or anywhere near Fast Foto, so we turned down Convention Center Drive and drove to the Landmark and parked in the hotel lot. Then, hand in hand, we walked back to the Strip. It felt good to walk off a big meal in the warm desert air. We were both still high from the gin and the puzzle, and Carol's hand in mine was the sweetest treasure I had ever held.

Fortunately, Fast Foto was a twenty-four-hour business, so we just walked right in. I pulled my claim check out of my wallet and handed it to the teenage girl behind the counter. She snapped her gum, opened a drawer, and withdrew a package of prints, and I paid with a MasterCard. I put the package in the inner pocket of my linen jacket, and we were out the door.

We passed a bus stop with a bench, and Carol said, "You want to sit down and have a look?"

"I can wait," I said. "I'd rather spread them out and take a look in better light."

"Good."

It's a ten-minute walk along Convention Center Drive from the Strip to the Landmark. We were strolling on the left side of the street when a taxicab pulled up alongside of us, going the wrong way. When I turned to wave it off, the driver jumped out of the cab and stood before us on the sidewalk. Yes. The same one. The pig nose, the knit cap. Oh shit. The same logo on the side of the car: LV-VIP.

"Okay," the cabbie said. "Just give them to me, and that will be fine."

"Give what?" I asked.

"You know perfectly well what, asshole. Less have 'em."

Carol said, "Get out of our way. You can't do this. We didn't come to Las Vegas to get mugged. Now—"

The cabbie gave her a backhand slap across the face with his right hand, then grabbed her arm with his left. In no time at all, a small knife was open in his right hand, and a long red line of blood popped out on the soft side of her forearm, which he had twisted for me to see.

"Ow!"

"That's right. It hurts. It's a real sharp blade, so you have to be careful with it, so it doesn't cut your arm or your face or something, right?" He still had a strong grip on Carol's arm, which he was twisting backwards so that she could barely keep her balance on one foot.

"Stop it," I said. I felt my hands turning into fists.

"What's that?"

"I said stop it right now." My fists dissolved. I pulled the package of photos out of my jacket pocket. "Here. You looking for these?"

"How did you guess?" He let go of Carol's arm and snatched the photos out of my hand and stuffed them into his hip pocket.

"How did you guess I had them?"

"Your other girlfriend doesn't like knives either."

He put his hand on Carol's sternum and shoved hard, forcing her against me so that we both ended up on the sidewalk. Then he quickly stepped back and folded himself into his taxi and slammed the door. As we pulled ourselves back up to our feet, we watched the cab squeal away across the oncoming traffic to rejoin the flow on the right side of the street. It bullied its way into the far lane, then turned right on Paradise Road and disappeared.

"Did you get the license plate?" Carol asked.

"No. You?"

"No. Shit."

"How's your arm?" I asked.

She pulled a yellow bandanna out of her purse and wrapped her forearm. "I knew this would come in handy some day," she said. "Not too bad. He didn't cut deep."

"Your face?"

"It hurts some. That little fucker!"

"Not so little," I said. "At least from my perspective."

"You gave him our photographs!"

"What else could I do? He wasn't interested in your purse or my wallet."

"Who is that man, Guy?"

"Same one who kidnapped Marjorie," I said. "But I don't know why he did it or who he's working for."

"Now what?" she said.

"I guess that's it."

"It? What do you mean, 'it'?"

"Well, Carol, we can't exactly go chasing that guy. I guess we could report this to the police. I still have Plumley's business card. But we'll never get those photographs back. But for now the important thing is to get back to our room and do something about your arm."

"Bull shit. We're going back to Fast Foto. Come on." She started walking back the way we had come.

"But, honey, that's not how it works," I said, struggling to keep up with my long-legged, stubborn partner. "They've sold us the prints and the negs. That's it."

"They may still have the film."

"Carol, the film and the negs are the same thing. They don't have anything there. It's gone."

"Maybe there were out-takes. Maybe they made duplicate prints by mistake."

"You're grasping at straws. Even if there were out-takes or dupes, they'd be thrown away by now."

"We'll dig through the Dumpster if we have to."

"Oh great," I mumbled. "They probably share a Dumpster with Arby's. That's going to be pleasant."

Carol stopped and faced me. She still held the bandanna to her arm, and it was now more red than yellow. "Don't go negative on me, Guy Mallon," she said. "Okay, it's a long shot, but it's a shot. That man hit me and cut me and threatened us both with a lot worse."

"My point exactly."

"Well I'm not quitting yet," she said. "And you aren't either. Come on." With that she was off again, and once again I was trotting to keep up with her. Her momentum seemed to make the impossible possible. That Carol Murphy was one amazing woman, and if she didn't get us both killed she'd keep us both young and hopping for a long, long time.

We reached the Strip, crossed it, and turned right. We walked a block and a half to Fast Foto. We ducked in, and there was the same clerk, who looked up at us with a red, fearful face.

"Omigod, I'm really, really sorry," she said. "I gave you the wrong pictures." She reached into the drawer and pulled out another package of photos. "These are yours. I didn't, like, did you look at the other pictures, I mean did you—"

"It's okay," Carol said. "We won't tell anybody."

"Can I have them back?" the girl said. "Here, these are yours." She handed me the package. "I mean can I have them back? Those other pictures?"

"We threw them away," Carol said.

"You promise?"

"They were repulsive," Carol insisted.

"You threw them away?"

"That's what I said. The trash can on the corner if you want to go digging."

"Oh that's all right," the teenager said. "I made two sets. Thank you! I'm really, really sorry."

"It's okay," I said. "Simple mistake. Will you do us a favor?"

"What?"

"Call us a cab?"

While we waited for the cab to arrive we spread the photos, the right photos, out on the counter.

Yup. These were all shots from the Random House party. There I was, arguing with Charles Levin. In the next shot Levin and I were both smiling at the camera. A shot of Taylor Bingham leaning into Linda Sonora's ear. Me again, holding onto Taylor's arm and leading him away from Linda's table, Casey and his trio; you could almost hear the music. Beatrice Knight leaving our table, her right hand cocked behind her butt to give Heidi Yamada the finger. Carol with her hands folded before her and her eyes rolled heavenward. Max Black standing behind Heidi's chair, glaring at the camera, and another shot of Max striding toward the dance floor. Two distant shots of Charles Levin lifting a champagne glass and speaking into a mike. A blond waitress approaching with a tray. Another. Another. The tray has three champagne flutes on it. Closer. Heidi accepting one of the flutes. Mitzi taking another of the flutes, her arm blocking Heidi's face. Heidi grabs the final glass. Heidi drinks, chugs one glass of champagne. Mitzi sips. The waitress backing away, a startled look on her face. Heidi starts on the second glass. Mitzi sips again, a smile on her lips. Carol and I glaring at each other, then Carol and I glaring at the camera. Heidi arguing with Mitzi; Heidi's eyes are at half mast, and Mitzi's grin is goofy. Both of Heidi's glasses are empty. So is Mitzi's. Heidi from behind, as she leaves the table; she's listing to the right, steadying herself with her hand on the back of my chair. My hand is on Carol's on the tablecloth, and Carol looks bored. Mitzi; her head is on the table. Another one of those, profile. Carol rising from the table. A facial portrait of Guy Mallon, proprietor of Guy Mallon Books, smiling for the photographer from *Publishers Weekly*. End of roll.

"Did anybody here call a cab?"

We turned around. The cabbie in the doorway was somebody I had never seen before. "That's us," I said.

On the short ride back to the Landmark, I asked Carol, "Did you see what I saw?"

"I think we've found our killer," she said.

When we got back to our room we found our suitcase dumped on the bed and our drawers messed up. As far as we could tell, nothing was missing.

"Are we going to report this?" Carol asked.

"To whom? The front desk? The police?"

"Well?"

"I don't mean to be gloomy, Carol," I said. "But the front desk lets things like this happen. I don't know why, and I don't think I want to find out. The police aren't very interested in this sort of thing either, as far as I can tell. I think we're on our own."

"So we're supposed to sleep in this room, knowing that some thug could just walk in here?"

I used the chain on the inside of our door, then blocked the door with the armchair tucked under the knob. "That's the best I can do till tomorrow. Tomorrow morning we check out."

"Look under the bed," Carol said.

I plopped down on the floor and peered. "There's no room to hide here, and there's nobody here." I got up and checked the closet and the bathroom. I threw back the shower curtain, and there—was nobody. "Just us chickens," I said.

Carol pointed at the phone on the bedside table. The message light was blinking. I picked up the receiver and dialed 2 to collect messages.

"Guy, honey, it's Mitzi. I've been waiting down here for fifteen minutes, and I came up and knocked on your door, and no answer. What gives? I guess you've left. Guy, we need to talk. I mean we really need to talk, and right now. When you get in I want you to phone my room. I'm in the Circus Circus. I don't have the number here, but you can get it and ask for me. If I'm not there, leave a message and the right time for me to call back. If all else fails, I'll see you at your booth tomorrow morning, first thing. This is important, Guy. I mean it. I'm trying to help you out. I think you're in danger."

"What should I do?" I asked.

"I want you to keep the light on in the bathroom," Carol answered.

We undressed and I helped Carol wash and dry her arm. Then got into bed and held each other tight until somehow we both fell asleep.

Lawrence Holgerson

The Jewel of My Collection

*My relationship with the late Heidi Yamada began on the day I received
the announcement of the publication of her first book,* And Vice Versa.
*I bought it, I loved it, I decided right then that this new poet would be
an important part of my collection. How little I knew. In fact, she has
become the jewel in the crown of my collection. I have given my life to
Heidi Yamada, and now she has given her life to us all.*

*As I think all of you know, I am a serious book collector. That's
different from being a book accumulator. Well, yes, once upon a time
I did accumulate books. But I have learned, painfully, that book
collecting, which emerged early in my life as a passion, precludes
accumulation. I think in fact that it was my infatuation with Heidi
Yamada that converted me from accumulation to collection.*

*By the time I found Heidi Yamada, I was already well stocked.
I had incredible holdings. Very well, I realize that my time on this
podium is not supposed to be spent describing my own achievements.
I'm getting there, believe me. Bear with me. You poets and literary
types are such wonderful, such sensitive souls.*

Very well, then.

*The first Yamada was easy to get. I was drawn to it largely by my
faith in Guy Mallon's taste; after all, here was a man who had at that
time what I considered the second most important collection of modern
American poets. I was absolutely sold by the endorsement of Arthur
Summers, whose books I had already collected. My collection of Summers*

was at that time complete and it remained complete for years thereafter. I had to have this new book by this as-yet unknown poet if simply for the fact that Arthur Summers' name was printed on the back cover.

I continued to collect Arthur Summers, and my collection of books by that poet is still complete, and although there's no way of determining the completeness of a poet's ephemera, manuscripts, and correspondence, I feel safe in saying my collection of those Summers materials is better than any other collection, including those held by the University of California, the poet himself, or even Guy Mallon. Some of the Summers letters would be of great interest to a number of people in this room, I can assure you of that.

No, wait. I hear you muttering and rustling, but this is important and it is about Heidi Yamada and my devotion to her. Really.

It is my belief, and I think this belief is shared with many of you, that Heidi Yamada kept the handwritten manuscript of her first book, And Vice Versa. *She referred to that manuscript often, even during the last weekend of her life.*

Friends, let me speak plainly. I want that autograph. I need it for my collection of Yamadana, and I feel that it rightfully belongs on my shelf, alongside every other book written by the hand of Heidi Yamada.

The manuscript has mysteriously disappeared. Ever since Heidi's death, I've searched and begged, and nobody can tell me anything about it. Some of you have denied knowing of its existence, but I believe every one of you who has spoken today knows about that manuscript, and I also believe that at least one of you knows exactly where that manuscript is.

I beg you. I beseech you. Come forward. Put that autograph in my hands. I am not a wealthy man, but I'll make it worth your while. I offer to anyone who gives me the original manuscript of And Vice Versa *my entire Arthur Summers collection.*

That's right. The entire Arthur Summers collection. As I said earlier, there are letters in that collection that would be of great interest to most of you in this room. I would dare to say that some of those letters would be as important to some of you as the Yamada autograph is to me. Let's make a deal.

Fair enough?

I've known Lawrence Holgerson since I was in college. I was at Stanford on a scholarship, working part-time in the Palo Alto Bookshop to make ends meet, and Lawrence was a graduate student in the English Department, an Yvor Winters/Janet Lewis groupie. He lived, and still lives, in a cheap garage apartment in College Terrace; he doesn't drive, and his tweedy clothes are all from Value Village in Redwood City. I don't say that to put him down, because I admire thrift. But in Lawrence's case the thrift is calculated: he spends lavishly on his book collection, which is why he has always scrimped on everything else.

As long as I was in Palo Alto, which lasted many years after I dropped out of Stanford, Lawrence was a fixture in the English Department, like a pencil sharpener. He was no longer enrolled, but he was supposedly working on a dissertation that would be the biggest thing since *In Defense of Reason*. Meanwhile, the department gave him a sinecure tending the Jones Room, the Creative Writing Program's private lounge in the main library. There he dusted furniture, catalogued literary magazines, and hung out with the best of the Stanford poets—Janet Lewis, Charles Gullans and Edgar Bowers and J. V. Cunningham in the early days, then on to Philip Levine and Ken Fields, and later the younger ones, Sharon Olds, Bob Barth, Thom Gunn, Tim Steele and those folks. I'm not sure why they tolerated him, but of course he posed no threat of competition.

"I don't write poetry," he used to confess. "I write *about* poetry."

Here it is 1990, that dissertation is still in the works (sup-posedly), and Lawrence Holgerson is still not a Ph.D. He may write about poetry, but nothing he's ever written has ever been published. I feel safe in saying that, because if Lawrence had gotten any essays or articles into print, he would certainly have let us all know about it.

In the interim, though, he has collected personally inscribed firsts from all of the Wintersian poets, and he's also built up an enormous collection of other postwar California poets, includ-ing such notables as Robert Hass and Dana Gioia and Arthur Summers, and of course Heidi Yamada and Maxwell Black. His personal library in College Terrace is legendary. Now that I've sold off most of my collection—and most of it went to him—I expect his is the biggest and best collection of postwar California poets in the world. That probably doesn't matter much to most people. It matters a lot to Lawrence Holgerson. I expect it has drastically reduced his living space, but nobody I know has ever been invited inside that garage apartment.

Arthur Summers dedicated one of his books to Lawrence Holgerson. One afternoon, when we were drinking wine in my office, I asked Art why he had done that. "I was hard up for cash at the time," Art said. "A girlfriend of mine needed an operation, and, well that's a long story. Anyway, Lawrence offered me a thousand dollars to dedicate the stupid book to him, and I took it. *Mea culpa.* It didn't hurt me much. I still got the MacArthur grant the next year, and now I'm up for Poet Laureate. My early books are starting to bring a pretty penny, so Lawrence got his money's worth."

As far as I know no other poets sold Lawrence a dedication, but some of his old friends started soaking him in other ways. They'd have letterpress broadsides printed by Clifford Burke in San Francisco in tiny editions and sell them to Lawrence for five hundred dollars. I know two of them who corresponded in longhand for a year, had the original letters bound, and then sold the volume to guess who. Holgerson didn't tell anyone how much he paid for that collection of letters; nor did he let anyone read it. He hinted that it was "significant" in both style and content, but a lot of us speculated that the correspondence was full of grocery lists and baseball scores.

Heidi Yamada was Lawrence Holgerson's downfall. He got suckered into buying that first book, *And Vice Versa,* because I published it and because Arthur Summers blurbed it. He could not admit that he'd made a mistake, so he continued to buy a first edition of each of Heidi's other books as they were published by Random House. That was still nothing to be ashamed of; he didn't have to say he read or enjoyed the poems, after all.

But when Heidi hooked up with Mitzi Milkin he knew he was being played for a sucker. Something about the man required that he buy a copy of every single edition of every single book of poetry published by the postwar Californians whom he collected, and Heidi was one of those. I used to be a book collector too, so I understand some of that madness. But even in my foolish youth I would never have bought an Ongepotchket Press book. Celestial Arts meets Victoria's Secret. Lawrence Holgerson couldn't help it. Nor could he afford it. Nor did he want it. But he was hooked.

He was hooked and he was desperate. There was only one way out of this addiction. There was only one way to ensure that he'd have a complete collection—the only complete collection—of Heidi Yamadana without having to spend any more money on crap.

Carol and I got out of bed early on Tuesday morning, after a mostly sleepless night. There were moments of slumber, perhaps, and some of those moments may have lasted minutes or even an hour, but there was no escaping the fear and the god damn it anger that washed over us like waves, whether we were thinking or dreaming, talking of murder and muggers, or merely holding onto each other until daylight came and reminded us that the only way to escape the panic was by being brave enough to act.

So by six o'clock we were showered, dressed, and packed. We took our last trip down the rattletrap elevator and shlepped our luggage—two suitcases, Carol's briefcase, and my Penguin bag—to the Landmark parking lot.

"Oh shit," we both said when we spotted our station wagon, two aisles away.

A yellow taxicab was parked next to us.

"You figure there's anybody in that cab?" I asked.

"You mean anybody armed and dangerous?" Carol answered.

"I guess we'd better find out," I said. "Let's put our suitcases and stuff under this car."

"Why?"

"If we have to make a run for it, I don't want to be lugging forty pounds of clothes, papers, and freebies."

Carol nodded, and we stashed our loot, then crept along the next aisle over until we could get a closer look at the cab.

No thugs. The cab was empty as far as we could tell. Carol said, "Thank God."

"We'd better have a closer look," I said. "He could be lying down on the seat."

"No, that's not the same taxi. This is just a Yellow cab."

"The one last night was yellow too."

"Yeah, but the company name on the door was different. That was LV-VIP Cabs. This is just Yellow."

"You're right. I forgot about that."

So we went back for our stuff and carried it to the station wagon. When we got it loaded into the back and locked the doors, Carol said, "Now can we get the fuck out of here?"

"Not quite," I said. "I have to go check out of the hotel. You want to wait here?"

Carol said, "No-ho way."

When we got back to the front desk we found my old friend Robert in charge. He acted as if we had never met. I paid with the company MasterCard and turned in the key, then said, "By the way, Robert?"

"Yes, sir?"

"Just thought you might be interested to know that somebody broke into our room last night while we were out to dinner."

"I'm sorry to hear that, Mr. Mallon," Robert said, his eyes focused about a foot and a half above the top of my head. "I hope your stay in Las Vegas was pleasant otherwise."

It was too early in the morning to come up with a retort that would keep this pleasant conversational ball rolling, so I snatched back my credit card, turned on my heel, and took Carol's hand. We left through the front door and went back to the station wagon.

The Yellow Cab was gone.

After checking to make sure our stuff was still in the station wagon—it was—we climbed in and drove across the street to the convention center lot, paid for a day's parking, and found a spot as close as we could to the loading docks around back.

We still had a couple of hours to kill before the convention center doors would open up for exhibitors, so we strolled back up Convention Center Drive to the Paddlewheel for breakfast. The weather outside was already blistering and the noise inside the casino was already turned up to nine. But the waitress in the restaurant looked as tired as we felt, and for some reason I found that reassuring. We thanked her for the coffee, placed our order, and began to plot our strategy for the day.

By the time we finished breakfast it was almost eight o'clock, so we walked back to Paradise Road and crossed over to the convention center. We could have gone straight into the building through the front doors, but Carol had left her briefcase in the back of the station wagon, and I wanted to get our hand truck, so we went around back. The lot back there was filling up with vehicles.

"Oh shit."

A yellow taxi was parked right next to the station wagon.

"Calm down," Carol told me. "We can't freak out every time we see a taxicab."

"I know," I said. "We only worry about the ones that say 'LV-VIP' on the side."

"Like this one," she added.

"Exactly. The hand truck can wait."

"I guess I don't need my briefcase right away either."

We changed our course and walked around to the front of the building and went through the main entrance just as they were opening the doors to exhibitors.

Just inside the door we were each handed a copy of the final *PW Daily*, which we carried through the labyrinth of tired aisles to our booth. Along the way we heard the Kindly Uncle give us our final pep talk.

"People, you have put on a spectacular show this year! Thank you all for making this year's ABA a stunning success. Now in a few minutes we'll be opening the doors one more time for those fabulous booksellers, the people we do it all for. Let me remind you, exhibitors, that the show is not over and will not be over until two o'clock this afternoon. The wonderful booksellers who come in this morning, wearing their honored blue badges, paid good money to see a full ABA. So remember, people, there is to be no breaking down early. The show is not over until two p.m. I hope you make lots of sales, lots of new friends, and lots of fond memories of our annual get-together."

Walking through the aisles, I looked right and left and saw publishers already hard at work knocking down their displays. Some were subtle about it, rearranging display cases by putting most of their samples into boxes. Others were piling up hand trucks with cartons and wrapping posters into tubes and crates.

Our aisle was fast becoming a ghost town. Half the exhibitors were already packing up their wares, and the other booths were unmanned. When we reached our booth I sat down and opened up the *PW Daily* to read the front-page story about Charles Levin and Linda Sonora. "Don't get too comfortable," Carol said. "Here she comes."

I stood up. Yes indeed, here she came struttin', in her flashy, flowery silk suit, a smile as big as the Tropicana painted on her face.

She kissed the air beside Carol's cheek, she kissed the air beside my cheek, she groaned out a big sigh and said, "Guy, darling!"

"Hello, Mitzi."

"You're a hard man to find all of a sudden," she scolded.

"It's a good man who's hard to find," said Carol.

"No, dear," Mitzi said. "Vice versa. Speaking of which—"

"Enough chitchat," I interrupted. "Mitzi, I want to know what that phone call was all about."

She plopped her briefcase down on top of our samples, patted it, and said, "Guy, I have here the beginnings of a book that you and I are going to publish together. It will be spectacular. It will be sensational in every sense of the word. It's going to be beautiful, as beautiful a book as I can design. It's going to put us both on the map—"

"Guy Mallon Books is already on the map," Carol snapped.

"—and, it will also make us both a ton of money," Mitzi continued. "What do you think of that?"

"Fine," I said, "but that's not the phone call I'm talking about. What were you talking about when you left a message that we're in serious danger?"

Mitzi groaned out a dramatic sigh. "Guy, honey, I just hate to play hardball."

"Go on."

"Well isn't it obvious? You're in danger of losing out on the publishing opportunity of a lifetime. I love you to death, Guy, but if you don't want to go in with me on this—"

"On what?" Carol demanded. "You can talk to me too, you know. I run this business."

Mitzi showed Carol the lipstick on her teeth, then turned back to me. "Let me be blunt," she said. "I have something you want, and you have something I want. Something to die for."

"That's what I'm afraid of," I said.

Carol said, "Oh Christ, to be continued. Here comes the Las Vegas Police Department."

Mitzi's face did a fast metamorphosis as she glanced over my head and down the aisle. She snatched her briefcase off the table, messing up our display. "Guy, honey," she said, "*and* Carol, I must be off. I have dozens of appointments, as you can imagine. But I'll be back. Or maybe we can do lunch tomorrow in Santa Barbara? The El Encanto? My treat."

"We're not going straight back to Santa Barbara," Carol said.

"No?"

"No," I said. "I promised Carol a night at the Nipton Hotel."

"Nipton?" Mitzi said. "That's way out in the desert."

"So's Las Vegas."

"I know, darling, but nothing's happening in Nipton."

"Exactly," Carol said, smiling.

"Well, I'll try to get back here to your booth before two, then. We have a lot to talk about. I won't make any commitments on this till I have your answer, and that's a promise!"

And she was off, down the aisle in the other direction from the one where Daniel Plumley and Perry Stone were approaching.

"I'm never going to get to read my newspaper," I told Carol.

◇◇◇

"Hey, Guy," Dan Plumley said when they reached our booth. Both cops whipped off their dark glasses and stuck them into their jacket pockets. Plumley grinned and we shook hands. Perry Stone nodded and stepped back. "Good to see you, Guy," Plumley said. "You too, Miz Maloney."

He set a full Penguin bag down on the display table, knocking over a stack of *And Vice Versa*.

"My name's Murphy," Carol said. "Good to see you, too. We were mugged last night, by the way."

The grin vanished from Dan Plumley's face. "You're kidding."

"She is not," I said.

"I'm awfully sorry. Where did it happen?"

Perry Stone whipped a notepad out of his pocket and got to work while Carol and I answered Dan's questions. On Convention Center Drive. About nine-thirty. A cab driver. Big guy, smashed-in nose, watch cap on his head. LV-VIP, a yellow vehicle. Knife, probably a switchblade...

Carol held up her arm and Dan inspected the wound carefully and whistled.

...No, he didn't seem to want our money. He was after something else, but he didn't say what. He cut Carol's arm, then
pushed us down on the sidewalk, then split. No, we didn't get the
license number. No, like I said, he didn't want our money....

"Gee, I'm awfully sorry," Detective Plumley said. "That kind
of thing is bad news for a tourist destination like this. We'll certainly look into this, although I'm not sure what we'll find."

"Probably nothing," I said.

"Just thought you'd want to know about it," Carol said. "Or
not."

"I appreciate that," Plumley said. "I really do. Well, listen, I
brought you this bag. It's the one Mr. Bingham had with him."
Plumley picked up the Penguin bag and handed it to me. "He
denied that it belonged to him. I don't know whether he was
telling the truth or not, but in any case he refused to take it
with him. So yesterday I had another look at all the books he
was carrying, and it turns out they were all published by you.
Thought you might want them back."

I looked inside the bag, and the first thing I saw was the
blond wig. Then the falsies. "They may be my books," I said,
"but I hope you know this isn't my bag."

Plumley laughed. "I didn't think it was. Just a little souvenir of
Las Vegas, so you'll remember what a good time you had here."

"Speaking of souvenirs," I said, "whatever happened to those
rolls of film you confiscated from Marjorie Richmond on Saturday night?"

"They're still down at the station," he said. "All but one of
the rolls were unexposed. The only one with any shots on it was
the one that was in her camera at the time. I can't release that to
you, because it belongs to Miss Richmond. She'll have to come
down to the station and claim it."

"Did you ever find out what happened to her?" I asked.

"I gather she checked out of her hotel room on Sunday afternoon. She must have gone back to New York."

"Oh by the way," Carol said, "somebody broke into our hotel room yesterday."

Plumley scowled at her. "You're pulling my leg, right?"

Carol stared at him for a moment, then gave him a huge smile. "Gotcha," she said.

Plumley laughed with relief. "Well, Perry, I guess we better move on." He shook our hands. "You folks have a nice trip home. Come back and see us again soon."

The cops wandered off, and I unpacked the Penguin bag. I set the books on the table, then stuffed the wig and padded bra back into the bag. As I was looking at the books—sure enough, they were all samples from our display table, including two advance reading copies of the Summers book, one inscribed by the author to Lawrence Holgerson—Carol peered into the bag.

"What's with the costume?" she asked. "Whose stuff is this, anyway?"

"Lawrence Holgerson's, obviously."

"What? Lawrence's? What do you mean 'obviously'? What's going on here, Guy?"

"Well? You saw the pictures, right? I thought we agreed we had a winner."

"Exactly what the hell are you talking about? I'm getting tired of this game. Which pictures?"

"The photographs," I answered. "The evidence. The proof that Lawrence Holgerson killed Heidi Yamada."

Carol burst out laughing. "Sometimes you amaze me, Guy," she said. "You and Lawrence used to be rival book collectors, and you still won't let that go, even though you're not in that game anymore. Now you're calling the poor man a murderer."

Huh? Hadn't she seen it? Was she blind? Or was I nuts?

I pulled the orange Fast Foto envelope from the breast pocket of my jacket. I was about to open it and spread the pictures on the table when I saw another visitor headed up the aisle.

"Oh boy," I said softly. "Phony females on parade." I set the envelope down on top of a short stack of *And Vice Versa*.

◇◇◇

Beatrice Wright flounced to a stop in front of our booth. "Well!" she exclaimed. "I suppose you've read all three stories?"

"All three?" Carol answered. "Which three? What stories?"

Beatrice pulled the *PW Daily* out of her tote bag and spread it out on the display table, covering the orange envelope and several stacks of books. Those poor display copies took another beating as she flattened the newspaper out.

"Ta-dah!" she sang, pointing at the page one announcement of the Levin-Sonora nuptials. "That's one. I guess my real talent is matchmaking, huh?" She turned to page two. "Ta-dah!" She pointed to the obituary of Heidi Yamada.

There she was, in the photo that still makes me weep and grow warm, that smile of starlight, those laughing eyes, the hair like black satin, the woman I had loved, if only briefly, on the cover of the book that put me in business and changed my life.

The article quoted me and it quoted Arthur Summers, and both of us sounded inarticulate and insincere, but I didn't care.

"What's the third story?" Carol asked.

Beatrice turned another page and jammed her forefinger down. "Ta-dah!"

"MAX BLACK TO EDIT RANDOM HOUSE ANTHOLOGY OF COWBOY POETRY." I scanned the article quickly. "*...Charles Levin Editions... mid-six-figure advance...San Francisco agent Beatrice Wright...*"

"Congratulations," I said.

As Beatrice folded up the *PW Daily* and stuffed it back into her tote bag, I picked up the Fast Foto envelope to put it back into my pocket.

"Pictures?" Beatrice said. "You have pictures?"

"You really want to see those pictures, don't you, Beatrice?" Carol asked.

"Well—"

"Because all you have to do is ask, you know. If seeing those pictures is so overwhelmingly important to you, ask politely, and—"

"Some other time, dear," Beatrice said, a plastic smile on her lips, her eyes darting back and forth between Carol and me. "Right now really must be off. I have a couple of deals to close before the fat lady sings. And I have a taxicab waiting for me out back with the meter running."

◇◇◇

"What was that all about?" I asked Carol after Beatrice had strode out of earshot.

"That's your killer, Guy," she said. "Forget Lawrence Holgerson. My money's on Beatrice Wright."

"But Carol, the photos—"

"Give me those photos."

I handed her the envelope and she pulled out the photos and shuffled through them till she found the one she wanted. She handed it to me.

There she was, and I had to admit there was murder in her body language. We couldn't read her eyes, because she was facing the other way, leaving the table in a thunderous huff. Her left hand was a blur beside her head, as if she were waving away gnats or the furies, but her right hand, in focus behind her butt, was a clear message of hatred. The middle finger was extended, the other three clenched back tight on either side: *Fuck you,* it said. *Fuck you out loud. Fuck you to death.*

"It looks pretty bad for the most powerful agent on the West Coast," I admitted.

"She's also the one who had us mugged," Carol said. "If she had known how fat this picture makes her butt look, she would have sent out two goons, maybe three."

"Okay, wait a second," I said. "Back up. I admit Beatrice looks dangerous in this picture, and that hand looks like a murder weapon. But honey, Beatrice Wright has been giving Heidi Yamada the finger, so to speak, for over eight years now, ever since Heidi fired her and stole her boyfriend."

"Motive, right?"

"Yeah, but that's old news. Why now?"

"Because she wanted Max." Carol reached under the table and brought out the *PW Daily.* She laid it on the table, open to page five. "Ta-dah!" she said, pointing to the article about the *Random House Anthology of Cowboy Poetry.* "Heidi was in the way."

"But—"

"It was just business, of course. Nothing personal."

"Right," I said.

"Right," Carol agreed.

"But look. Let's get real. The finger doesn't kill people. Heidi was poisoned."

"And who told Heidi to drink two glasses of champagne?"

"But how did she know the champagne was poisoned?"

"I don't know, but she did," Carol answered. "What you see here is a murderer leaving the scene of the crime. Sayonara, sweetheart."

I looked again at the photo, focusing this time on the victim. The smile that had captured my heart was gone forever, replaced by a goofy grin. Her eyebrows struggled up on her forehead, as if to hold her slender eyes open for the brief rest of her life.

Then back at Beatrice's back. The big butt. The finger.

"So where's Beatrice off to?" I asked. "In this picture, I mean."

"Gone. We didn't see her the rest of the evening. My guess is she knew what would happen and she wanted to be gone by then. Alibi City."

Carol grinned like someone who has plunked down the winning tile: all seven of them, with an X and a Q and a triple word score.

I gave her about thirty seconds to enjoy the triumph and then said, "Now can we talk about Lawrence Holgerson?"

"What for?" The look on Carol's face morphed from gloat to glower.

"Because he's the one who poisoned Heidi Yamada," I said. "Wait—I'm not saying Beatrice wasn't happy about it, and maybe she knew what was happening, but it was Lawrence who gave Heidi the cocktail of death."

Carol squinted. "Prove it."

I squinted back. "Easy." I pointed at the stack of books I had taken out of the Penguin bag that Plumley had given me. "Lawrence's books, right?"

"Maybe."

"Definitely. All our freebies, some of the samples we were not giving away but he took anyway because he's a thief—"

"A thief maybe. I'll grant you that."

"—including one he had inscribed to him at the party on Saturday night. It has his damn name on it, Carol."

"Okay, so Taylor picked up Lawrence's bag by mistake. The bags all look alike."

"And the bag also contained this." I pulled out the wig. "And this. Or these." I pulled out the stuffed bra. "Now what do you say?"

"We've already had a discussion of Lawrence's sexuality," Carol grumbled. "That's really none of our business."

I stuffed the costume back into the bag and stowed the bag under the table. Then I picked up the photos and sorted through them. I selected six shots, which I held in front of my face like a poker hand.

"Pick a card," I said. "Any card."

"Quit playing games."

So I laid my cards on the table.

"Jesus," Carol whispered after she had studied the photos for a full minute. "Oh Jesus, Guy. I'm so sorry, but you're—"

"I'm what?"

"You're *right*. That's him. Her. Whatever."

"Speak of the devil," I said. I gathered up all the photos and slipped them into the orange envelope and put the envelope back into the breast pocket of my jacket. I looked up into his shit-eating grin and said, "Hello, Lawrence."

He looked chipper, and he even seemed to have gotten that horrid linen jacket pressed. Smiling like an innocent child, har har. "Greetings, friends," he said. "This place is a morgue this morning. Have you had any traffic, any traffic at all?"

"Come to think of it, no," I said.

Carol added, "The only people to drop by our booth have been people we already know."

"That's what I figured," Lawrence said. "So I thought I'd better come around now, in case you're planning to close down early. I want to be available in case you can use some help."

"Such a gentleman," Carol commented.

Lawrence shrugged and blushed. "Well, of course I have ulterior motives." He let his gaze wander across our display panels, resting on the posters for Heidi's first book and Arthur Summers' most recent.

I took the orange envelope out of my pocket and placed it carefully on the table. "Lawrence," I said, "you and I have to have a talk."

His eyes widened. "Oh?"

"On Sunday and again yesterday you were asking us if we knew where Taylor Bingham was."

"Was I?"

"Why were you looking for Taylor?" I asked. "Hmmm? How come?"

"God," Lawrence sputtered. "Lighten up."

"Just answer my question."

Lawrence pulled a pack of Salems out of his shirt pocket, looked up and down the aisle, then put the cigarettes back in his pocket.

"Lawrence?"

"Well," he said, "I seem to have taken his Penguin bag home with me from the Random House party. By accident, and I wanted to return it to him. It had his appointment book and some advance reading copies and stuff, and I figured—"

"You figured maybe he took your bag by mistake, too."

"Yes, well."

"Yes, well you came to the right place." I picked up the stack of books he had lifted on Saturday and said, "Any of this look familiar?" I plopped the stack on the table in front of him.

Lawrence dropped his cool. He caressed the books with his hands, and when he looked up there were honest-to-God tears in his eyes. "Bless you, Guy," he said softly.

"You're welcome," I said. "That is you're welcome to some of those books. Not all of them."

"But they're mine," he whined. "You said—"

"Some of these were giveaways," I said. "You're welcome to those. Some were put out for display only. As you well know."

"Well, at this point, I can't see as it matters," he said. "They're extras, right? I mean you don't really want to shlep them back to Santa Barbara, do you? Don't be so uptight. My God."

"Uptight?"

"Yeah, uptight. Anal."

"You're the anal one, Holgerson."

"What the hell do you mean by that?" His face was the color of raw liver.

"Anal," I repeated. "As in asshole."

"Boys!" Carol scolded. "Calm down, both of you."

Lawrence and I went back to our corners, without moving an inch. When I regained control of my fury, my breath, my voice, and my wits, I said, "Those books weren't all that I found in your Penguin bag, asshole."

Lawrence chewed on that for a while. "What are you accusing me of now?" he asked.

I took a deep breath. "I'm accusing you of wearing a blond wig and big boobs," I said.

"Oh shut up."

"I'm accusing you of impersonating a waitress," I continued.

"Is this some kind of sick joke? Honestly, Guy!"

"I'm accusing you of serving poisoned champagne to Heidi Yamada," I concluded. "Lawrence, my man, Lawrence, you asshole, I'm accusing you of murder."

Whew. Big breath. I unclenched my hands, never removing my glare from his florid face.

"You're out of your mind," he sputtered. "You're out of your *fucking mind.*"

I reached under the table and retrieved the Penguin bag. I pulled out the tricks, like rabbits from a magic hat. "Here's your wig, blondie," I said. "And here's your treasure chest." I pointed at the Fast Foto envelope on the table. "These are photographs of you in costume, the cocktail waitress from hell."

Lawrence reached toward the envelope and I slapped his hand away. "I'm not done yet," I snapped. I reached into my hip pocket for my wallet and got out Daniel Plumley's business card. "And here's the police detective who has asked me to help him figure out the meaning of what's obviously a disguise concealed in the Penguin bag. Perhaps you have something to say about that? If so, say it now, because I have an appointment with Detective Plumley at two-thirty this afternoon."

Lawrence Holgerson looked from me to Carol, then back at me. Then up the aisle one way, then down the aisle the other way. Then back up the aisle, and his face broke into a big grin.

"Max!" he called. "Hi, Max! Over here!"

Carol and I both looked up the aisle, and sure enough, along came the cowboy poet, the darling of the day, moseying slowly in our direction. I was glad to see him coming our way; the tension was getting to be more than I could handle on my own, and I needed a breather.

Max finally reached our booth, and while he was giving Carol a hug, I turned my attention back to Lawrence.

Lawrence was gone.

So was the orange envelope from Fast Foto.

"Holy shit!" I shouted. "That little asshole took off!" I looked down the aisle, and there he was, way down at the other end, just turning the corner into the main aisle, the one that ran down the center of the convention hall. "He's got our photos!"

"What's up?" Max asked.

"Go get him, Max!" Carol begged. "Guy, I can't believe you let him get away with that. Hurry, Max!"

"Get who? Why?" Max grinned and scratched his head.

"Lawrence Holgerson," I shouted, then added, *sotto voce,* "He killed Heidi, and I can prove it. Don't let him get away! Run!"

Max lost the grin, nodded once, and took off, full speed. As we watched him turn the corner into the main flow of traffic, Carol said, "You'd better go too. It wouldn't do to have Max dragging Lawrence back through the crowd, kicking and screaming."

"But I'll never—"

"Go," she insisted. "Now. As quick as your little legs can carry you."

"Shut up about my little legs."

She turned me around and gave me a shove. "Go!"

By the time I reached the main aisle, Max was nowhere in sight. I charged forward anyway, stopping to look right and left at every cross aisle. The crowd was sparse, but there were still dozens of people in each aisle. No Lawrence. No Max. Next aisle—no Max, no Lawrence. Next aisle, no—oops, I saw Mitzi coming my way, waving to me and flashing a toothy smile. I quickly moved on. Next aisle…

It was hopeless. I'd never find them. They were gone. Max would wander back to the booth empty-handed, and Lawrence would be back in Palo Alto, pasting Marjorie's photos into his scrapbook before any of us heard from him again.

I'd blown it.

The exercise felt good, though, so I kept up the trot to the end of the long main aisle, which led to the doors that opened out to the receiving area and loading docks.

I decided to go ahead and get that hand truck from the station wagon. Might as well accomplish something useful, I figured. So I went through the rear door to the receiving area, and that's where I found them.

"Hey, Guy," Max said, an angry grin on his face. "Look who I found trying to steal books out of the Coffee House booth." He had Lawrence's left arm bent back in a hammerlock behind his back, and the little creep was squirming like a caught trout.

"I'm going to scream," Lawrence threatened.

"Okay," Max said. "If you want a broken shoulder. Then you'll scream for real."

"Lawrence," I said, "look at me."

Lawrence looked away.

"I said look at me."

He still wouldn't do it.

"Max?" I said.

Max gave Lawrence's arm a yank and Lawrence did as he was told. He showed me his face and his eyes were full of pain. "What are you going to do with me?" he begged. "Please, you guys, let me go!"

There was no air-conditioning back there in the receiving area, and sweat was pouring off all three of us. My undershorts were bunched up like a twisted damp rag.

The doors to the main hall opened and a fork lift passed through, surrounded by a cloud of cool air. The fork lift was carrying a full load. Things were breaking down in there.

"What do you want me to do with him, Guy?" Max asked.

"Out back," I said. "My car."

We followed the fork lift out onto the loading dock and I led the way down the cement steps and across the blazing asphalt to where the station wagon was parked.

The LV-VIP cab was nowhere to be seen.

I unlocked the door on the driver's side and flipped the switch that unlocked the other three doors, walked around to the passenger side, and opened the door.

"Get in, Lawrence," I said.

"Why?" he whined. "Where are we going?"

"Get in."

Max gave Lawrence a little shove as he released his arm, and Lawrence crawled into the passenger seat. I slammed the door and said, "Thanks, Max. I'll explain all this later. Just keep him inside the car till I get in and lock the doors."

Max nodded.

I went back to the driver's side and got into the car. It was an oven in there. I slammed the door shut and flicked the switch that activated the child-proof lock on all the doors.

Lawrence was panting like a rabid dog. His clothing was a wet wreck. "Jesus Christ, Guy," he said. "Get this thing started and turn on the fucking air-conditioner!"

I cranked on the ignition. "Fasten your seat belt, Lawrence. We're going for a drive."

He did as he was told and I buckled up too. I released the brake and put her in drive. We rolled slowly through the parking lot toward Paradise Road.

"Will you please put on the fucking air-conditioner?" Lawrence said. "Now, for Christ's sake?"

"I don't think so, Lawrence. I kind of like it warm like this." I pushed the button that rolled down my window, then drove out of the lot and onto Paradise, heading east.

"God damn it," Lawrence snarled, "my window doesn't work."

"It works," I said, "but I control it. It's so bad little children don't jump out and get hurt."

Lawrence pulled a Salem out of his pocket and stuck it between his lips. As he was digging in his pants pocket for a lighter I said, "What are you trying to do, smoke me out? Give me those cigarettes."

"Fuck you."

"Have it your way." I rolled up my window and drove on, the oven on broil.

"Jesus Christ," he said. "Here!" He handed me the pack.

I put it between my legs. I took the unlit cigarette from between his lips and stuck it behind my ear, then opened the window and turned left onto Sahara, heading toward I-15. When I got onto the freeway, pointed west, I threw the pack of Salems out my window.

"Hey! God damn it, Mallon, what do you think you're doing?"

I took the last cigarette from behind my ear and said, "Would you like this one?"

"Yes. Give it here."

"Hand over my photographs," I said.

"Fuck you."

"Your call," I said. I flicked the cigarette out into traffic and zoomed on.

"You're a real sadist, you know that?" Lawrence cried. Cried. He was actually crying.

"Lawrence, are you really crying over lost cigarettes?"

"Fuck you."

"Because we could stop and buy more cigarettes."

"Oh God, Guy, *please* stop this car. I'm dying. This is killing me."

"Don't talk to me about killing," I snapped. "Just shut up till I tell you to talk."

We drove on in silence, past a bunch of future casinos under construction, until we were out in the desert, sailing through blazing waves of heat and watery mirages.

"Will you tell me where we're going, at least?" he whined.

"Yeah. Sure. We're going to stop for a cold beer, and then we're going to turn this station wagon around and drive back to the Las Vegas Convention Center."

"Thank God."

"Just as soon as you answer a few questions," I added.

He groaned. "I don't have anything to tell you," he said.

"I have a full tank of gas," I told him. "Should get us to Barstow, maybe even Victorville."

He groaned again. "Okay. What do you want to know?"

"Number one," I said, "why did you kill Heidi Yamada? You told me you loved that woman, in your own sweet way. So why, Lawrence? Why in the world—"

"I didn't kill her," he answered.

"Oh for—"

"It was an accident," he insisted.

"I see," I said. "You just accidentally dressed up like a stacked, blond waitress, and you just happened to be carrying three glasses of poisoned champagne, and you just accidentally happened to carry them straight to our table and offer them, by accident, to Heidi Yamada. Of all the rotten luck."

Lawrence was sobbing now. "It was an accident!" he insisted when he caught his breath. "She was only supposed to take one glass." He buried his face in his hands and howled, "Oh, God, oh Heidi!"

We drove. Westward through the salt flats, the valley between the mountains of southwest Nevada. I opened Lawrence's window for him—for both of us—and the hot wind buffeted our sweaty faces. Lawrence cried like a child ashamed. His head was flung back against the back of his seat, his eyes streaming with tears, his jaw wide like the mouth of a trout gasping in the harsh dry air.

When he quit whimpering I said, "Lawrence, maybe you'd better tell me all you have to say. I'm going to quit grilling you. Just tell me what happened. The truth can't hurt you now."

He sniffed. He snorted snot and sighed. He took off his soaking linen jacket and rubbed his face with it, and I drove on, westward, eighty-five miles an hour.

Finally he spoke. "What do you want to know?"

"The poison. Your idea?"

"Of course not."

"Whose?"

Silence.

"Whose, Lawrence?"

"Charles Levin," he answered. "His idea. 'Knock the bitch out,' he said. I don't think he meant to kill her. I know he didn't."

"So he hired you to dress up like a cocktail waitress and slip Heidi a mickey? A roofie?"

"That's right."

"And how could you do such a thing?"

"The price was right."

"He must have offered you a lot of money."

Lawrence was silent for several minutes, several hot miles.

"Well?" I said.

"Well what?"

"How much did Levin pay you?"

Lawrence laughed, a dry hot cackle. "Not a cent. God, Guy, it's not all about money, you know."

"What, then?" I looked over at my passenger, and my passenger was gloating back at me.

"I now own a first edition, signed and limited, of twenty priceless books published by Charles Levin Editions. Copy number one, every one of them. Signed by the author, inscribed to the publisher. Twenty books, pal, by the most collectible poets in the land. Alan Tate. Louis Simpson, Karl Shapiro, J. V. fucking Cunningham! The Cunningham's been on my want list for ten years. I never thought I'd get a first, let along a signed number one. I don't need to tell you what such a collection is worth in dollars, or what it means to me. Don't tell me you're not jealous, Guy Mallon, because you are. You of all people know what such a score is worth. Let's just say my position in the world of book collecting is pretty much locked in for life. Wouldn't you say? So eat your heart out, Número Dos."

I let him gloat while it sank in. Yes, as a matter of fact I *was* jealous. The only New York editor to make a name for himself by publishing modern poets had given up his collection of autographs to this shlemiel—for what?

"For *what?*" I asked. "What was he thinking? He offered you a collector's dream just to have Heidi knocked out for one evening? That doesn't make sense."

"Nope," Lawrence agreed. "Doesn't make sense. But he did it. It was Linda Sonora's idea. Or anyway he did it for her. The man's in love, can you imagine. It was her big night, right? Her debutante ball? She was nervous about that speech she had to make. I'm told it was a stupid speech anyway, but I didn't hear it. By that time I'd left the party."

I didn't answer because I hadn't heard Linda's speech either.

"I was a back-up plan, a contingency," Lawrence went on. "Linda told Levin to keep Heidi away from the party and Levin tried to do that. But just in case she wangled an invitation, he hired me to do the waitress thing with the knock-out drops.

Cross-dressing isn't my thing, but hey, I earned a lot of first-class books, wouldn't you agree?"

"Great books," I agreed. "A collection to die for. But to kill for?"

"Guy, I didn't kill her. Levin didn't kill her either. Nobody murdered Heidi Yamada. She grabbed two glasses before I could stop her—"

"Why were you carrying three, all poisoned?"

"I didn't want it to look like I was forcing a drink on her. The idea was to offer her a glass, and as soon as she took one I was supposed to leave or spill the tray. But then Mitzi grabbed a glass, and then Heidi grabbed another glass, and I knew things had gotten out of my control, so I got the hell out of there. I'd done my job, earned my reward. I had no idea what was going to happen. Nobody told me what was in those drinks, exactly."

I drove. The casinos of Stateline were looming on the horizon. "So you were pretty glad to see Heidi show up at the party, weren't you?" I said. "So you could earn those books." I glanced over.

He grinned back. "I made sure she had an invitation."

"So you're the one who stole the invites from Levin's desk on Saturday morning?"

Lawrence shook his head. "I'm done confessing," he said. "I've told you a lot, and I think you should turn this car around."

We had a beer in Whiskey Pete's at Stateline, and Lawrence bought a pack of Salems. Then we drove back to Las Vegas with the windows closed and the air-conditioning going full blast. Lawrence chain-smoked all the way back, which was disgusting, but I let him have that in exchange for a few more answers.

No, he had no idea who had ransacked Marjorie Richmond's room. Who was Marjorie Richmond anyway?

He was shocked and sorry to hear that Carol and I had been mugged. I believed him.

It was Levin himself who gave him the tray with the three champagne glasses. Levin then made his announcement, telling everyone to get ready to toast Linda Sonora, and that was

Lawrence's cue to go across the room and give Heidi the champagne. "One glass, but it got out of my control," he repeated.

"So if I were to ask Charles Levin—"

"He'd deny it all, of course. And so will I. So you can quit trying to be a crime solver. Give it up, Guy."

"Except that I have proof," I reminded him. "Speaking of which, before I let you out of this car I expect you to give me back that envelope of photos you stole when you ran off this morning."

"What envelope?" Lawrence responded. "What photos?"

"Lawrence, quit being an asshole."

He put out his cigarette and lit another. "Sorry, Guy, those photos are no longer available."

"Fuck do you mean by that?"

"While you were chasing me I deposited that envelope in a trash bin."

"What trash bin? Which one?"

"I don't know which trash bin. There must be over five hundred trash bins in the convention center. I threw it in one of them, but I have no idea which one. I was in such a hurry. I'm sure if you look through all of them you'll find it, if they haven't all been emptied by now."

"Fuck you, Holgerson."

He laughed. "So it's really just your word against mine that this conversation ever happened. You have no proof that I ever wore a blond wig."

"And falsies," I pointed out.

"Right," he agreed. "The evidence is gone. Case dismissed."

I tried to look pissed off and heartbroken, but I couldn't hold it. I started to giggle.

"What?"

"You threw away the prints," I said. "Smooth move, Ex-Lax. I still have the negatives. They're in my suitcase."

"Oh shit." Lawrence lit another cigarette.

"Would you quit smoking up my car?"

"Give me those negatives and I will."

"Fuck you," I countered. "Those negs are worth a lot more than that."

"How much?"

"Huh?"

"How much?"

"What did you say?"

"You heard me, Guy. How. Fucking. Much do you want?"

"For what?"

"For all the prints and all the negatives that show me prancing around in drag. God."

I grinned. This was great. "Give me all those Charles Levin Editions signed firsts," I told him. "Every one of them. All twenty, including the J. V. Cunningham. Do that and the negatives are yours."

"Fuck you, Guy Mallon."

"Up yours, Lawrence Holgerson."

"You sawed-off little shrimp."

"Shut up, you flaming fag."

We both started to giggle. I put my hand on his knee and he covered my hand with his and squeezed. We broke out laughing and we laughed out loud, tears streaming down both of our faces, till we reached the Las Vegas Convention Center.

Laughing? Why laughing?

Well, I don't know exactly. Heidi was still dead and I was still sad about that. We all were. But it felt so good to know that nobody had actually meant to take her life.

That made all the difference.

We parked in the lot, around back near the loading dock. I opened up the back of the station wagon and got the hand truck out. I started rolling it toward the building and Lawrence scurried after me.

"One more thing," he said.

"What's that?"

"Um—"

"What? I'm in a hurry, Lawrence. Carol's probably worried sick. What do you want?"

"I'm sorry I stole your photos, Guy," he said.

"Forget it," I told him. "No harm done."

"Um..."

I stopped wheeling the dolly and faced him. "What, Lawrence?"

"Can I still have those posters?" he asked. "For my collection?"

Carol Murphy

Closing Remarks

Thank you all for coming. Some of you have come quite a distance to say good-bye to Heidi, which is quite fitting. She is someone who touched every one of us in this room. I know she would appreciate your presence on this occasion, and your good wishes and fond memories.

You are all welcome to join us at the Santa Barbara Cemetery for the placement of Heidi's ashes after the service, followed by an informal gathering with refreshments at the office of Guy Mallon Books, downtown. You'll find a map to both locations on the back of your programs.

Thank you.

Carol didn't say a word to me until we were at least ten miles west of the city limits and Las Vegas was just a small pile of toys on the horizon in my rearview mirror. Our air-conditioned station wagon was the quietest place on earth. We were putting the miles between our car and a certain yellow taxi, but I could feel the miles between me and Carol, too.

She wasn't letting me into her thoughts and feelings, but I had plenty of thoughts and feelings of my own to stew in. Heidi was gone. Forever. Marjorie, that poor pathetic child, was out there in the evil world somewhere, being battered, and I had no way to stop it. I felt like a first-class chickenshit leaving town like this, but what more could I do? I had to protect Carol. I had to protect myself. I had to feel like shit.

"I am so glad to be out of there," Carol said, finally. "That is one weird city, and that was one grueling convention. What a bunch of thugs."

"I'm glad it's over too," I said.

"Over?" she responded. Her voice was sharp and high. "Over?"

I glanced across the seat and saw a look on her face like fish gone bad. She turned to me and said, "What are you talking about?"

I watched the road before me, the mountains on either side, and my fellow escapees driving west along the highway. I took another glance into the rearview mirror, where the city had disappeared altogether. "Over," I repeated. "The ABA. Done for another year. That's all I meant."

"It's not over. Heidi Yamada's still dead."

"That isn't going to change," I said.

"So we should just get used to it?"

"Carol, what's eating you? You weren't in love with Heidi Yamada."

"That's right, Guy, but you were. And now you don't care that she was killed."

"I do care, Carol. You have no idea how much I care. But will you please allow me to take some comfort in the fact that she wasn't actually murdered? That it was an accidental overdose?"

"That's what Daniel Plumley said. The big detective."

"And Lawrence," I reminded her. "He explained things pretty well, I think."

"You are so full of shit, Guy Mallon. So full of shit."

"What?"

"You didn't hear me?"

"I heard you."

"Daniel Plumley and Lawrence Holgerson. Two of my favorite people. Okay, let's take their word for it. Accidental death. So Heidi had an accident, right? How careless of her."

I sighed. "All right, it wasn't *her* accident. Somebody else's accident. But at least it wasn't murder, and I, for one, am relieved to know that. I don't know why, but there it is. I feel better. Not perfect, but better."

"Sorry to bum you out," Carol said. "Sorry to remind you that just because it may not have been a murder, technically, some person or some people committed a major crime, as a result of which somebody else is dead. She was killed. Okay, maybe not murdered, but what's the difference? Same malice, same result. Pardon me if I'm not feeling a lot better."

"I'm not sure about malice," I argued. "Or about major crime."

"If you don't think feeding drugs to people without their knowledge is a major crime, I don't want you mixing my drinks, ever again. It might not have occurred to you, but most intelligent people would stop to think about what might happen if Heidi were already on Valium or something incompatible with whatever that poison was. That was highly irresponsible, and whoever was behind it all didn't really care one bit if Heidi was out for the evening or moved to the morgue. I call that malice. Come to think of it, it's a lucky thing Mitzi Milkin wasn't on some incompatible drug either, or we'd be missing two people as a result of some careless, malicious accident. Some unforgivable, selfish risk. But you don't care about that anymore. You're full of shit."

So much for feeling any kind of better.

So much for my self-esteem.

Well, I thought, watching the dotted line before me and the dotted line behind me, and the steady stream of westbound traffic, at least we're out of Las Vegas. Or at least that's what I thought until I saw a yellow taxicab, also traveling west, pass me going maybe eighty miles an hour.

LV-VIP.

I didn't point it out to Carol, who had her head back against the head rest, her eyes slammed shut.

There's not much to Nipton. The town was once owned by Clara Bow after she quit acting, but even then there was nothing much there. Nowadays Nipton is just a couple of buildings. One is a general store and post office, which also has the "front desk" for the hotel, which is the other building, right next to it. The hotel itself consists of four tiny bedrooms off a common sitting room, with one bathroom in the back of the building. The scenery is alarmingly beautiful, especially in the early morning and late afternoon, when the light on the skyline of the New York Mountains makes you think that nature took lessons from Maxfield Parrish. In front of the hotel is a cactus garden, a beautiful display of living torture instruments; behind is a man-made pond surrounded by willows and cottonwoods. On the other side of the pond are a couple of trailers that nobody lives in and a scattering of big rusted machines that may have had something to do with mining or ranching long ago, but they've become landscape. The place is eerily quiet except for the buzz of insects in the afternoon, the croaks from the pond at night, and the glass-rattling explosions that happen about once an hour, sometimes more, round the clock, as the freight trains thunder through, only a few dozen yards from the hotel.

Carol and I have been to Nipton several times, because she likes to hike in the East Mojave, and I like to be wherever she is. Every time we've gone, we've been the only guests in the hotel, which has no locks and no clocks.

It was three in the afternoon when we got there. We hadn't spoken to each other since we left the state of Nevada. I was hoping that after we left I-15 we might have something to talk about along the way, like a dead jackrabbit in the road or a Joshua tree in bloom, but nothing happened and neither of us said a word. We were the only ones on the Nipton Road, and the silence in our station wagon was charged with anger and remorse.

I parked the car in front of the store. I turned to Carol and she turned to me. We both said it at the same time: "I'm sorry." She offered me her right hand and I shook it as if we were making a deal, and then she pulled me across the seat, into her arms.

"I really am," she whispered. "So sorry."

I couldn't speak, but I nodded into her shoulder.

"Let's go check in," she said. "We need a nap."

We got out of the air-conditioned station wagon and into the bright Mojave afternoon. The temperature was no doubt just as hot in Nipton as it had been in Las Vegas, but there is a big difference between a hot desert and a hot city. We held hands and walked into the dark general store, which smelled of old wood and tobacco from yesteryear. I tapped the silver call bell on the desk and we thumbed through the postcards on the rack until the old lady who ran the place shuffled through the back door and smiled at us. She wore a pink bathrobe and fuzzy slippers.

"What can I do you for?" she asked.

"We're staying in the hotel tonight," I answered. "Name's Mallon."

She pulled the book off the shelf and opened it up. "That's you all right," she said. "You folks been here before?"

She asks us that every time. "Yup."

She slid a 3X5 index card across the desk. "Fill that out," she said. "Name, address, license plate. Cash or charge?"

Carol gave her our business credit card.

"Want to buy a lotto ticket?" the old lady asked.

"Sure," Carol said. "What's it paying?"

"Who knows? But a lot of folks are coming over from Vegas this week to buy them. Must be high. You folks will be in the Senator's Room."

"You usually put us in the Clara Bow room," I said.

"Somebody already has that room," she told us.

"You mean we'll have company?" Carol asked. "I hope they don't snore. The walls in that hotel are pretty thin."

"Well, she may not stay the night, she told me," the old lady said. "Said she just needs a place to get some work done. What kind of work is what I want to know but it's none of my beeswax. There's no key. Make yourself at home. You folks been here before?"

"Thanks," I said. "You too."

As we were getting our suitcase out of the back of the station wagon, Carol said, "Bummer. I was planning on making you sing out loud, all night long."

"You're the one who makes all the noise," I said.

"Let's call it a duet. Don't worry, we'll still sing, just *sotto voce.*"

We kissed, and then we shlepped our stuff through the cactus garden, careful to stay away from the balls of fine spines, and up the steps to the hotel porch.

We walked through the screen door, and there she was, stretched out on a divan like the Queen of Sheba, in her hot pink pants and and white silk blazer. She sat up when she saw us and gave us that huge Neiman-Marcus smile. "There you are," she said. "I wondered when you were going to show up."

"Hello, Mitzi," I said.

"What brings you here?" Carol asked.

"We had an appointment, remember?" Mitzi answered. "But you left the ABA before it closed. You're not supposed to do that. Shame on you. We have work to do."

Carol kept walking across the sitting room, carrying her suitcase toward the Senator's bedroom. As she walked she said, "Well I'm sorry to disappoint you, Mitzi, but we're done working. Welcome to Nipton, but we're not talking business. We came here to unwind."

Mitzi laughed out loud. "Don't worry, Carol darling. It's not you I want to talk with anyway. Guy, honey, come sit down and maybe we can get through this quickly, so you and Carol can have a nice vacation. How long are you staying in this God-forsaken place?"

I shook my head, picked up my suitcase, and followed Carol across the sitting room and into our bedroom. I closed the door behind me.

"Of all the fucking nerve," Carol said. "What a bitch!"

"Careful," I said. "These walls are paper-thin."

"Good. Maybe she can take a hint. Where are you going?"

"Out there to get it over with," I said.

"You're a sap."

"I'll get rid of her," I promised.

"I want that hellcat out of Dodge by sunset."

I nodded and went back out into the sitting room, where Mitzi was calmly reading a *National Geographic*. She put the magazine down on the rough-hewn coffee table and smiled at me. "Don't worry, I'm sure we can conclude our business long before sunset. Have a seat."

So I sat in a chair across the table from her and said, "What's up?"

As Mitzi opened her mouth to speak, the air was split with the scream of a train whistle, followed by the din of the train itself, empty freight cars whamming by in a percussive procession that lasted and blasted for a full two minutes.

"God," she exclaimed when the noise died down. "I don't know how you can stand this place."

"We come here to feel the earth move." I said. "So. Get to the point."

"Guy, I have the most marvelous idea," she began.

"Don't try to sell me anything, Mitzi. Just tell me what this is so I can give you a simple answer."

"I can't help it, I'm so excited," she gushed.

"My answer's getting simpler by the minute," I said.

"Okay, listen," she said. "Heidi Yamada is dead, right?"

"Oh for Christ's sake."

"Darling, we have to put on a memorial service. We have to. She was important to us. To me, to you, to all of us. It's the right thing to do. We must."

"Okay," I said. "I'm with you so far. So what's in it for you, I wonder."

"May I be frank?"

"Be frank," I said. "Frank and fast."

She took her time with a lingering smile. "I'm thinking *festschrift,*" she said. "A collection of eulogies. A *festschrift* is an anthology of—"

"I know what a *festschrift* is."

"So? What do you think?"

"Of what?"

"We have a memorial service, we invite lots of Heidi's colleagues and associates, you know, people who matter, and get them to give eulogies at the service, and we publish a volume containing all those speeches, and we fill it full of beautiful pictures—I have some sensational photos—and of course wonderful design, and we sell it to them all, because they'll all want lots of copies, and we'll charge plenty because it will be the most elegant, elaborate—"

"Ongepotchket," I said.

Mitzi grinned. "Exactly."

"You go ahead, Mitzi. Fine. But I don't want anything to do with it. That's not the kind of publishing I do."

"Of course, dear. It's my book. But I want you to arrange the memorial service. That's more your department."

"Why don't you do it?" I asked.

"It wouldn't be appropriate," she said. "It might look self-serving."

"Of course. That would be self-serving. So you want me to arrange the funeral. Sorry to sound self-serving, but what's in it for me? I assume you expect me to pay for all this?"

"I should think you'd want to do this memorial service for Heidi, Guy. After all, she was so special to you."

"It might cost quite a bit," I said. "I mean there's the flowers, the venue—"

"The Mission," Mitzi said. "It has to be the Santa Barbara Mission. Heidi would want that."

"Reception afterwards—"

"The El Encanto," she said. "Such a lovely view of the harbor from there."

"You've got this all thought out," I said. "How long have you been planning this affair?"

"Let's just say I have a certain flair," Mitzi said. She smiled at me. I swear to God, Minnie Mouse meets Eleanor Roosevelt.

"I still don't know why I should spend all this money," I said. "I don't have that kind of money."

"Sweetheart, I paid you ten thousand dollars for those poems you ghostwrote for Heidi. Come on, now."

"Heidi paid me for those, not you."

"I paid Heidi," Mitzi snapped back. "The money came from me and it went to you and you wrote the poems and the poems are now with me. The point is, you have ten thou to spend, and I'm telling you how to spend it."

I took a deep breath. Little people get pushed around a lot. Mitzi was a big person. I am a little person. That meant she could tell me what to do. Right?

"Forget it," I said. "You're a ghoul."

She took her briefcase off the coffee table, opened it up, looked inside, then apparently changed course and closed the briefcase. "Well," she said, "that's that. You're making a big mistake, Guy Mallon. A big mistake."

"I'll live with it. Shall I show you to the door? Do you have things to pack?"

"Oh I'm not quite ready to leave," she answered. "My ride won't be back here till six o'clock. We have another couple of hours together. Let's try to make them pleasant."

"How did you get here?" I asked. "Didn't you drive?"

"Oh Lord no," she answered. "I came in a taxi."

Carol walked out of the bedroom, closing the door quietly behind her. "I'm going next door to buy a sixpack of beer," she announced. "Guy, can I have your wallet?"

I fished in my pocket and pulled out my billfold. I tossed it across the room and she snagged it out of the air. She nodded to me and left the hotel.

"I don't think your wife likes me," Mitzi said after Carol was gone.

"She's not my wife," I said.

"Well that's okay. It'll give you and me a chance to talk privately."

"I think we've finished talking," I said.

"Think again," she answered. "You have something of mine, and I want you to give it to me now, whether or not we plan to publish this book together."

"I don't have anything of yours," I said. "I earned that ten thousand dollars, and I'm going to keep it."

"I'm not talking about the ten thousand dollars," she said. "I'm talking about a certain roll of film. According to Lawrence, you still have that roll of film packed in your suitcase, and now it's time to hand it over." She held out her hand.

I didn't move.

She dropped her hand, sighed, and fished in her briefcase. She brought out an orange Fast Foto envelope and threw it on the coffee table. "You can have those back," she said. "I never imagined, Guy, that you were into that sort of thing."

I picked up the envelope and pulled out the photos. They were bedroom shots of the clerk at Fast Foto, conjoined in various ways with somebody who looked like Mr. T, or at least what I imagine Mr. T looks like with his clothes off: built like the *Normandie* and sporting an erection the size of the Chrysler Building.

"I don't have to ask where you got these," I said.

"No you don't. Now let's have the other roll."

"Which roll is that?"

"You know perfectly well what roll I'm talking about."

I didn't move and I kept my mouth shut. I hoped she couldn't hear my pounding heart or smell my fear.

But she appeared to be just as nervous as I felt. Her smile had vanished. She said, "Let me level with you, Guy. I'm in trouble. I have presold a lot of copies of *Out of My Face* which I won't be able to deliver as advertised."

"You can't still publish the book?" I asked.

"I can publish it, and I intend to. But I sold *autographed* copies, and that bitch refused to autograph them. Now there's no way she can sign the fucking things, so I have to come up with something else, something even better."

"Go on."

"In a way I have an excuse for not being able to deliver. How can a dead poet sign books? So I'm off the hook as far as that goes. But a lot of my customers are going to want their money back, and the money's already spent. See what I'm talking about?"

"And how will some pictures help?" I asked. "And why do I care?"

"I want to combine *Out of My Face* with the *festschrift*. It's going to be fantastic! It won't have the autograph, and that's too bad, but it will have so many other goodies I can't stand it! Pictures of most of the people Heidi wrote about, all taken during the last weekend of her life, some of them even taken during the last evening of her life. And on the cover—oh this is so terriff—*a beautiful photo of the poet at rest.* What do you think?"

I did my best to control my gag reflex. The horror of this woman! "How long have you had this planned?" I asked.

She was back to the coy smiles. "Well, when Heidi said she wouldn't sign the books—actually she said she'd sign them if I paid her another ten thou, but fuck that—I knew I had to do something. That's how I decided on the photos. The ABA photos of all the principal players, the people those poems are about."

"And your cover idea?"

"Let's call that a happy accident. Heidi at rest. On Elvis Presley's bed! Can you beat it?"

"So—"

"So let's have that roll of film."

Another freight train filled the sitting room with its roar, and that gave me a little time to think, but it wasn't easy to think under the circumstances.

I wondered what could be taking Carol so long to buy a six-pack of beer.

Mitzi had her hand out again, palm up, fingers tickling the air. "Film, Guy. My film."

"Your film?" I said.

"Lawrence told me you have it."

"*Your* film?"

"Gimme."

"That's Marjorie Richmond's film," I said. "She gave it to me and told me to hold onto it. It doesn't belong to you."

Mitzi stood and towered over me. "Guy, wake up. I paid Marjorie to take those pictures. That photography was work for hire. The pictures, the film, and all the rights to same are *my property.* Give me my property."

"You hired Marjorie?"

"Quit stalling. Let's get this over with."

"Where is Marjorie now?" I asked.

"I have no idea. She left town."

"In a cab," I guessed.

"Yes, in a cab."

"LV-VIP."

"I'm tired of small talk," Mitzi snapped. She began to pace. "I'm going to have that roll of film, and it will be far pleasanter if you just hand it over."

"Or?"

"You don't want to find that out."

226 John M. Daniel

Carol walked into the hotel and set a six-pack of Heineken on the coffee table. She took a seat in the other armchair and said, "Who wants a cold one?"

"Mitzi, if you don't mind, I'm going to bring Carol up to speed, so she'll understand why I'm so tempted to give you a roll of film."

"What?" Carol responded. "You can't give that away. That belongs to Marjorie. You're holding it for her, not for—"

"The film is mine," Mitzi said, her voice feigning weariness. "I don't want to go through all this again."

I soldiered on. "So here's the deal. Mitzi hired Marjorie to take a bunch of embarrassing pictures, which she wants to put into *Out of My Face,* which will also contain tributes to Heidi by a lot of the same people, and it will also have a picture of the poet on the cover, a picture of her dead." I turned to Mitzi for confirmation, and she nodded. "If we don't give her the roll of film, which she claims is hers anyway, there could be some unpleasantness. I'm guessing a certain cab driver—"

"My dear friend Booter," Mitzi said. "You've met him, I believe. He'll be here at six to pick me up. Me and the film."

"Wait a minute," Carol said. "You hired Marjorie to take pictures of Heidi?"

"Let's don't go through all this again," Mitzi answered.

"And what about the poison? Your idea?"

"I'm done talking," Mitzi said. "I'm not answering any questions, so don't bother to ask."

"So Charles Levin had nothing to do with that," I said. "Lawrence's story about all those signed and numbered firsts was a total lie?"

Mitzi asked, "What do you mean, signed and numbered firsts?"

I exchanged nods with Carol: confirmation. Levin and Sonora weren't involved. It was Mitzi's doing. Lawrence was her lackey.

"Good work, Mitzi," I said. "So you forced Heidi to drink two glasses of champagne, knowing full well that would be her last drink."

"I never forced anybody to do anything," she shot back. "I drank a glass of that stuff too, remember."

"Right," Carol said. "That was the glass you were going to offer her for seconds, but since she had already polished off two you didn't need that option. You drank your glass to give the impression that you had no idea what was in it. Put you to sleep, but you knew it was temporary. You also knew Heidi's dose was permanent."

Mitzi stopped pacing and responded with an icy stare. I checked my watch. Quarter to five.

Mitzi sat back down. "Really, you two," she said. "Be kind to yourselves. Just hand over the film, so Booter doesn't have to extract it from your bowels. Do you know what he does for fun? He likes to smash beer bottles against his forehead. Please don't make him mess up this cute little hotel just because of your foolish pride."

We sat in silence for a while and then I said, "Don't you have enough pictures? Marjorie was shooting all weekend long, and your friend Booter has all of those pictures, right? He busted into Marjorie's room and tore it apart and left with all of her film. Why do you need one more roll?"

Mitzi looked at me as if I were part naive, part dumb, part sneaky. "The cover shot, obviously."

"You mean Heidi dead?"

She nodded wearily.

"Mitzi, I'm sorry to tell you this, but I don't have that roll. The police have that roll. That's the truth."

"That's not what Marjorie told me," Mitzi said.

"Marjorie lied to you," Carol said.

"You stay out of this. I have no intention of being double-teamed."

"It's true," I said. "Marjorie's last roll of film was in her camera, which she handed over to the police. They gave her back the camera, but they kept the roll of film. That's the roll with the dead poet. Sorry."

"Who wants a beer?" Carol said again. "I'm going to have one. Anybody else?"

"I'm in," I said. "Mitzi?"

"Okay."

Carol twisted the tops off of three Heinekens and handed them around. We drank in silence. We were done by the time the next train came through.

Carol opened up the other three bottles. I checked my watch. Five-fifteen. We sipped our beers. There was nothing to say. The afternoon was as quiet as a grave until we heard an automobile pull up outside, tires crunching in the gravel parking lot next door.

Mitzi rose and went to the front door of the hotel. She looked out and waved, then turned back to us. "Booter's here early," she announced. "Are you going to give me that film, or shall I tell him to come in?"

◇◇◇

The man named Booter walked through the hotel door wearing a Stanley Kowalski tee shirt with the words BITE ME across his chest in black block letters.

Mitzi said, "Booter, darling, you've met these nice people."

He nodded and cracked his knuckles. There was something different about him. No watch cap today, and his skull was bald and shiny. Same pig nose, though, and same eyes: all business.

"I've seen you before," I said.

"I remember it well," he answered.

"No, I mean before that. Back when you had a mustache."

"Mitzi told me to shave it off."

"It was tacky," Mitzi said. "And recognizable. I heard that security was looking for him at the convention center after that little prank in the Random House aisle. Looking for a big bald man with a big bushy mustache."

"Hence the watch cap," I said.

"That thing's hotter'n hell," Booter said.

"So that was you at Julia Child's demonstration," I said. "Made the explosion and then slammed a custard pie in Charles Levin's face."

He grinned.

"That's my Booter," Mitzi said. "He's a man of many talents, aren't you darling?"

Booter shrugged and said, "You got that film?"

Carol said to Mitzi, "So you're the one who stole all those invitations to the Random House party."

"No, I was at your booth at the time, as you may remember," Mitzi answered. "Lawrence took the invitations. I distributed them of course, made sure everyone had one. Everyone who mattered."

"To have lots of suspects in case Heidi just happened to die?" Carol asked.

"To get more photographs of more people," Mitzi explained. "For the book. Speaking of which, would one of you two like to go get Booter that film so we can be on our way?"

"I've told you, Mitzi, that the roll of film with the dead body pictures is at the police station in Las Vegas. That's the truth."

Mitzi rolled her eyes and pointed at the Senator's Room. "That's their room, Booter dear," she said. "You'd better go through all their luggage. I believe it's two suitcases, a briefcase, and a Penguin bag. Do your stuff and then let's go back to Las Vegas where the buildings are air-conditioned and people tell the truth."

Booter strode across the sitting room and reared back as if to put a shoulder through our bedroom door.

"That won't be necessary," I told him. "There's no lock on the door."

"Shit." Booter opened the door as if he wished it were locked. He left the door open while he got to work disassembling our luggage.

"So you've known Booter a long time?" I asked Mitzi.

"We go back a long ways," she answered. "Back when I lived in Las Vegas he was my partner in crime, you might say. My manager."

"He's still your partner in crime. What was he, your pimp?"

"Don't be vulgar."

Another train barreled across the desert, its noise filling the hotel. Mitzi put fingers in her ears and looked, for a few seconds, like a tired old woman.

"Wow," Carol said. "Lot of traffic out there."

"So Mitzi," I asked, "how did you get home on Saturday night after that party? You were really out of it."

She chuckled. "I have no idea how I got home. I suppose some kind soul took care of me. I hope I wasn't taken advantage of, but if I was, I'll never know."

"What about Sunday morning? What was it like waking up from a bender like that?"

"I didn't wake up till noon. I haven't slept that late since I used to stay up all night. I was supposed to meet Marjorie inside the convention hall at ten, but I didn't get there till two."

"By which time she had left?"

"No, she was there. She was sitting on a bench out in the lobby, crying. She had your badge on. She said you had walked off with her camera case, her wallet, her room key, her everything. She was furious."

"Shit. Poor woman. I had to go down to the police station."

"So I took her with me back to my suite at Circus Circus."

"That was good of you."

"I got her in my room and locked the door and started asking her some questions. She told me what had happened the night before. Damn shame about poor Heidi. Told me she got some great shots. That's when she informed me that you had the roll of photographs taken at the party—including the shots of Heidi dead on Elvis' bed. I practically wet my pants!"

"You've got strange taste, Mitzi."

"The rest of the film was in her room, she said. But you had the room key. And you had the most important roll. That's when I'm afraid I got a little out of sorts and slapped her around a bit."

"You hit Marjorie?"

"Well, she was beginning to annoy me. I mean that was careless of her, giving you the roll of film. She said it was to keep it away from the police, but that was before there were cops on the scene, and I could see she was shining me on. I wouldn't put it past her to keep those shots for herself. But I hit her hard enough that I'm sure she wasn't lying to me about where that film was. That's why I know Booter will find it, and we'll be out of here. After Booter takes you two for a walk in the desert. He loves the desert. Collects rattlesnakes."

I glanced at Carol. She had no expression on her face. I know that expression. "Then what happened?" Carol asked.

Mitzi ignored Carol and spoke directly to me. "Well, finally Marjorie told me she knew where you'd be that evening, the Ingram party. So I gave her instructions: go find Guy, get your wallet and camera case and room key and that roll of film, and then go to your room and get the rest of that film, and bring all the film to me personally, back at my suite."

"And so—"

"So, after we had a nice dinner thanks to room service, I called her a cab. The cab driver came to our room, and Marjorie left with him."

"Booter."

"That's right."

"Did Marjorie know who Booter was?

"Of course not."

"And she never came back to your suite."

"No. According to Booter she tried to leave town with some piano player, then she tried to get you to steal all of my film. Booter did the right thing, bless his heart. He drove her outside the city limits. And left her."

"Dead or alive?"

"Goodness, Guy! Booter's not a murderer."

"Likes rattlesnakes, though, right?"

Mitzi smiled. Someday I hope I stop having nightmares about that smile of hers.

"Then Booter returned to Marjorie's room and took the film that was rightfully mine, except for the one roll that he's getting right now as we speak."

"How did he get into Marjorie's room?"

"He's a professional. I don't ask him questions like that. Ah, here he comes now."

Booter came out of our bedroom slapping an orange envelope against his hand. It was the inner envelope from the Fast Foto package, the one that contained the negatives of the prints Lawrence had thrown away. "This is all there is," he told Mitzi. "I looked through it all. This is it. I have to go get something out of my cab, and then I'm taking these people for a nice walk."

I got up from my chair and followed Booter out onto the porch in front of the hotel. He turned and pointed a thick finger at my right eye. "You stay put," he said. "Don't go anywhere. It would just mean extra work for both of us. I'm bigger than you, obviously, and I'm faster, and I tend to get real mad real easy."

He turned, walked down the steps, and out into the cactus garden on the way to his cab.

I suppose if I'd had any time to think about it, I might have wimped out again and I probably wouldn't be alive today. But I didn't have any time for making decisions. I let him get to about the middle of the cactus garden and then I tore off after him, down the porch steps and along the path as fast as I could run. He must have heard me coming, because he picked up speed, but that worked to my advantage because when I dove the last few feet and caught his ankles in my arms, he had enough momentum to send him down, face-forward, into a large barrel cactus. His heels kicked my face and that felt great.

You should have heard the scream.

I backed away and watched him rise and turn toward me. There was blood popping out all over his face and his throat and his arms and hands. He howled and started toward me, his arms outstretched and his eyes shut tight from the pain. I whistled and he picked up speed. I let him get as close as I dared, then dropped to the ground and rolled into his lower legs so that he tripped again, this time onto a tall cholla cactus, which broke off and went down with him into the gravel and dust.

He disengaged himself from the cholla and tried to rise, but his hands were too full of spines to support his weight. He rolled over onto his back, and he had spines all over his body. He was leaking blood. His BITE ME shirt was a war zone. His face was the worst though. And he couldn't touch it with his hands, because they were covered with spines too.

I knew he'd be back on his feet eventually, and I hadn't figured out what to do when that happened. At the moment, my attention was caught by a little orange envelope that had dropped from his hand with the first tackle.

I picked it up.

Off in the distance I heard the approach of a freight train. I ran the fifty-odd yards to the track and looked back.

He was on his feet. He was coming toward me. He was trotting, even though I could tell that every step was excruciating.

I looked to the right. The train was barrelling in at a fast-paced crescendo. I crossed the track and waited. *Come and get it.*

Booter and the train were both only a few feet away from me when I laid the yellow envelope on the track.

The whistle screamed bloody murder and the freight train charged between us. *BLAM BLAM BLAM BLAM RATTLE BLAM RATTLE BLAM RATTLE BLAM RATTLE RATTLE RATTLE RATTLE BLAM BLAM BLAM BLAM RATTLE BLAM RATTLE BLAM RATTLE BLAM RATTLE RATTLE RATTLE RATTLE BLAM BLAM BLAM BLAM RATTLE BLAM RATTLE BLAM RATTLE BLAM RATTLE RATTLE RATTLE RATTLE rattle rattle rattle rattle rattle....*

The train rattled away down the track. On the other side, I saw Booter heading back toward the hotel, walking carefully but purposefully. Slowly. He had murder on his mind, I knew. He wouldn't be able to outrun me, he knew that. He was going for easier prey.

This time I wouldn't be able to tackle him. He'd be on guard, and who wants to hug a porcupine anyway? So, duh, I picked up a board that was lying by the tracks, and when he got to the cactus garden again I charged like a knight.

Right in the back. Down he went. He missed the cacti this time, but the spines he already had were driven deeper into his flesh.

I took a big chance and kicked him in the balls. Ouch. I ruined my right shoe, and I'm still limping, but it was worth it.

That's when I heard the wail of a siren and looked up to see a California Highway Patrol car turning into the hotel lot. The vehicle stopped, the siren shut off, the doors opened. Out of the driver's side stepped a tall officer in his tan uniform.

And out of shotgun stepped Detective Daniel Plumley, Las Vegas Police Department.

Poor Booter was on his back whimpering, with his knees spread apart. He tried to hold his crotch but his hands were useless. So I kicked his crotch again, this time with my left foot. I'm right-handed so this wasn't as strong a kick, and Booter's scream wasn't as loud as the first one.

It took about twenty minutes for the ambulance to get there. The late-afternoon shadows turned the New York Mountains purple while we waited. Booter lay bleeding into the dirt. The highway patrolman had made him as comfortable as he could, but there was no dealing with those wounds without moving him, and it made sense to wait for the paramedics to do that. So we stood around the body—the patrolman, the detective, and I—listening to it twitch and whimper.

"That was really a stupid thing to do, Guy," Plumley said, when the patrolman went back to his car to call in his report.

"Because I might have killed him?"

"Shit no. I wish you had killed him, since I'm not allowed to. No, all I mean is, you might have gotten hurt."

"I figured I was going to get hurt anyway," I said. "I didn't think I had any options."

"It was also stupid for you to kick a man when he's down, right in front of two officers of the law. Fortunately Mr. Chips was looking the other way."

"How about you?" I asked.

"I didn't see anything either," Dan said.

The old lady from the store shuffled over to us in her bathrobe and fuzzy slippers. She had a tumbler of wine in her hand.

"What's all the racket?" she asked. "Looks like this fella got careless with the cactus. Should I go get some Band-Aids?"

"We've called an ambulance," Dan told her.

"Well, I'll leave it in your hands," the old lady said. She took a sip of her wine. "I got to get back to 'Miami Vice.'" She turned and shuffled away, back to the store.

The ambulance showed up and the team of paramedics got to work on the human pincushion. He cried out at every touch until they gave him an enormous shot of something to shut him up. It took them about half an hour to cut off all his clothes, dress his wounds, wrap him in a clean sheet and a blanket, place him on a gurney, and hoist him into the back of their vehicle. They handed Booter's wallet and keys to Dan Plumley, who said, "I'll be driving that cab back to Las Vegas and I'll check in with the suspect at the hospital. You taking him to Sunrise?"

One of the paramedics nodded and said, "Suspect?"

Plumley corrected himself. "Patient."

The patrolman, the detective, and I went through the cactus garden to the hotel, where Carol and Mitzi were standing on the porch.

Carol was grinning at me.

Mitzi was weeping.

"Are you okay, ma'am?" the patrolman asked.

Mitzi nodded.

"Did you know that man?" Dan Plumley asked her.

"Of course not," she answered. "He's a cab driver."

"But you're crying."

"Only because now I don't have a way to get back to Las Vegas. I'm stranded here without my ride." She looked at me and Carol, then back at the detective. "This is not a place I want to be."

The highway patrolman said, "Ma'am, I have to go back to Las Vegas now anyway. I can give you a lift."

Mitzi looked at me as if for permission. "I guess we've concluded our business," I said. "Thanks for coming all the way out here. We'll see you in Santa Barbara and we can iron out the details there."

"And those, um, negatives…?" she asked.

"I'm afraid they got run over by a train."

She turned to the patrolman. "Can you wait just a minute? I'll go inside and get my briefcase."

While she was in the hotel Carol said to me, "What's going on?" Then she turned to Detective Plumley. "Didn't you come out here to arrest that woman? She's the one who—"

"I can't arrest anybody outside the State of Nevada," Dan said. "And I know this will disappoint you, but I still consider the death of Miss Yamada an unfortunate accident. No, Miss Maloney, I came out here to arrest that cab driver. I've been looking for him since we talked this morning. Since yesterday afternoon, actually. And by the way, thanks a million for that phone call. Of course I couldn't arrest him here, technically, but by the time he wakes up he'll be in a hospital in downtown Las Vegas. That's my turf."

"You want us to make a statement about that mugging last night?" I asked.

"No, that won't be necessary for the time being. If that becomes necessary I'll contact you. Meanwhile, we have a bigger charge to nail him on. Attempted murder."

"Who?" I asked.

But before he could answer Mitzi came smiling out of the hotel. She shook my hand and said, "Guy, thanks a mill." She offered Carol her hand, but Carol didn't take it. Mitzi told Plumley, "Thank you, Officer." Then she turned to the patrolman and said, "Shall we?"

The CHP grinned back at her, his eyes drifting down over her body, and the two of them walked across the cactus garden, got into his vehicle, and drove off into the evening.

◇◇◇

I went to the store to buy a bottle of gin and some ice.

Plumley went to the cab to check it out.

Carol went inside to freshen up. Long day.

We met back on the porch and I served cocktails. Plumley said, "Miss Richmond's clothes are all in the trunk of his cab.

Just like she said. And there was a loaded pistol in the glove compartment."

"What happened to Marjorie?" Carol asked. "Where is she?"

"Sunrise Hospital," he said. "I hope they don't stick that cabbie in her room, come to think of it."

"What happened?" Carol asked again. "My name's Murphy, by the way."

"Miss Richmond came into the station yesterday afternoon," Plumley told us. "She was wearing a yellow slicker and nothing else. Not even shoes. Fortunately I was out in the lobby when she showed up, and fortunately she remembered me, because I would never have recognized her. She was a mess, frankly. Poor woman."

"What—"

"That cab driver," he answered. "Took her out in the desert Sunday night and left her there, naked. And barefoot. He had beat her up pretty bad. It took her till almost noon yesterday to get back to the highway. Lucky for her, the first person to come along was a Mormon kid with an old slicker in the back of his pickup. She had him bring her to the police station. Like I say, damn lucky I was out in the lobby when she got there or they'd have just thrown her in the tank or back out on the streets."

"She was lucky," I agreed.

"If you want to call it that. Anyway she told me what had happened, told me about the cab. LV-VIP. He's an independent, not even registered, so he was hard to trace. Thank God you called me. Lucky for you, too."

"Is that what you were doing when you were supposed to be buying beer?" I asked Carol.

"That's why I needed your wallet," she answered. "I needed this man's business card, which you're so fond of flashing around."

"How did you know we were in such trouble?" I asked. "I had no idea."

"It came through loud and clear to me," she said. "Even though I was in our room with the door closed. She said she had some photographs—'sensational photos,' she called them—and

I thought those might be Marjorie's. Then when she said she'd come here to Nipton in a taxi cab, well shit." She turned to Plumley and said, "You didn't seem all that glad to hear from me at the time."

Plumley chuckled. "My mistake. But as soon as you mentioned the cab I was all ears. You told me this morning you'd been mugged by a cabbie driving a yellow vehicle with the logo LV-VIP on the side. That matched the description Miss Richmond gave me. You had me hooked on that one."

"You didn't waste any time getting here," I said. "Thank God."

"I called CHP and arranged to have someone meet me in Stateline. I took a helicopter there."

"We're sure grateful," I said. "You want another drink?"

"No, I've got a long drive ahead of me," Plumley said. "And cab drivers aren't allowed to drink."

◇◇◇

Carol and I were the only guests in the Nipton Hotel that night, so we moved our stuff into the Clara Bow room, our favorite. Then we drove over to Searchlight, Nevada, twenty-five miles south of Nipton, for cheeseburgers and beer in a combination coffee shop and casino.

Driving back afterwards, though a forest of Joshua trees in the moonlight, Carol held my hand, called me her hero, and sang me our private love song. I won't tell you what it is.

Later, standing on the hotel porch, she said, "I'm not pissed off anymore. But I guess we're just going to let her get away with it, right? With killing Heidi?"

"No way," I said.

"But Detective Plumley doesn't have any interest in opening up the case, so I guess there's not much we can do about it."

"Mitzi Milkin won't get away with it," I said. "Believe me. I've got her nailed."

"You're not the law," Carol reminded me.

"I'm better than the law," I answered. "I'm a publisher."

To receive a free catalog of Poisoned Pen Press titles, please contact us in one of the following ways:

Phone: 1-800-421-3976
Facsimile: 1-480-949-1707
Email: info@poisonedpenpress.com
Website: www.poisonedpenpress.com

Poisoned Pen Press
6962 E. First Ave. Ste 103
Scottsdale, AZ 85251